THE CHAMBRION

Borgo Press Books by P. A. PONSON DU TERRAIL

The Chambrion and Other Stories

THE CHAMBRION AND OTHER STORIES

PIERRE-ALEXIS

PONSON DU TERRAIL

Translated by Brian Stableford

THE BORGO PRESS

MMXIII

CLASSICS OF
FANTASTIC LITERATURE
NUMBER SEVEN

THE CHAMBRION AND OTHER STORIES

THE CHAMBRION

CONTENTS

INTRODUCTION
by Brian Stableford

Le Chambrion, histoire mystérieuse by Ponson du Terrail, here translated as "The Chambrion: A Mysterious Story" was first published as a feuilleton in the *Monitor du Soir* in 1865 and reprinted in book form in the same year. It was then reprinted again in the annual omnibus *L'Écho des Feuilletons* in 1866—that is the version I have used for translation, thanks to its availability on the Bibliothèque Nationale's *gallica* website.

1865 was one of Ponson's busiest years;[1] his long-running series chronicling the boyhood adventures of King Henri IV was still in full swing, and that was the year that he resurrected his most famous protagonist, Rocambole, for a new series of adventures in *Le Perit Parisien*, He also published several other serials of various lengths. *Le Chambrion* passed virtually unnoticed, although Alphonse Baralle, writing in the 24 May 1866 issue of *Le Foyer*, mentioned it briefly as an item of particular interest in an article defending Ponson against a scornful attack mounted by Gustave Vapereau, who used Ponson as the primary target in a polemic against the alleged contemporary "decadence" of the *roman feuilleton*.

---

1. A more detailed account of Ponson's life and career can be found in the introduction to the Black Coat Press edition of *The Vampire and the Devil's Son* (2007; originally *La Baronne trépassée*, 1853). I hope to translate his other two vampire novels, *La Femme immortelle* (1868) and *L'Auberge de la rue des Enfants-Rouges* (1866) in the course of the next two years, and, if I live long enough, will undoubtedly find the temptation to tackle all 1,500,000 words of the Rocambole saga eventually irresistible.

Le Chambrion is, in fact, quite atypical of Ponson's work, departing from the casual flamboyance of his "Dramas of Paris" and from the historical settings he used in almost all of his other works. It is a contemporary rural drama that devotes some effort to protesting about the plight of the rural poor, and analyzing that plight, albeit rather crudely, in terms of economic exploitation and oppression; it also advertises itself as a "mysterious story" and its plot is organized around a murder mistakenly attributed by stupid agents of the law, whose true circumstances are in dire need of clarification.

What we now think of as the genre of "murder mysteries" was fully gestated by 1865 and merely in need of a literary midwife to lend a final helping hand in bringing it to light—a role played by Émile Gaboriau during the next few years. It is hardly surprising, however, that Ponson—who was sometimes writing as many as five daily serials simultaneously without any clear idea of how long they might be able, or required, to last—missed out on an apparent opportunity to be that midwife. Mystery stories require considerable and careful planning if they are to work properly, but Ponson never had more than the vaguest idea of where his stories were headed, and always had to be ready to change direction in response to editorial whimsy. In the event, the murder mystery supposedly at the heart of the plot of *Le Chambrion* was eased toward the wings rather than taking center stage. The novel now seems primarily remarkable for two striking features of its narrative method: the extreme streamlining associated with its then-distinctive use of dialogue—a method now familiar, but which Ponson helped to pioneer—and the acute contest that develops between the conflicting moral requirements imposed on the author by what he believed to be the pattern of reader demand.

By the 1860s, narrative melodrama had evolved to such a high pitch that its villains were very villainous indeed, but its heroes were still hamstrung by the limitations on what they could do in response while remaining within the guidelines of moral behavior. This is a problem that has not gone away today, of course—it still causes unease and controversy if and when heroes in TV series resort to proactive violence and torture to achieve their supposedly just ends—but Ponson felt such pressure much more keenly, and all the more awkwardly because the various editors for whom he was working simultaneously sometimes had different views as to what it was permissible for heroes to do in contesting the cunning and violence of villains. That is one reason why ambiguous characters like Rocambole, part-villain and part-hero, first came to the fore in that period.

When the narrative of *Le Chambrion* abandons slick dialogue to go inside the heads of its characters and analyze their decisions—as it does more often than most of Ponson's works— what it finds there is a moral labyrinth in which it is exceedingly difficult to navigate reliably, and which seems to have no center or exit. If the results of that authorial struggle seemed inept or absurd to refined critics like Vapereau—although it clearly did not to the readers who followed Ponson's serials avidly— it was not entirely the author's fault, and the fact that we can now examine the struggle from a more distanced and objective viewpoint allows it to take on an interest that was less obvious at the time.

Although the Chambrion is set up as a much less ambiguous hero than Rocambole, and is a character for whom the author obviously has a lot of sympathy, the consequent fact that he is compelled thereby to take the question of what he ought to do, and what it might or might not be morally justifiable for him to do, very seriously indeed, creates knotty difficulties that have no easy narrative solution. Modern authors, with far more license to contend with the logical requirements of melodrama, have a lot more freedom to negotiate such questions than Ponson had—or thought that he had—and the Chambrion might therefore seem to be a rather weak-kneed character to modern readers, but that is precisely what makes him interesting in his historical and narrative context. At any rate, the predominance of such difficulties helps to explain why *Le Chambrion* turned out, in the end, not to be much of a mystery story—although it remains more mysterious than it seems, for reasons that are best left for discussion in an afterword.

The same struggle between the logical demands of melodrama and the moral demands of the literary context can also be seen in the three shorter stories that I have added to the short novel—which therefore help to provide a context for it, as well as to add necessary bulk to what would otherwise be a rather slim volume. The conflicts are eased in each of the three cases by social and historical settings that impose a seemingly-unquestionable moral code on the stories' protagonists, but in each case the apparent simplicity is recomplicated by an adventurous story-line that illustrates the difficulties involved in adhering to those moral codes in sticky situations.

"La Fée, conte de Noël," here translated as "The Fairy: A Christmas Story," which I have taken from the version belatedly reprinted in *Écho des Feuilletons* for 1884-5, had been previously a published in pamphlet form as *La Fée de Noël* in 1854, presumably having appeared in the Christmas issue of a newspaper before that. It dates from the early years of Ponson's career, before he began mass-producing serials simultaneously and threw all hope of attaining literary respectability to the winds. By that time the genre of Christmas fantasies was well-established, following the enormously successful precedents established in England in the 1840s by Charles Dickens, and Ponson's faithfully reproduces both the sententious moralism and the three-step narrative process typical of such tales—but with typical Ponsonian excess, he doubles up the three steps, and takes the second set in a far more problematic direction than the first.

"Une légende fatale," here translated as "A Fatal Legend," was originally published in the *Bulletin de la Société des gens de lettres* in 1854 and was reprinted in *La Presse Littéraire* in the same year (I have used the latter version, although both are available on *gallica*). The story uses the same doubling technique as "La Fée," embedding a melodramatic tale of the Age of

Chivalry modeled on Christian legends within a contemporary story, thus providing the same kind of binocular vision as its counterpart, with a similar slight unease—although the story's most spectacular, and arguably most interesting, element is its flamboyant recomplication of the long but then still-unpolished tradition of tales of diabolical pacts.

"Le Castel du diable," here translated as "The Devil's Manse," was one of Ponson's earliest attempts at serial fiction, first published as a feuilleton in *Le Journal des chasseurs* in 1852, and it was the first to go manifestly awry. It was reprinted as a pamphlet, as *Le Castel du Diable, histoire cynégétique* [i.e. a hunting story] in 1853, included in *L'Écho des Feuilletons* in 1860, and then reprinted again in a volume by Dentu in 1865 which only bore the title *Le Castel du diable*, even though the story was followed therein by two further novellas. Both are quite unrelated to it, although they share a common setting themselves and had previously been published as *Le Trou de Satan* in 1863.

When Ponson was interviewed about his writing methods for *Le Journal* in 1861 he claimed that he would approach editors and offer them a serial, asking them to give him three episodes to get it under away, and that if the readers liked it he would undertake to extrapolate it indefinitely, but would bring it to a swift conclusion if they did not. It is possible that when he boasted of his versatility he had "Le Castel du diable" ironically in mind, as it changes direction abruptly and completely no less than four times, starting out (as might be expected, given its origin) as a straightforward tale of hunting mania, transforming itself into a legend-based tale of the supernatural, backtracking to become a flirtatious tale of frustrated sexual conquest and finally giving up the ghost after feigning, briefly, to become a tale of cunning military double-dealing.

There is no better illustration than "Le Castel du diable" of the hazards of attempting to respond to reader demand on the hoof, or of the extreme absurdities that can result from trying to do so with bold ingenuity. Even so, Ponson contrived to publish the story four times, so it must be regarded as a success in purely professional terms, and perhaps as a triumph of sorts. Although it is now more interesting as an exotic narrative specimen than as a story in its own right, it does retain a certain stubborn charm, and certainly illustrates Ponson's avid determination to master the art of crowd-pleasing. He did that more successfully than any of his contemporaries in the latter part—some might say the decadence—of the Second Empire. It is a pity that he was condemned to feature in subsequent literary history merely as an example of the follies of his era; he was considerably more interesting than that, as this volume will hopefully illustrate.

THE CHAMBRION
A MYSTERIOUS STORY

I.

"What is a Chambrion?"[2]

In those villages lost in the depths of the forest, as hunters say, a Chambrion is a peasant who has made a tacit vow of solitude and celibacy.

If he has a little land, he cultivates it; if he has none, he works as a journeyman, either as a laborer, a vine-grower, a barn-worker or a woodcutter.

The Chambrion lives alone, in a small house almost always distant from any other habitation, usually situated in the woods. He does his own housework and cooking, and repairs his own garments; and in winter, when the snow forbids him any other work, he does not disdain to spin a little wool in order to knit socks.

Almost invariably, the Chambrion is a person over whom some mystery hangs, or upon whom some painful memory weighs. One is a child of the hospice, another had parents who had a bad reputation. Some are even accused of practicing a

---

2. The term *chambrion* does exist in other texts than Ponson's (and he used it again himself as a trivial noun in *Memories d'un gendarme*, 1867) but it is exceedingly rare; the noun is derived from the verb *chambrer*, one of whose meanings is forcibly to isolate someone in a single room—like, for instance, someone put in quarantine...or, of course, someone obliged to produce four or five daily serial-episodes six days a week.

little witchcraft. Others are reputed to have remedies against anthrax, rabies or the pox. If, on Sunday, they take the risk of going to the village inn, they are greeted with astonishment mingled with dread. At a ball, the Chambrion does not often find a girl who will consent to dance with him. There are few examples of Chambrions who have ended up getting married.

On the other hand, he is generally a good worker, honest, obliging and hospitable. A hunter caught out by the rain can find shelter with the Chambrion, a log fire and a pitcher of something to drink. Some accuse him of being a poacher—and, in fact, who is better placed than he is to exercise that illicit industry? His house is on the edge of the forest; he knows its trails better than anyone, hears the partridges calling, sees the hares leaping and the rabbits in their warrens at dusk. He can tell, by the eastward flight of a roe deer lightly marked in the mud of a forest trail, whether it is a doe or a buck. The droppings, tracks and lairs of wild boar are familiar to him.

The Chambrion, however, has never been brought to court. The rural policemen smile when someone tells them that he is a poacher; purely out of condescension for a neighboring landowner jealous of his hunting, the police have searched his house for traps, bait, the classic noose and the no-less-classic decoy bird, but they have found nothing. The Chambrion has been slandered.

One last characteristic trait: the Chambrion generally has a more cultivated mind than other peasants. He can read and write; he borrows books from the curé and the schoolmaster. Sometimes, he even composes naïve songs, both words and music, while going through the woods that surround his dwelling.

II.

The traveler who leaves Paris in Autumn by the morning train[3] will see rapidly passing by, to the right and the left, the beautiful nature of the banks of the Seine of which the sensitive Madame Deshoulières[4] has sung in hexameters. Soon, the green hills, the meadows bordered with poplars, the elegant villas built on the slopes and the white villages, advances sentinels that seem to say "the great city is there, just over the horizon" all disappear.

When the gray belfries and ruined tower of the pretty town of Étampes have disappeared behind him, the traveler feels his heart contract.

Here is the wilderness! A wilderness of cultivated fields, a desolate horizon of fertile terrains, where everything has been sacrificed to speculation and profit. It is the Beauce!

The Beauce, without a tree or a ripple in the ground, without a stream or a pond; the Beauce, scorching in summer, frozen in winter.

For more than a hour you traverse that ocean of clods of earth and bare fallow land; then, finally, a black line fringes the horizon. It is the forest of Orléans.

But you do not have time to breathe and gather courage, for, after the forest comes the city: a sad city, deserted, abandoned,

---

3. Although Ponson does not specify which train he means, it is obviously heading southwards. The French railway network expanded very rapidly between the late 1840s and the early 1860s, but many places were still inaccessible by rail in 1865, and the track to and through Orléans was one of the most heavily used. During the time-period covered by the story the region in which it is set was, in effect, transformed by the railway from a remote and little-known wilderness to an area ripe for commercial development.

4. The poet Antoinette du Ligier de la Garde Deshoulières (1638-1694), prominent at Louis XIV's court for some time, although she subsequently fell on hard times. She was described by Voltaire as the best of female French poets. Ponson, who was no feminist, probably thought that was damnation with faint praise, but it was not.

populated with old town houses in which grass paves the court-yards. A Thébaïd of roofs and streets, as the Beauce is a waste-land of fields and farms.

Fortunately, your soul will soon expand. The train has passed rapidly over the Loire. It emerges from the vale; it arrives in the Sologne.

There is no need to be an artist or a poet to admire that melan-choly landscape, The Sologne is a vast territory of an adorable and charming sadness. It is covered in large woods, streaked by small watercourses, dotted with ponds, and here and there, through the stands of fir-trees, the setting sun draws myriads of sparks from the flamboyant windows of an old château built in red brick.

It is in this region that our story will unfold.

III.

"Go along there, Gendarme, and carry on straight ahead to the house."

Thus spoke a boy of fifteen or sixteen years, one morning in the month of October 186*, on the edge of a wood not far from Salbris, the major town of the canton of Sologne. He was addressing a dog, which undoubtedly understood marvelously, for it turned on its heels, put its tail between its legs, and, instead of going across the fields, slipped into a ditch, which it followed in the manner of a fox.

As for the boy, he hid his rifle in a bush and plunged into the wood, running flat out and saying to himself: "If I can get to the Chambrion's before that damned Maupert, Clappier's policeman,[5] catches up with me, I'll be safe.

---

5. The boy refers to Clappier's gamekeeper as a "policeman" because the *gardes champêtres* who shared the task of policing rural areas with the town-based gendarmes in the nineteenth century had started out as royal gamekeepers, accumulating other responsibilities as time went by and governments changed, and private gamekeepers still had certain policing privileges in 1865—as the plot of the story makes evident.

And while running, he wrapped in his shirt a hare, still warm, which he had just killed, and which he did not want to abandon. The wood was dense, but the boy crawled, ran, slid and leapt over young hedges and bushes like a rabbit chased by speedy beagles.

In less than a quarter of an hour he arrived on the edge of a clearing, in the middle of which stood a small house, from the roof of which a thread of smoke emerged.

It was still daytime, but night was not far distant—a cold, damp night such as October brings to the feverish and melancholy region of Sologne. The young poacher went across the clearing in three bounds, arrived at the door of the cottage, put his hand on the latch and launched himself inside, shouting: "Save me, Chambrion!"

A man was seated in front of a fire of oak-twigs and fir-branches, which was flaming sufficiently to illuminate the interior of the house in collaboration with the last rays of the dying day, and the pages of a book that the man was turning slowly when the boy entered his home so precipitately. He put his book down on a block of wood placed beside him and got up.

"Oh, it's you, Brocart," he said. "Some policeman's chasing you, you're afraid of being hauled up in court, perhaps sent to prison...and you think that by taking refuge here you'll be out of danger."

"You can save me if you want to, Chambrion," said the child.

"That depends. If it's a government policeman..."

"No, no," said the boy to whom he had given the singular name of Brocart, "it's Maupert, that old rogue Père Clappier's gamekeeper."

At that name, the owner of the small house shivered; a cloud passed over his forehead, and a glimmer of somber hatred shone in his eyes.

"Sit down there," he said, "and get warm."

"But if Maupert comes...."

"Maupert never comes in here."

"But my hare...." And the child let the hare fall upon the

earthen floor of the cabin.

The Chambrion picked up the hare, took a knife from his pocket, made an incision in the left foot between the tibia and the tendon, passed the right foot through that opening, and then hung the hare under the mantle of the fireplace.

"Well," he said, "don't I have the right to have a hare in my house, since the owners of the château have given me permission to hunt, and we're in the woods dependent on the Sapinières here?"

As the Chambrion said that, there was a noise of confused voices and hurried footsteps outside.

"It's Maupert," said the child, trembling lightly once again.

"If it's him, he's not alone."

Indeed, the footsteps and voices were coming closer, and the Chambrion, sticking his face to the window-frame garnished with oiled paper that served his house as a window, looked outside.

Two men armed with rifles were jut coming into the clearing. One had a beard that was already going gray; he was dressed in a blue smock, over which there was a broad sash ornamented with a gamekeeper's badge. The other, who was a young man of twenty-seven or twenty-eight, wore a hunting-jacket in bottle-green velvet with a matching game-bag, long leather gaiters coming up to his knees and one of those hats, also in velvet, that is known in the profession as a "melon."

Having arrived a hundred paces from the house, the two men appeared to confer, and the Chambrion, whose hearing was as keen as his sight was piercing, heard the ensuing conversation.

"Monsieur Hector, I'll put my hand in the fire to swear that that little bandit the Brocart is in the Chambrion's house."

"Well then, we'll have to go look for him there," replied the man in the melon.

"Go on, then—you go, Monsieur Hector; you know that I never go into François Véru's house."

"Why's that?"

"We've had our differences in the past."

"Which is to say," said Monsieur Hector, "that you went looking for a quarrel one day, and he gave you a thrashing."

"That's as may be," said the gamekeeper in a surly tone.

"Well, I'm going there, and if the Brocart's in there, I'll drag him out by his ear."

"This time," the gamekeeper muttered, "I'll make my sworn statement in such a way that he'll go to prison. He's a recidivist."

The young-man in the hunting-jacket took a few steps toward the house.

Then the Chambrion turned round and silently showed the young poacher a ladder leaning against the wall, which put the ground floor of the house in contact with the hay-loft.

The child climbed up, as nimbly as a cat, and disappeared into the loft, whose trap-door he replaced.

When the trap-door of the loft had closed again the Chambrion moved the ladder, laying it down horizontally behind the door; then he went to sit down calmly by the fire, and picked up the book that he had been holding in his hands a little while before.

The Chambrion, who answered to the name of Fançois Véru, was a young man of about twenty-eight or thirty, of medium height, with broad shoulders, a high forehead and calm blue eyes, with energetic features that were also full of a gentle melancholy.

He was a peasant, but a peasant less coarse than the others, to judge by the slimness of his hands and the care he lavished on his long chestnut-colored beard.

His cottage, which comprised a single room, was a model of neatness and respectability. The bed, set up in a corner, was enveloped by curtains in Rouen cloth with a floral pattern; a dresser in old pear-wood enclosed plain crockery sparkling with whiteness; a few pieces of wrought brass were hanging on the walls, and above the fireplace there was a rifle and a hunting-knife. Finally, and rather exceptionally, there was a set of shelves in one corner that supported a dozen volumes of various sizes, some of them bound and others with paper covers.

The Chambrion was literate. He occupied himself in learning

a host of things from books during the long winter evenings, when there was no work.

The young man who answered to the name of Hector knocked on the outside of the door—two discreet little raps that seemed to betray a certain hesitation.

Francois Véru, alias the Chambrion, got up and went to open the door.

"Oh, it's you, Monsieur Hector," he said, in a tone of perfect indifference. "Are you thirsty? Or has some young boar that ran at your dogs and stood up to them, wounded you?"

"That's not why I've come," Monsieur Hector replied, awkwardly.

"In that case," the Chambrion continued, impassively, "perhaps you're cold. The weather's rather harsh this evening. Sit down—I'll get you something to drink."

And the Chambrion threw another armful of fire-branches into the hearth.

But Monsieur Hector remained standing, while darting rapid glances around him.

"Are you looking for something?" asked the Chambrion.

"No, but...it's odd, all the same...."

"What is?"

"I thought you weren't alone."

"Well, as you can see...."

Monsieur Hector darted one last glance under the bed, but did not even think about the hay-loft.

"It's that animal Maupert," he said, "who claimed that the Brocart was here."

"What roebuck?" asked François Véru, playing on the word.[6]

"The old Malbéque woman's boy," Monsieur Hector replied.

---

6. *Brocart* usually means "brocade" nowadays, but *Larousse* also gives it as one of the alternative spellings of *brocard* [roebuck], both terms deriving from the Old French *broquard*, and the latter meaning is clearly the one intended here. Indeed, the French text occasionally renders the nickname as Brocard, although I have unified the spelling to comply with the more frequent version.

"The diabolical little poacher who's killing our rabbits."

"Oh, but, excuse me. Monsieur Hector," the Chambrion interjected, naively, "you don't know your boundaries very well, for the woods around my house are the demoiselle's, and if the Brocart was hunting here, it's my business."

"It's not for having been hunting here that I'm after him," the young man said.

"Why, then?"

"It's for having taken a hare under the windows of the Meunerie. He ran away, but Maupert saw him. He went into the wood, and I thought...."

"Monsieur Hector," said the Chambrion, "Maupert's a bad man, and you're wrong to trust him."

"But he saw him, I tell you!" said Monsieur Hector, imperiously.

"Well, let him run after him then."

"But Maupert claims," Hector persisted, "that the Brocart's in your house."

The Chambrion laughed delightedly, showing his white teeth. "Call Maupert, then," he said, "and let him come and look."

Monsieur Hector called Maupert, but the gamekeeper did not budge. One might have thought that he dared not approach the Chambrion's house.

"Well," the latter shouted to him, ironically, "arcn't you coming?"

The gamekeeper's only response was to turn his back and go away. Hector saw him disappear into the fir-trees. Instead of following him, though, he turned back to the Chambrion.

"I need to talk to you," he said.

"Oh, that's different. Go on then, Monsieur Hector—I'm listening."

Hector at down again by the fireside, hesitated momentarily, then appeared to make an effort.

"Tell me, Chambrion," he said, "you know the demoiselle don't you?"

"Of course I know her," François Véru replied, frowning.

"You see her often."

"Oh, nearly every day...wasn't I born in the château myself?"

"That's true. Then you've spoken to her."

"As I'm speaking to you."

"Well, what do you think of her?"

"Well," said the Chambrion, "that might be asking a lot."

"Why? I want to know whether she's pretty."

"What does that have to do with you?"

"Answer me—is she pretty?"

"Pretty enough to kneel before."

"Really!" said Monsieur Hector, marveling.

"Ah!" said the Chambrion, with a mocking smile. "That lights up your imagination, does it?"

"Perhaps."

"But what does it have to do with you whether the demoiselle is ugly or pretty?"

"It's just that I have a plan in mind...."

"Really?" said the Chambrion, still ironic.

"She has property, doesn't she, the demoiselle?"

"Perhaps three thousand acres, and woods, and houses in Paris...and money in the bank. But what are you trying to get at, Monsieur Hector?"

"This: Père Clappier's a miser...he doesn't want to give me my marriage-portion. If I married the demoiselle, I'd have no further need of it, and could wait patiently for him to die."

The Chambrion was still smiling.

"Come on, what do you think, François?" Hector continued.

"Well, it's necessary to consider...."

"You know very well that I don't have any prejudices."

"Oh, as to that, no!" sniggered the Chambrion.

"People can say whatever they like about her...that doesn't frighten me...."

"But people have only ever talked about one thing," the Chambrion said, dryly. "Her parents' misfortune—that's all. That's not her fault."

"All the same," sniggered Hector, "the amorous aren't thick

on the ground hereabouts...."

"Pooh! Who knows?"

"And suitors aren't rallying to the call," the young man continued, sardonically."

"And that's why you want to enter the lists?"

"Well, you can imagine that it would suit me very well to have the Sapinières and the rest of the dowry. I just need to see the demoiselle."

"That's easy," said the Chambrion.

"You think so?"

"Well, all you have to do is pay her a visit," the Chambrion sniggered. "She'd let you in. Go."

The young man did not perceive the peasant's muted irony. "Do you often go to the château?" he asked.

"That depends. I'm going there this evening...the demoiselle has asked for me."

"Well," said Hector, "mention me to her. See what she thinks."

"I won't forget," the Chambrion replied.

"And I'll come back tomorrow," the younger Clappier added. "You can tell me what she says."

"Yes, Monsieur Hector."

"Goodbye, then...until tomorrow. As he left, the young man added: "You'll swear to me, won't you, that the Brocart isn't here?"

"Well," said François Véru, laughing, "you certainly don't pay any heed to the proverb that says 'he who chases two hares at the same time will find an empty bush.' Since you're concerned with the demoiselle, leave the Brocart alone."

"You're right, after all," said Hector, who resumed thinking about the mysterious heiress, whom it was said that no one wanted, but who nevertheless had a fine dowry. And he went away, repeating: "Until tomorrow."

François Véru, alias the Chambrion, remained standing on the threshold of his door until he had seen the other disappear on the far side of the clearing; then he went back in and closed the door. No longer giving any thought to the child he had hidden in the loft, he sat down by the fire and fell into profound thought.

"An unexpected fatality!" he murmured, eventually. "Why did such a thought have to germinate in the mind of that imbecile? He's capable of presenting himself at the château...to make his request of Madame Gertrude! Should I say something? The son of that brigand Clappier...never!"

The Chambrion stopped, wiped away a few drops of sweat that had suddenly formed on his brow, and then, remembering the Brocart, replaced the ladder under the trap-door to the hay-loft.

The Brocart, who was on the alert, lifted the trap-door and showed his cunning face.

"Have they gone?" he asked.

"Yes—you can come down."

"They won't come back, will they?"

"No, don't worry. Come and get warm. When it's dark you can go."

"As long as Maupert isn't watching out for me nearby."

"I'll go with you to the edge of the grounds of the Sapinières, and give you a message for Monsieur Horace."

"That's fine by me," said the boy.

The Chambrion put his smock on over his shirt, and picked up his game-bag—an indispensable item of equipment for any Solognot—and his rifle, which he posed on his shoulder like a soldier on the march.

"Come on," he said to the Brocart.

"What about my hare?" said the boy. "Are you going to keep it?"

"You would have sold it, wouldn't you?"

"Yes, to Chambolle the poulterer, who goes to Romorantin every Saturday, and gets provisions from us."

"How much does he pay you for a hare?"

"Forty sous."

"I'll give you three francs. Here, take them." And the Chambrion took three twenty-sou coins from his pocket.

"That's too much," said the child, who was conscientious.

"No," said François Véru, "not if you'll promise me one thing."

"What?"

"I'll tell you on the way—let's go."

But the Brocart put his hand on François' shoulder. "No," he said. "I want to know now. What do I have to promise?"

"Not to hunt tomorrow."

"And why's that?"

The Chambrion looked at the boy sadly. "I'd like to find you some honest work that will provide you and your mother with bread."

"That's not possible," said the Brocart, boldly. "I have the soul of a poacher; game is my enemy. You could give me white bread to eat every day, but if it were at the price of not touching a rifle again, I wouldn't want it."

"What if I were to place you as a kennel-groom somewhere?"

"Oh, that would suit me...provided that one could go out hunting occasionally."

"We'll see about that. Come on."

The Chambrion put the hare in his game-bag and, after letting the Brocart go out, closed the door, turned the key and hid the key under the window-shutter.

Then, as they set out, taking one of the little forest paths known as "false roads" the Chambrion said: "You detest Maupert, then?"

"Oh, that brigand," said the child. "It's because of him that my father died in prison."

A cloud passed over the Chambrion's face at the word "prison," but he continued: "And Père Clappier?"

"That man," the boy said, "I'd like to see skinned alive, for he forced my poor mother and me to sell our last chair for the hundred francs we owed him. We've been living on charity for a year. So, when I kill a hare on the Meunerie's land, it seems to me that I'm getting two for one."

The Chambrion seemed to take nourishment from the hatred that the child formulated with such naïve crudity. "That's unfortunate," he said.

"Why?"

"Because I might have been able to place you with him."

"With Père Clappier? Thanks. I'd rather die of starvation... and he doesn't have any dogs."

"Monsieur Hector has some."

"Oh, well," said the boy, "if I were in his service...I believe I'd set fire to the kennels."

"All right," said the Chambrion. "Come and see me tomorrow, and we'll see."

They arrived at the broad edge of the forest, beyond which fields could be seen, over which a residue of daylight still shone.

"Here's a road," said François Véru. "You don't have a rifle and it's a public road. Run along."

"Aren't you sending me to Monsieur Horace?"

"Listen, and you'll see that there's no need...." The Chambrion extended his hand toward the depths of the forest.

The shrill and strident sound of a horn was heard, and then a young and sonorous voice calling: "Here, Ramoneau! Here, Ravaude! Here, my little dogs!"

"Monsieur Horace," the Chambrion said, "is hunting over there, by the Mare aux Chevrettes[7]—can you hear him calling his dogs?"

"Yes, that's his horn and his voice," the child replied.

"Well I'll deliver the message myself by going to meet him."

"But say, François," the child persisted, "since you want to make me a kennel-groom, why don't you place me with Monsieur Horace?"

"We'll see about that. I have an idea—come to see me tomorrow."

The child shook hands with the Chambrion, to whom he owed his salvation, and ran off, cutting through the fields along the edge of the forest, along the by-road.

---

7. *Chevrette* is a diminutive of *chèvre* [goat], but it is also used to refer to a female roe deer, and the pond in question obviously has that name because roe deer go there to drink.

The Chambrion, by contrast, went back into the woods, and headed through the oaks that had now replaced the firs, toward the hunter whose horn continued to resound.

Ten minutes later he arrived at the edge of a pond; it was the Mare aux Chevrettes.

The hunter was sitting at the foot of a tree, and had set his rifle down beside him. One of his dogs was running around the rim of the pond; the other was barking madly in the wood a short distance away.

It was nearly dark, but a crepuscular gleam was reflected in the dormant water of the pond, and the hunter saw François Véru emerge from the forest. "Bonjour, Chambrion," he called to him.

"Bonsoir, Monsieur Horace. I heard your horn and I've come...aren't you going to call your dogs back?"

"Yes—Ravaude is there, and Ramoneau has heard me...and since you're here, François, you can give me a hand to carry away this fellow..."

The Chambrion then perceived a magnificent roebuck extended at the young hunter's feet—for the hunter was a young man of twenty-five or twenty-six, elegantly dressed and with an open, honest face that was not unhandsome.

"Aha!" said the Chambrion. "That makes a good thirty this year, doesn't it?"

"Very nearly. Where were you going when you heard me?"

"To the Sapinières,"[8] said the Chambrion.

Monsieur Horace shivered. "You're very lucky," he said, to be able to go into the château whenever you like."

"You think so?" said the Chambrion, in a melancholy tone.

"Alas!" sighed the hunter. "Whereas I...."

"You, Monsieur Horace, go there too often...."

"What do you expect? If you knew how much I love Denise...."

The Chambrion sat down next to the hunter in a familiar fashion and said to him, sadly: "Have you ever thought about

---

8. A *sapinière* is a fir plantation.

what would happen if the demoiselle knew the truth?"

"Shut up, Chambrion, shut up!"

"But she will know, some day...no matter how hard it is for people to get to her. The local people are wicked."

"I've often thought of taking her away, a long way from here...."

"Madame Gertrude doesn't want that," said the Chambrion. "She's like me and you, Monsieur Horace. She knows full well that your father...."

"Oh. I'd swear," said the young man, vehemently, "that my father was innocent of the infamous action for which he's reproached!"

"Certainly, yes," murmured the Chambrion, in an emotional voice. "I think as you do, but the entire neighborhood thinks otherwise...and it's as if there were an abyss between the demoiselle and you."

"And yet, you know how I love her...."

"Oh...yes...!" stammered the Chambrion. Then he stood up and picked up the roebuck, which he placed over his shoulders. "Come on, Monsieur Horace, let's go," he said, "And prepare yourself for some bad news that I have to give you."

"What do you mean?" said the young man, in an anguished tone.

"A suitor has appeared for the demoiselle."

"So? What does that matter to me? Denise will refuse him...."

"Yes," said the Chambrion, "but that suitor will tell her who you are, and then...."

"Shut up! Shut up, François!" cried Horace, in a strangled voice.

The Chambrion had set out *en route*, at an abrupt and unsteady pace. "I should have told you that later," he said. "Come on, it's a long way from here to your house."

"Yes, but we're not far from the Sapinières, and you can take the roebuck there."

"All right," said the Chambrion, "and when I leave, I'll come to your house, because I want to talk to you...."

The hunter extended his hand to the Chambrion, and whistled for his second dog, which emerged from the undergrowth and ran around the pond. The two of them separated at a fork in the path.

Then the Chambrion, who was carrying the deer on his shoulders as if it were a hare, increased his pace, went sideways through a large thicket, and arrived at a gap in a hedge. That hedge enclosed the grounds of the Château des Sapinières.

The Chambrion went through the breach and, talking to himself, he murmured: "Well, wretch, don't you have the courage to speak?"

IV.

What was the story of the Château des Sapinières, the "demoiselle," Père Clappier and Monsieur Horace? That is what we are going to tell you, by recounting a terrible and mysterious drama that had unfolded in the locality fourteen years earlier.

In May 1840, the diligence providing a service between Orléans and Vierzon deposited a traveler at Salbris. He was a man of about thirty, of distinguished appearance; you could tell that he was a gentleman from a mile away.

As he had arrived at eight o'clock in the evening, he took a room at the modest inn where the diligence changed horses, and waited for he following day to seek out Maître X***, notary of Salbris.

"Monsieur," he said to him, "the commune of **** is attached to your notariat, and you are instructed to sell the Château ds Sapinières. I desire to visit that property, and to buy it, if I find it suitable."

The notary took him to visit the property; its price was four hundred thousand francs.

The traveler did not haggle. He handed over two hundred thousand francs to the notary, who gave him a receipt in the name of the Baron de Méreuil, retired officer, and agreed that the two hundred thousand francs that would complete the purchase of the property would be delivered at the end of the following year—which is to say, in the month of December 1841.

Now, the Château des Sapinières, which Monsieur de Méreuil had just acquired, had for a vendor a certain Monsieur Clappier, a local man who had amassed his fortune by buying and selling property.

Maître Clappier, as he was known, was the son of a timber merchant, who had left him a fairly sizeable fortune. He was a tall, stiff, thin man, nearer forty than thirty, avid for profit, as hard as a peasant, and a peasant himself, spending the winter at Romorantin, a little sub-prefecture as tedious as a rainy day, and the summer at a property of his known as La Meunerie.[9]

The Meunerie was a hovel built in the middle of three farms, successively bought, which constituted Sieur Clappier's estate. An old house with old timbers, a meager kitchen garden, an orchard planted with apple-trees, and a seed-nursery of acacias that was decorated pompously with the appellation of "the park"—such was the property that Madame Clappier, née Jousserand, called, on her days of vanity, the Château de la Meunerie.

In the vicinity of Orléans, the name "château" is applied to the meanest dovecot. It is the sole luxury of that avaricious population, which refuses itself all comfort for the excellent reason that words alone cost nothing. One has to pay wages to domestics, and horses need oats, but one can, without opening one's purse, have one's letters addressed to any old building, which immediately assumes the denomination of *château*. Thus, one said "the Château de la Meunerie," as one said "the Château des Sapinières"—but the Sapinières was an authentic château, built at the end of the reign of Henri IV, with a moat, turrets, a park a league square, and a residue of attractiveness. The worthy Clappier had bought it in order to break up the property, and that would have been done if Monsieur le Baron de Méreuil had

___
9. Literally, "the miller's house."

not arrived in time to save the pretty estate.

The deed of acquisition having been drawn up, Monsieur left the same evening, announcing his imminent return. Indeed, he was seen to return in early January, not in the diligence this time, bit in a post-chaise, accompanied by a pretty young wife and a two-year-old-child, and escorted by two domestics and a nurse.

Monsieur de Méreuil took up residence at the Château des Sapinières.

He adored his wife. He shunned society, having a taste for solitude. He put together a small hunting pack, equipped his stables, and from the very beginning he led the life of a country gentleman.

Fort fifteen leagues around Orléans, however, to the north or the south, one is not a stranger with impunity. Monsieur de Méreuil was a man well-born and well-educated, rich and affable; his wife was beautiful and charming. That was enough. The gossips of the province began to work overtime.

Where did these people come from? Were they not adventurers? Did people who had nothing to hide, nothing for which to reproach themselves, come in that fashion to a region that was not their own?

The town of Romorantin was in turmoil. The president of the tribunal talked about it in session; the Maire discussed it with his municipal council. The worthy Clappier was questioned. The worthy Clappier replied that Monsieur de Méreuil's money had seemed to him to be a sound alloy. But Madame Clappier opined that Monsieur de Méreuil was an ill-bred man and that his wife gave the impression of having been an actress—which is the supreme insult in the mouth of a stupid and evil-minded provincial woman.

In any case, Madame Clappier had reasons for not liking the proprietors of the Sapinières, and to understand those reasons, we shall permit ourselves a rapid sketch of that individual, who will not be one of the least salient in this story.

Mademoiselle Lucinde-Fortunée Jousserand, the daughter of

a Orléans ironmonger, had spent her youth reading romances of chivalry and persuading herself that she would one day marry some Knight of the Round Table—but Père Jousserand, an ironmonger in the Rue du Bourdon-Blanc, at the sign of the Clef-d'Or,[10] had married her off to the Clappier son, and from then on, the poetic Lucinde had had to renounce "entering the nobility."

However, when Maître Clappier bought the Château des Sapinières, with a view to breaking up the estate and selling it off piece by piece, his wife had had a dream: the dream of leaving the Meunerie to go and live in that beautiful residence, reserving herself the privilege of one day calling her son Monsieur Clappier des Sapinières.

A decisive man, but something of a Norman, the worthy Clappier had never said yes or no to that, in order to avoid domestic quarrels—but one fine morning, he had sold the Sapinières to Baron de Méreuil, and Madame Clappier, disappointed, had sworn a violent hatred for the stranger who had thus smashed her dreams of grandeur.

Monsieur and Madame de Méreuil paid little heed to the gossip of the province and, entirely occupied with the cares of their installation, limited themselves with regard to their neighbors to chilly conventional visits. Within a league of the Sapinières, however, there was a small property inhabited by a keen hunter, who immediately forged a link with the Baron de Méreuil. The property was named Le Sausseux,[11] its owner was Armand de Verne.

Monsieur de Verne was a widow, although he was scarcely thirty-five years old; he had a son from his marriage, who was being brought up by his wife's parents in Artois, where they lived.

Monsieur de Verne, who lived in Paris during the winter, spent the summer and autumn at the Sauuseux. He did not take

---

10. Approximately, "the sign of the Golden Key in Busy Bee Street."

11. In a slightly unorthodox version, "The Willows."

long to become a regular visitor at the Château ds Sapinières, and the province, which had nothing to do, sharpened its charitable tongues, and the rumor went around that Madame de Méreuil had accepted a courtship from him that was not very respectable.

These calumnies, muffled and vague at first, took on a certain consistency toward the end of November 1841, thanks to a journey that Monsieur de Méreuil made to Paris.

The Baron had gone to liquidate a considerable sum of money, with which he intended to pay the balance of the price of the Sapinières. When he came back, his first visit was to the Clappier family. He spent a part of the evening at the Meunerie and did not return home until very late. The domestics who saw him come in found his expression somber and anxious; then, shortly afterwards, they heard him go into the Baronne's room, where she was in bed, and reported thereafter that he had quarreled with her violently—after which, everything reverted to silence and sleep.

The next morning, however, a sinister rumor spread with lightning rapidity throughout the surrounding region. Madame de Méreuil had been found dead in her bed, and her neck bore the marks of strangulation.

As for the Baron, he was found in his study, his throat cut with a razor, and gave no further sign of life. The window was open; beneath the window footprints were found, which headed through the kitchen garden toward the bushes of the park.

The agents of the law, who hastened to the spot, did not interpret that indication as evidence of a murder. They gathered the rumors of the province, which burst forth like a thunderclap. They thought that they had discovered the truth in its entirety: Monsieur de Méreuil's study communicated with his wife's bedroom. When the husband had arrived home, Monsieur de Verne had made his exit through the window. Monsieur de Méreuil had strangled his wife, and had then cut his own throat.

By virtue of an unfortunate fatality, Monsieur de Verne had left the Sausseux during the night, and had gone to Paris. It was there that he learned about the terrible drama at the Sapinières, and of what he was accused. He was gripped by a fit of fever, got hold of a pistol, and blew out his brains.

From then on, the facts of the matter were not even debated, and from Orléans to Romorantin, and Vierzon to Blois, it was averred that Monsieur de Méreuil had killed his wife, that he had then killed himself, and that Monsieur de Verne, over-whelmed by remorse, had not had the courage to survive them.

Monsieur and Madame de Méreuil left a three-year-old child, a charming little blonde girl, who had only one remaining rela-tive, an old aunt of her mother's, who hastened to take care of her. That aunt was named Madame Gertrude, and she was a widow. A woman of determination and energy, she decided to brave opinion; instead of leaving the Sapinières, she stayed there and brought up her niece there.

Denise grew up under that funereal roof. She spent her child-hood in that solitude, henceforth a limitless desert for her, for it was as if the death of her parents had traced an iron circle around the château that no one wanted to cross.

Only once had a considerable man of the locality crossed the threshold of the Sapinières since the terrible event. That was Maître Clappier, who had come to claim his two hundred thousand francs—to the great amazement of the Baron's former valet, who had sworn by all the gods that, on the eve of his death, Monsieur de Méreuil had left for the Meunerie with the two hundred thousand francs in banknotes in his wallet.

As it was impossible to present the receipt that the worthy Clappier ought to have given him, however, it was necessary to pay. That circumstance was not widely known, however.

The Château des Sapinières had become a tomb, from which nothing emerged, and in which Mademoiselle Denise de Méreuil grew up, ignorant of her parents' misfortune. In fact, strangely enough, Madame Gertrude had trained her domestics so well, sending away all those of whom she was not sure, and had accepted with a kind of savage joy the ostracism with which her niece was afflicted, that Denise arrived at the age of eighteen without knowing anything positive about the catastrophe that had bloodied the château fourteen years before.[12]

All she had been told was that her father and mother had died suddenly.

One day, however, she had expressed astonishment at the fact that no one ever visited the Sapinières. Madame Gertude had explained to her that the inhabitants of the region were unsociable, badly brought-up, and that there was no one to see in the vicinity. Denise had contented herself with that explanation, but hazard had taken charge of enlightening her.

One morning, about three months before the day when we saw the young poacher nicknamed the Brocart seek refuge in the Chambrion's house, the staff of the château having gone to work in the fields and Madame Gertude having gone to Romorantin to see the lawyer in charge of her niece's affairs, Denise went for a walk in the park.

She was riding a pretty iron-gray pony of the Morvandell breed, which leapt over hedges and ditches like a true Scottish hunter. Denise was an intrepid horsewoman, and all the paths, "false roads" and woodlands comprising the estate around the château were familiar to her.

Having arrived at the enclosure of the park, she had given free rein to her pony, which had jumped the hedge and taken a path that it had obviously followed frequently, for it began to trot more rapidly, and then to whinny contentedly when, after a quarter of an hour, it perceived the Chambrion's hut in the middle of a clearing.

The Chambrion was Denise's friend. Although he was seven or eight years older than her, they had played together at the

---

12. These figures, and various others recorded in the course of the story, are not entirely consistent, probably because the chronology of the story became confused as Ponson wrote it—presumably in a tearing hurry—but perhaps because the version in the *Écho des Feuilletons*, published some time after the serial version in the *Moniteur du soir*, was subjected to few incompetent editorial changes in a failed attempt to reconcile the dates in the story with a different "present day."

Château des Sapinières. It was not until the Chambrion had turned fifteen that he had left the château, where his father had long been the gardener, to come and live in his little house lost in the woods.

At the sound of the horse's hoofbeats, the Chambrion, who was at home, had emerged precipitately and run to meet her.

"Bonjour, Fronçois," Mademoiselle de Méreuil said to him. "It's always necessary to come to see you, isn't it? Why do you so rarely come to the Sapinières now?" But she said it cheerfully, in a tender voice.

The Chambrion stammered a few words by way of excuse. "I've been working," he said.

"Not today, though."

"You must excuse me, Mademoiselle, I was busy recaulking a barrel."

"My aunt has need of you, though."

"Why is that, Mademoiselle?"

"To come and prune the trees in the kitchen garden."

"Well, I'll come tomorrow."

Denise had let herself slide to the ground, and the Chambrion had knotted the reins of the bridle on the horse's neck.

Behind the cottage there was a quarter of an acre of land converted into a garden. Beautiful moss-roses were swaying in the morning breeze there. The young woman set about making a bouquet, chatting and laughing with her childhood friend— but all of a sudden, she pricked up her ears.

"Do you hear that?" she said, extending her arm toward the heart of the forest. "There's a hunt passing by."

"It's only two dogs," said the Chambrion, "but they're chasing hard. Oh! They're holding firm—a boar has turned to face them."

Scarcely had the Chambrion finished than a gunshot rang out.

"Someone has killed the vile beast," said the young woman.

"No, Mademoiselle, the dogs are still giving voice."

Another gunshot rang out—followed, immediately afterwards, by a cry of distress: a cry of agony uttered by a human voice.

"Oh, my God!" cried the Chambrion. "The boar has undone the hunter!" And he had run into his house, unhooked his rifle, and raced off, saying: "As long as I get there in time...."

Denise had leapt nimbly on to her pony, and she followed the Chambrion through the woods—but the Chambrion seemed to have wings; he leapt over ditches, bounded from thicket to thicket, and the pony had difficulty following him.

The injured hunter as still shouting, and the dogs were howling. Then the Chambrion reached a clump of thorny bushes, stopped, raised his rifle and fired.

Suddenly, the dogs fell silent, and when Denise arrived on the scene of the strange battle, she saw a handsome young man, bloodstained and covered with mud, unconscious. Beside him lay the dead boar. The Chambrion had killed it outright.

As for the two dogs, they had been scored by the boar's tusks, and one of them had its entrails dangling from its gashed flank.

The Chambrion had knelt down beside the hunter and had taken off his hunting-jacket.

Denise approached tremulously.

"Fortunately," the Chambrion said to her, "the thrust of the tusk hasn't penetrated very far. The young man's trousers are thick...but three inches further, and he'd be dead."

The Chambrion and the young woman did not exchange any unnecessary words thereafter. They placed the unconscious young man over the saddle, and Francois Véru maintained him there while Denise, taking the pony by the bridle, said: "Let's go to the Sapinières—it's nearer."

When the young hunter, whose wound was not serious, recovered consciousness, he was lying in a bed in an unfamiliar room. A man and two women were at his bedside: François, Denise and Madame Gertrude.

He spent a month at the Sapinières, and emerged healed in the body but mortally wounded in the heart. He was in love with Denise.

Now that young man, who was unknown to them to begin with, took it into his head to reveal his name in the presence of Madame Gertrude and François Véru—and they both went pale. His name was Horace de Verne, and he was the son of the unfortunate Armand de Verne, who had blown his brains out on learning that he was being blamed for the death of the Baron and Baronne de Méreuil.

And the young man also began to tremble when he learned that he was at the Château des Sapinières.

"Monsieur," Madame Gertrude said to him, "I am firmly convinced that your father was an honest man and that my poor niece has been slandered, but in the name of Heaven, try to prevent Denise finding out what you, alas, know as well as we do."

Monsieur de Verne made the promise that was asked of him, but, driven by his heart, he returned to the château, initially at rare intervals, but then increasingly often....

Then Madame Gertrude, who shuddered on seeing the nascent love of the two children, between whom fate and society's slanders seemed to have raised an insurmountable barrier, thought of leaving the region and taking them both away. Madame Gertrude had distant relatives in Switzerland, with whom she had maintained communication. They lived in Lausanne. She wrote to them, and asked them to buy a small property on the shore of the lake on her behalf, telling them in her letter that she intended to spend the following spring there in the company of her newly-married niece and her husband.

Unfortunately, as you shall see, events were about to move with giant strides, and render that project impossible to realize.

V.

We left François Véru, alias the Chambrion, in the first chapter of this novel striding over the palisade of the park of the Sapinières and heading for the château. Even though he had a heavy burden—for the roebuck that Monsieur Horace had killed was a large specimen, and very heavy—he began to run.

He did not take the main driveway, however, which was the shortest route, but a more tortuous path that followed the hedge of the enclosure for some distance and arrived at a small rustic building with a thatched roof, whose windows were fitted with colored glass.

A trickle of multicolored light filtered out, and the gray spirals of a fire in the heart were escaping from the summit to climb into the ashen-blue sky, already full of stars.

When he was ten paces from the building in question, François stopped running, paused momentarily to catch his breath, and then advanced slowly on tiptoe and stuck his face to one of the window-panes.

Inside, the pavilion was round in shape. It was a pretty work-room and reading-room, furnished in bamboo upholstered in twill, in the middle of which could be seen a round table laden with books, fashion magazines and elegant periodicals, along-side a work-box. There was a piece of tapestry-work beside it.

In front of the table, Mademoiselle Denise de Méreuil was sitting and reading.

The Chambrion contemplated her, under the spell of a mute ecstasy.

She was a tall young woman, with a lithe and muscular figure, with broad shoulders, and a high forehead crowned with abundant blonde hair—not the ash-blonde praised by poets but that blonde with tawny gleams, reminiscent of bronze or copper, which antiquity attributed to the hair of Juno.

Large blue eyes; an aquiline nose; lips redder than roses; a mouth garnished with dazzling teeth; a long and flexible neck of irreproachable whiteness—such were the principal charac-teristic features of Mademoiselle de Méreuil's beauty.

She had a harmonious voice and an adorable ingenuous and impertinent smile.

How beautiful she is! thought the Chambrion, whose expres-sion became somber.

Then he rapped gently on the window-pane.

Denise looked up, made an eye-shade of her hand, recognized the Chambrion, and smiled at him.

The Chambrion went in, the roebuck over his shoulders.

"Oh!" the young woman said. "You've brought off a fine coup there, François."

"It's not mine, Mamzelle—it's Monsieur Horace's."

Denise blushed slightly. "Why didn't he come to bring it to me himself?" she said.

"I don't know," the Chambrion replied.

"His ears must have been burning today, though," the young woman continued, "for my aunt and I were talking about him. Sit down, François."

"It's not worth the trouble, Mamzelle. So you've been talking to Madame Gertrude about Monsieur Horace?"

"Yes, certainly. And do you know what we agreed?"

"No," said the Chambrion, curiously.

"Well, it appears that my aunt and I are going traveling."

"When?" demanded François, vehemently, his voice changing.

"In the spring, in four months time. We're going to Switzerland. Monsieur Horace will come to in us there. And then, you see, we'll be married, for he loves me very much... and I him."

"Ah!" said the Chambrion. "You're going to marry."

"It seems that in the region we're in," the young woman continued, naively, "nasty stories have been circulating about Horace's father, which are lies. In order not to give rise to gossip, however, we're going to marry a long way away...and if we find a nice house, either on the shore of Lake Geneva or in German Switzerland...."

"You'll settle there, will you?" said François, sadly.

"Yes, but we'll take you with us, my good Chambrion," the young woman went on, taking the peasant's hand and squeezing it gently. "You'd like to come with us, wouldn't you?"

François Véru made no reply. He lowered his eyes, and

furtively wiped away a tear with the back of his sleeve. Then, abruptly, he said: "Excuse me, Mademoiselle, but I'm a little pressed for time this evening. I'll carry the roebuck to the kitchen and be on my way." And without giving the young woman time to protest, François fled, and resumed his course toward the château.

"A strange fellow!" Denise murmured. "Always sad, always preoccupied, and only ever responding distractedly."

Then she picked up her book again—and did not give any thought to closing the door, which the Chambrion had left open when he went out.

A few minutes went by; then sudden footsteps sounded on the gravel of the pathway near the cottage.

At first, Denise thought that it was the Chambrion coming back; then she raised her head and uttered a cry of alarm. A man who was unknown to her had just stopped on the threshold of the pavilion.

He was armed with a rifle, which was slung over his shoulder, but his hunting-jacket and velvet cap immediately reassured Mademoiselle de Méreuil, all the more so as he took off his hat and bowed respectfully.

"A thousand pardons, Mademoiselle," he said, "for daring to present myself thus without having the advantage of knowing you."

Denise had risen to her feet, somewhat nonplussed. She replied, however, without overmuch embarrassment: "You've doubtless gone astray while hunting, Monsieur, and as the hedge of the park is in a poor state...."

"No, Mademoiselle," the unknown man interjected. "I know perfectly well where I am and to whom I have the honor of speaking."

Denise bowed, and waited for the strange visitor to explain.

"Mademoiselle," he continued, coming into the pavilion, "my name is Hector Clappier, and I'm your neighbor."

"Your name is not unknown to me, Monsieur," Denise replied. "In fact, I believe that it was you who sold the Sapinières to us."

"That was my father, Mademoiselle."

"Then please excuse me," the young woman went on, "if I refer you to my aunt, who takes care of our business affairs, for I know absolutely nothing about them."

"Forgive me, Mademoiselle, but it's to you that I desire to speak...."

"It's not a business matter, then?"

"It's a very serious matter," said the chubby young man, adopting a sprightly manner, "but a matter that only concerns you."

"But Monsieur, in truth...."

Hector Clappier had the aplomb of a rich bourgeois who does not beat around the bush. He deposited his rifle in a corner and sat down before Denise, confused as she was, had thought to offer him a seat. Then he continued, while she remained standing before him, utterly nonplussed.

"I don't want, Mademoiselle, to remind you of painful memories. However, you must know how you stand in the opinion of the region where we live, regarding your misfortune."

These words astonished Denise, but at the same time, awoke a keen curiosity in her heart. "Apart from the misfortune I had," she said, "of losing my parents when I was still in the cradle, I do not see, Monsieur, why I should be of any interest to the region where we live."

"It's a region full of prejudices, Mademoiselle—prejudices that I don't share myself. Ultimately, though, hereabouts, people stubbornly weigh the sins of parents upon children."

"I don't understand you, Monsieur," said the young woman, with a cold dignity. "I have always been brought up to respect my parents."

"It's not possible, however, that you don't know about their tragic end," said Hector Clappier, who displayed great astonishment.

"I've been told that they died suddenly."

Confronted by that naïve belief, another man would have retreated into silence, but the Clappier son was a savage and cruel churl, and he replied: "You've been deceived, Mademoiselle. Your father committed suicide..."

Denise uttered a scream.

"After having killed your mother," the executioner concluded, with a composure that merited capital punishment.

Denise leaned on the wall in order not to fall over, but God doubtless gave her courage at that moment, for she did not faint, and she looked Hector Clappier in the face. "Monsieur," she said to him, "I have never been told that, and I'm tempted to believe that you're lying."

"I'm telling the truth, Mademoiselle."

"And with what atrocious objective have you come to make such a revelation to me?" exclaimed the young woman, indignantly.

"I'm telling you this, Mademoiselle, because I'm critical of the opinion that people have of you, and I want to give the lie to it resoundingly."

Stunned by amazement, Denise looked at the young man wildly.

He went on: "My father is rich. One day, I shall have more than a million. I thought of putting a stop to all the gossip of the province and becoming your protector."

"My protector!" she said, in a tone that was close to madness.

"Yes. I have the honor of asking for your hand...."

That was the final straw.

Denise, terrified, let herself fall back into her chair, and hid her face, red with shame and indignation, in her hands.

Hector Clappier remained calm and cheerful, and imagined, for ten seconds, that the poor child was about to kneel before him and thank him for his generosity—but the illusion did not last long.

Denise stood up again, sublime in fury and dolor. "Monsieur," she cried, "if you do not leave this instant, my fiancé will come to slap your cheeks tomorrow."

"Your fiancé!" stammered Hector, astounded.

"Yes, Monsieur Horace de Verne, whom I love, and who is to

be my husband."

But Hector, cowed momentarily by the young woman's explosive indignation, straightened up at that name, and loud laughter emerged from his throat.

"Oh, indeed!" he cried. "There's a marriage that will be superb! You don't know either, then, that Monsieur Horace de Verne is the son of your mother's lover?"

Denise uttered a scream, and fell to the floor.

At that moment, too, a man came into the pavilion like a thunderbolt—and that man sent Hector sprawling with the back of his hand, and began kicking him furiously.

It was the Chambrion.

VI.

Two hours later, Mademoiselle Denise de Méreuil, prey to a delirious fever, was in danger of death.

Madame Gertrude and Horace, warned in all haste, were weeping by her bedside.

A man standing in the corner, as pale as a ghost, seemed to personify despair.

The doctor, who had been summoned in haste from a nearby village, arrived and examined the patient, who was laughing and crying by turns, and suffering from an ardent fever. "Until tomorrow," he said, "I can't guarantee anything—but a great joy might save her.

The Chambrion heard these words. Then he emerged from his statue-like immobility and went straight to Horace, abruptly seizing his hand. "Come with me," he said.

His tone was harsh and imperious, and there was something authoritative therein that impressed Monsieur de Verne greatly. Horace followed him.

The Chambrion drew him into the park and leaned on a tree. "Monsieur Horace," he said, "Mademoiselle Denise will die if she does not marry you."

"That's impossible now," Horace replied, in a despairing tone."

"It won't be, if I succeed in making the truth victorious."

"Ah!" said the young man, explosively. "You believe, as I do, that my father was innocent—but how can we prove it?"

"I shall prove it," said the Chambrion, with a sob in his voice. "And after fourteen years, it's high time that the truth came to light!"

"To light!"

"Yes, to light, Monsieur Horace—and I've been cowardly and cruel in not speaking sooner. Alas, if you knew...."

"What do you mean?"

"The entire region has been deceived. Your father is innocent, and Monsieur de Méreuil did not strangle his wife."

"Oh! Well...," Horace murmured, bowing his head.

"Monsieur and Madame de Méreuil were murdered!" cried the Chambrion.

Horace stifled an exclamation in his turn.

"It's the truth," said the Chambrion. "I was only a child then, but the terrible events of that night remain engraved on my memory."

Beads of sweat were forming on the young man's brow; he looked at the Chambrion with a kind of stupor.

The latter continued: "You see, Monsieur Horace, the demoiselle, you and I are all poor creatures that have been put in quarantine. It's necessary to get out of it. People call me the Chambrion because, since the age of fourteen, I've lived alone here, in the middle of the woods, and never asked for a young woman in marriage...." The Chambrion sighed. "Ah!" he went on. "Would you believe that I too would have liked a small house in the village, with a wife sitting by my hearth and children playing outside the door?"

"Well," said Horace, "why aren't you married? You're a good worker, François, you have a little land; everyone knows that you're an honest man...with that one can find a good hardworking girl who'd consent to become the mother of your children."

But the Chambrion, bowing his head, replied in a dull voice: "When you know the story that I'm about to tell you, Monsieur Hector, you'll understand why I'm not married."

"Is the story very terrible, then?"

"I was only eight years old then, but when I think about it, I felt my hair standing on end.

"My father worked by day at the Château des Sapinières as a gardener. He was already working there in the time of the former owners; Père Clappier had kept him on, and after him, Monsieur de Méreuil. He was a widower, and didn't want to marry again; we made our own soup. I went to the village school and I already had the taste for independence and liberty that has made me a Chambrion.

"My father, whose name was Jérôme, was somber and taciturn, bad-tempered since the death of my mother, whom he had loved dearly. He was avid for money, like the Marchois he was, for he had come to this region twenty years before, with a gang of stonemasons. He had left his original profession to become a gardener, but he often regretted it, saying that masons earned higher wages.

"He had bad instincts with regard to the bourgeois, especially when he'd been drinking, and he drank a lot. 'Why,' he often said, striking his fist on a table in a tavern, 'don't the bourgeois work like us, and have their living ready-made? God isn't just!'

"He read bad books, in which there was always question of the rights of man, but never of his duties. He didn't know A-B-C himself—but he frequented Old Mère Malbèque's tavern."

"Isn't that the beggar-woman who sometimes comes to the Sausseux?"

"The same. It's the Clappiers who ruined her, when her husband, who was a poacher, died in prison. In those days she kept a tavern, where a few bad lots met in the evenings, talking politics and reading a heap of books in which the poor were promised that the day was nigh when everyone would have ten acres of land, vines and a meadow, and would eat white bread every day.

"My father listened to all that, and while listening, he drank, and when he was drunk, he broke things, or picked a quarrel and got into a fight. He was hard and wild, and only one man could master him whenever he wanted—that was Monsieur Clappier, who wasn't called Maître Clappier yet. He could have made my father walk through fire—and the reason for that influence was very discreditable.

"My father had bought a little plot of land in the forest. For that, he'd needed money, and Maître Clappier had lent him fifty pistoles, at an enormous interest for poor folk like us. The interest was difficult to pay. My father worked hard, but never paid it off.

"Père Clappier had a mortgage on the property, and he only had to call in his loan to dispossess my father within twenty-four hours. That thought made him crazy. Sometimes, when he was in his cups, he became furious and shouted: 'I believe I'd commit murder in order not to owe anything to Père Clappier!'

"Hereabouts, everyone poaches; my father, like the rest, went out hunting in the evenings. He was caught one night in the estate woods, and a charge was laid against him. The Baron de Méreuil hadn't yet bought the Sapinières. The tribunal in Romorantin was severe. It took into consideration a previous conviction for the same offence, and after ordering the confiscation of the weapon it sentenced my father to two months in prison and a hundred franc fine.

"When he came out of prison, Père Jérôme—that's what people called him—found a bailiff who had a warrant against our house and had come to seize our poor possessions.

"I was all alone there, and I was crying.

"Fortunately, my father no longer had his rifle, for he'd have killed the bailiff who had come to collect the fine and the court costs—but the misfortune was that a hunter was passing by at that moment. That was Maître Clappier. He took my father aside and said to him: 'I don't want to let them sell your house, and I'll pay.'

"And he did, indeed, pay—but he made my father sign a paper in which the latter admitted that he owed him forty-five louis, payable on demand. The bailiff went away, but from that moment on, my father's temper became even worse, and I often hear him utter sinister words.

"Whenever he met Maître Clappier, the latter would say to him: 'I'll leave you in peace for now, Père Jérôme, but you'll have to pay me one day.' Then despair would grip the unfortunate man; he'd abandon his work, go to the tavern and get drunk. When he looked at me, though, his face softened, and tears came to his eyes. Oh, I swear to you that he loved me dearly, Monsieur Horace; he was harsh with everyone else, but he became good and tender with me. Perhaps he loved me too much...."

The Chambrion paused momentarily, and the young man saw a large tear roll silently down his cheek. He continued, however: "But I have to tell you about that terrible night of the twenty-ninth of December 1841.

"Ah!" said Horace. "Wasn't that the fateful night?"

"Yes—listen." The Chambrion made an effort to level his emotional voice, and continued: "My father was working in the park of the château; he was coppicing a stand of young fir-trees on the day that the Baron de Méreuil came back from Paris. The Baron was preoccupied, and a trifle pale, and a valet told my father that he had quarreled with Madame la Baronne. However, he came to see my father in the park and said to him: 'Go to the Meunerie and tell Monsieur Clappier that this evening after dinner, I'll mount my horse and bring him his money.

"My father left his work, put his smock on over his shirt, took me by the hand and took me to the Meunerie. As I said, I was eight.

"From the Sapinières to the Meunerie, as you know, it's scarcely a quarter of a league across the fields. When we arrived in Père Clappier's poultry-yard, we found him cleaning his rifle on the bottom step of the staircase. 'Oh, there you are,' he said. Have you brought me my money?'

"'Mine, no,' said my father, who began trembling, so much fear did his creditor inspire in him, but I've come to tell you that the Baron will bring his to you.'

"'When?'

"'This evening.

"'Money's always welcome,' muttered Maître Clappier, whose face lit up, suddenly radiant with good humor. At the same time, he patted me on the cheek amicably. 'He's growing well, the kid,' he said.

"Having delivered his message, my father turned to leave, but Clappier held him back. 'Come and have a drink in the kitchen,' he said. 'I need to talk to you.'

"Père Clappier had never been known to offer anyone a glass of wine; my father was astonished, and thought he hadn't heard correctly—but the property-dealer went into the kitchen first and said: 'Hey, Jeanette, get us a bottle of white Saint-Jean de B.' The maidservant, no less astonished, went down to the cellar.

"Then Clappier said to my father: 'I've got the devil of a thirst, and we'll clink glasses together.' Jeanette came back with two bottles of wine instead of one. 'Bring three glasses,' said the Maître.

"'Oh, excuse me, Bourgeois,' my father said. 'It's not necessary to make the youngster drink—that always comes too soon!'

"'Bah!' said Père Clappier, 'this little white is like sugared water.' And he handed me a glass.

"We drank water at home. When my father wanted wine, he went to the tavern—but I'd never tasted it, red or white. I emptied the glass in a single draught, though.

"Père Clappier was sitting by the fireside and he was chatting to my father, talking to him about the last harvest, the timber he'd cut and the hay—in a word, making a naïve and brutal display of his wealth. The two bottles were emptied.

"'That's odd,' said Père Clappier, 'I'm still thirsty. Fetch some more wine, Jeanette.'

"While my father was drinking, he had no further thought of going away. While he was talking to Maître Clappier, the farmhands arrived, one by one, for they ate at the Meunerie. Jeanette laid the table and ladled the soup into the bowls.

"'You can eat supper, since you're here, Jérôme,' said Maître Clappier. And he sat me down on a stool himself. The wine had gone to my head; everything around me was spinning.

"As the servants finished supper, the sound of hoofbeats was heard in the courtyard. Monsieur de Méreuil had arrived. 'Come on, kid,' my father said to me. "We have to go.' He stumbled as he stood up, but he was in a hurry to go. Maître Clappier's generosity frightened him.

"As we were about to out, a door opened at the back of the kitchen and Maître Clappier stuck his head around it. 'Don't go, Jérôme,' he said. 'I have to talk to you. Jeanette, give Jérôme another bottle.'

"Either be inadvertence or calculation, Père Clappier didn't close that door, which led to the dining-room. Now, the dining-room at the Meunerie is also the property-dealer's office, and it was in the corner of an old desk that he kept his money and his papers. It was, therefore, into the dining-room that Monsieur de Méreuil was introduced. And through the partly-open door, my father, who had resumed drinking, saw him place in front of him, on the desk, a heavy bag and a wallet.

"There was no one else in the kitchen any longer; even Jeanette, having washed the dishes, had gone to bed.

"Monsieur de Méreuil opened the bag, and my father, who was dizzy with the drink, saw gold coins piled up on the table. As I said, the wine I'd drunk had dazed me so much that I was only seeing things through a kind of cloud, and everything seemed to be spinning. Even so, I remember quite clearly that, after having displayed the gold, Monsieur de Méreuil counted out, one after another, thick wads formed of small pieces of paper, which resembled images, and which I later knew to be banknotes.

"Then Père Clappier locked all that in a drawer, which he double-locked—and only then did Madame Clappier come in. She bowed to the Baron and started chatting with him—which permitted Maître Clappier to come back into the kitchen briefly and speak in a low voice to my father.

"My father was drunk, but his eyes shone with a dark gleam. When Maître Clappier had finished talking to him, he got up abruptly and said to me: 'Come on now, boy.' He dragged me out of the kitchen' we went through the yard and the garden and soon found ourselves in the depths of the woods.

"My father was walking as if he had the gendarmes on his heels; he picked me up in order to jump the ditches. We passed through the copses and the undergrowth like phantoms. Finally, we arrived at the house. My father lit a fire and sat down beside it, putting his head in his hands. His expression was so grim that I kept behind him and didn't dare speak to him. 'Go to bed,' he said to me, brutally.

"I obeyed, and was so stunned that I didn't take long to fall asleep.

"A bright light woke me up, at the same time as the sound of voices, but I didn't dare part the bed-curtains. My father had lit a resin candle and he was talking to a man whose voice I recognized immediately. It was Maître Clappier. 'Yes,' the latter said. 'I'll give you back your note and you won't owe me anything. In addition, I'll give you one of those piles of gold coins that you saw shining on my table.'

"My father replied in a muffled voice, blurred by drunkenness; 'Are you the Devil himself, then?'

"Maître Clappier burst out laughing; then, after a pause, he added: 'Otherwise, my lad, it'll be necessary to see you dispossessed in a week. I have the right, and I'll send young Maupert after you, who's the best bailiff in Romorantin.'

"The name Maupert exasperated my father. Maupert was thirty-five then; he's fifty today. He'd been a bailiff for fifteen years, and he'd thrown more than one poor family into terror and mourning. He didn't so much do his job as savor it. Where one of his colleagues would take six weeks, he'd arrive to throw you into the straw in a fortnight. Unfortunately for him, he was a drunkard and a debauchee; what he earned, he ate. He ended up having his license revoked; then he sold his practice and fell into poverty. Today he's very happy to eat the Clappiers' bread, having become their private policeman.

"The name of Maupert caused my father such terror that he got up and went out. Maître Clappier followed him. What happened between them? Only God and Maître Clappier know. Drunkenness had me in its grip and didn't take long to close my eyes again—but I was woken up with a start for a second time. It was my father, coming back. This time he was alone, and I understood by his pallor that he was no longer drunk.

"His shirt was torn, and he had the bag that I'd seen Monsieur de Méreuil put on Maître Clappier's desk a few hours earlier slung over his shoulder. I drew back the curtains abruptly, and as I looked at him in terror, he stared at me with eyes crazed by madness. 'Look at me!' he growled. 'Take a good look—for you'll never see me again....'

"Then he lifted up the stone in front of the fireplace, where the fire had gone out, and he started digging a hole with his hands and fingernails. When the hole was big enough, he put the bag in it and let the stone fall back on top of it. After which he got up, ran to the bed, and took me in his arms—and I felt fiery tears on my forehead.

"'Look, boy,' he said to me, 'when you're a man, you'll lift up that stone, and you'll take what's underneath it. It's your father's blood!' He hugged me one last time, stifled a strangled sob, and fled.

"I've never seen him since—but I can't get rid of the idea, you see, Monsieur Horace, that he went to drown himself in the Saule, which flows a league from here. Remorse had taken possession of him, as soon the crime had been committed!"

Horace de Verne had listened to that strange tale without interrupting the Chambrion. When the latter had finished, Horace remained pensive momentarily. Then he said to him: "So you're convinced that Méreuil and his wife were murdered by your father."

"My father was only the instrument, Monsieur," the

Chambrion replied, in a dull voice. "The real murderer is Maître Clappier."

"But what if your father isn't dead?"

"Ah!" murmured the Chambrion. "It's that dread, Monsieur Horace, that has condemned me to silence until now...and then again, sixth months ago, what imperious interest did I have in denouncing the guilty party? You weren't here, the demoiselle was happy as she was...and yet, sometimes, remorse entered into my heart and gripped me by the throat. Did I really have the right to keep such a secret? But every time the confession rose from my heart, it died on my lips. By delivering Maître Clappier to justice, wouldn't I be denouncing my own father, to my shame?"

"Alas, that's all true," said Horace.

"But the time for hesitation is past," the Chambrion went on, gradually becoming more animated. "It's necessary to act...I don't want the demoiselle to die!" And he added, in a more emotional voice: "Since you love her...."

Horace took his hands. "Listen to me, François," he said. "There's no need to deliver that man to justice. Denise will believe you...and after that, what does it matter to us? Aren't we going to leave this accursed country...to live a long way away... abroad? I'll change my name. We'll be happy, and you won't be dishonored."

"But Monsieur Horace," said the Chambrion, firmly, "that's impossible now."

"Why?"

"Oh, you don't know the Clappiers! That brute named Hector has a plan in mind—he wants to marry the demoiselle."

"The wretch!"

"If we keep quiet, he'll talk. He'll make a noise, and such a scandal that the entire province will resound."

"And you think his father will back him up?"

"Doesn't he have an interest in the truth never being discovered?"

"But you don't have any serious proof to offer to the law, you poor fellow...."

"Oh, you're mistaken," the Chambrion replied, "and if you put the Maître, yourself, Madame Gertrude and the demoiselle in my hands, I'll deliver Père Clappier to justice personally...."

At that moment the old aunt's voice was heard, calling to Monsieur de Verne from the perron.

The young man ran toward the château, and the Chambrion stood there motionless, leaning against a tree, gripping his pale forehead in both hands.

"Now, wretch," he murmured, talking to himself, "now that you've given up your secret, dare you confess that you're in love with the demoiselle yourself?"

VII.

The Meunerie, the property inhabited by the Clappier family, which was situated scarcely half a league from the Château des Sapinières, had not changed its appearance since the day when the Baron de Méreuil had crossed its threshold for the last time, except for the fact that everything had aged, from the trees in the garden to the gates of the poultry-yard—and not a single item of furniture had been replaced. Whenever a chair broke, Maître Clappier limited himself to saying: "Take it up to the attic!" Mère Clappier had had dust-covers in yellow damask made for the drawing-room furniture, which was scratched and greasy. Those people, the extent of whose fortune no one knew, but who were reputed to be rich, had ended up, as they grew old, erecting a colossal monument to avarice.

Their son had grown up in the midst of that deprivation. He had been refused any money, and had had all the difficulty in the world obtaining a horse, two basset-hounds and a hunting permit.

Maupert, the former bailiff, now a gamekeeper, was given every kind of job to do; he raked the garden paths, looked after the horse, pruned the trees, lent a hand in harvesting the crops, repaired the planks of the henhouse and served at table on ceremonial occasions. The man, who had gradually fallen into the most complete abjection, had only one satisfaction: ministering to be harsh and terrible desires of his master. With what zeal he drew up a legal complaint! And how he could extort money from the farmers and the tenants! Sometimes he served as a front man for Père Clappier's usurious dealings, which involved lending money at eleven per cent, and nine commission.

Now, on the day when his son and Maupert had launched themselves in pursuit of the Brocart, Maître Clappier had a tranquil dicussion with his wife beside a meager fire in the little dining-room, which also served as a drawing-room and business office.

"We ought to think about setting our son up, though," said Mére Clappier.

She was a fat, vulgar and red-faced woman, inquisitive and spiteful, who had an evil laugh and walked around the house with a bunch of keys that would have made a criminal tremble.

"What?" said Maître Clappier, dryly. "I'm a little hard of hearing."

Mère Clappier, who, in spite of her avarice, had not forgotten her ideas of grandeur and her vocation for the nobility, went on: "Hector's twenty-six; we'll leave him a fine fortune, and there's more than one heiress in the département who wouldn't ask for anything better than...."

Maître Clappier shrugged his shoulders. "To begin with," he said, "one doesn't marry at twenty-six. Secondly, I'm perfectly healthy, and I've no desire to die in order to leave our son a fine fortune."

"It's necessary, however, to give him a marriage portion."

"Never!" said the property-dealer. "No one gave one to me. I worked—and what I've amassed, I intend to keep."

As he expressed that determination—which was, in him, absolute—Maître Clappier heard footsteps behind him. He turned round and saw his son crossing the threshold of the dining-room.

Hector had an animated complexion, shining eyes and a blissful smile on his lips. "What's that you're saying, Father?" he said, in a mocking tone. "You don't want to let go of the écus, eh?"

"I keep what's mine," Clappier replied, brutally. "It's quite enough that I keep you...you cost me the eyes in my head."

"That's what I've been saying to myself," Hector replied, insolently, "So I think I'll keep myself."

"Do," said the property-dealer, looking his son up and down with the disdain the businessmen have for idlers. "What are you good for?"

"Getting married!" said Hector, who, at that moment, straightened up and stuck out his chest.

"A son whose father gives him nothing finds a daughter who has nothing," replied Père Clappier. "And as no one's ever got blood from a stone, I advise you to hold your peace."

With these words he got up and picked up his hat—a brown straw hat that he wore in all seasons—making as if to go out, but Hector held him back.

"Listen, Father," he said. "I'm not asking you for a sou, and if I want to, I can marry a rich girl."

That word made Père Clappier tremble.

"Go on!" he said. "Rich girls aren't for folk who have nothing."

"That's the way it is, though."

"Who are you going to marry, then?"

"Mademoiselle des Sapinières."

Madame Clappier uttered a screech of horror. As for her husband, he went as pale as death, and launched himself toward the door without saying a word. From the corridor he went into the yard, crossed it with large strides and did not stop until he reached the far end of the garden. There he found a bench and sat down, as if exhausted.

Père Clappier was, however, still a robust man, in spite of his sparse white hair and his sixty years. Tall and stiff, with broad and knotty hands, small, extremely mobile gray eyes, a thin ironic mouth that one might have thought sliced with a knife, and old loose yellow teeth: such was the man, in physical terms. Always badly dressed, he obstinately retained a black frock-coat as long as a soutane, and trousers of the same color, which allowed a glimpse of dirty white socks and disreputable lace-up shoes that were only polished on Sundays.

The name of the Demoiselle des Sapinières had been like the blow of a sledgehammer for that man, and doubtless, at the sound of her name, bloody specters had loomed up before him.

For a few minutes he remained weighed down by a profound prostration; then, all of a sudden, like a wild boar momentarily stunned by a hunter's bullet sensing that it is only wounded, he got up again, shook his head, shrugged his shoulders and let slip a single brutal phrase in a low voice: "All this is stupid!"

And he began striding back and forth the garden purposefully, no longer irregularly, like a man overwhelmed by passion or terror, but with the precision of a man who is thinking hard. *After all*, he said to himself, *why not? She's rich, that girl...and who knows the truth today? No one.*

Then he went back to the house. As he went in, he met his son.

Hector had picked up his rifle and his game-bag, and put on his hunting-cap in a very deliberate fashion.

"Where are you going?" his father said, stopping him as he passed.

"To seek my fortune," replied Clappier junior, insolently.

His father stopped him with a cold, calm stare that reduced him to obedience. "Not before talking to me," he said. And he took him into the garden again, to the bench he had sat down on a little while before.

"So," he said, "you want to marry the Demoiselle de Sapinières?"

"Yes."

"Does she want you?"

"I've made arrangements for that."

"Oh yes!" said the property-dealer. "And what do you intend

to do?"

"Well, I'll simply go to her house and say to her: no one wants you, but I, who am more courageous, do want you."

Père Clappier shrugged his shoulders. "You're a churl," he said. "It's not like that that it's necessary to catch her."

"And how would you do it?" Hector sniggered. "You who have such a golden tongue."

"Me?" said Père Clappier. "That's different—but that's not your concern. So you're determined?"

"Yes."

"And what if I refuse my consent?"

"I'll get a legal sanction."

"Ha ha!" sniggered the property-dealer. "You do well, when you put your mind to it. And what if I disinherit you?"

Those last words had the same effect on Hector as a cold shower. "Oh!" he said. "Who will you leave your property to, then?"

"To no one."

"You can't take it with you, though."

"Perhaps not...but anyway, I'm in good health."

"Yes, but you can't live forever."

"I'll try, said Père Clappier. "In any case, I can consume my wealth if necessary."

Hector uttered a burst of laughter that was by no means respectful to his father. "Go on!" he said. "I can see that you're joking. You, consume your wealth, Papa? You'd rather die of starvation."

Père Clappier was one of those men who never come straight to the point. "But at the end of the day," he said, "if the demoiselle wants you, where will you find the money for the expenses of the marriage?"

"I'll borrow it."

"Against what?"

"Against the dowry of my marriage."

"That's possible," said Pere Clappier, softening slightly, "but it's still not enough...."

"Ah! What else is it necessary to do, then?"

"If you marry without my giving you a marriage portion, people hereabouts will talk about you."

"That's true, but what's it to you?"

"Oh," the property-dealer said, naively, "I'd rather people talked, after all, than give you my money—but perhaps we can come to some arrangement...."

"Go on—I'd like nothing better."

"We'll say, then, that you need my consent."

"Yes."

"Well, what if, in exchange, you give me a receipt for a hundred thousand francs, which you declare that you've received from me?"

"You're a hard man, Papa," Hector murmured, "but that's all right with me...as long as you don't try to get in the way of my plan."

"Wait a minute, boy," the voracious property-dealer continued. "The demoiselle has a hundred acres of woodland that are enclaved in ours."

"So what?" said Hector, frowning.

"It's poor wood," Clappier continued, disdainfully, "not worth a hundred francs an acre...."

"But its all mature oak and beech!" protested Hector, already defending Mademoiselle de Méreuil's property as his own.

"Pooh! That's not worth much...."

"Well then, why bring it up?"

"Oh, I'm merely observing that you won't be making any great sacrifice."

"Eh?" said Hector. "Do you want to buy those woods from me?"

"Just to round my land out."

"Well," said Hector, "we'll see about that. We'll have them valued, and if we're in agreement...."

Père Clapier looked at his son with untranslatable irony. "I thought that you were less stupid," he said.

"What's that, Father?"

"The woods I'm asking for are my commission—for I want one."

"A commission? Why?"

"Well, if you marry, it's because I permit it."

"Agreed."

"And if I permit it, it's as if I were giving you a pat on the back—so, I require a commission."

Hector laughed, in a coarse manner that, on the part of a son, would have wounded any other father than Père Clappier."

"It must be said, Papa," he said, "that you're worse than an Orléanais in matters of money. Not only won't you give me anything, but it's necessary that I give you something."

"It's always like that, my lad, in these parts," Clappier sniggered. "Look—you know our cousin, Père Janisset, of Mothe-Beuvron? Well, he hasn't given a sou of dowry to his daughter, but he has himself nourished by his son-in-law, who's a poor bureaucrat."

"Well, Papa," said Hector. "If you want a commission, you'll have to earn it."

"How's that, my lad?"

"You'll have to ask for the demoiselle for me."

"Ask who?"

"Her aunt, of course."

"Where do I do that?"

"At the Sapinières."

Père Clappier went pale. "Never!" he said. And he got to his feet abruptly. "I'm going to bed," he added, as he went away.

"That's odd!" Hector murmured, when he was alone in the garden. "I wouldn't swear that my father hasn't committed some villainy against the people at the Sapinières in his time. I've always had an idea that he got his money twice, and I believe that the Chambrion knows more about it than he wants to say...."[13]

---

13. I have let this reflection remain, in order to be faithful to the printed text, although it might have been better to take it out, given that Hector appears to have no such suspicion hereafter and seems to be unaware of the

With that reflection, Hector Clappier left the garden in his turn—but instead of going back into the Muenerie he headed toward the woods.

An hour later, as we have seen, he made his stupid declaration to Denise, informing her brutally of the story of her parents and falling under the rude fist of the Chambrion when the young woman fainted....

* * * * * * *

That night, Père Clappier did not sleep well beside his corpulent spouse, whom the peasants of the neighborhood designated simply, and rather irreverently, by the name of "the fat one." He slept on his left side and had a nightmare—a nightmare that went like this:

He found himself seated in the large drawing room of the Sapinières, illuminated as if for a ball, and he had a table in front of him laden with papers. Sitting at the table was a man dressed in black with a white cravat, who appeared to be a notary.

Around the notary were several people, Hector among them, dressed for a celebration. The notary was drawing up the marriage contract, and they were only waiting for the fiancée. She soon appeared, smiling and dressed in white—but as she took the pen to sign the contract, a door opened and a man covered in blood appeared, extending his hand toward Clappier.

The property-dealer uttered a cry and woke up. The bloody man he had seen in his dream was none other than the unfortunate Baron de Méreuil.

"What's the matter?" he wife said to him, having woken up on hearing the cry.

"Good...I was asleep...," replied the property-dealer, wiping away the sweat that was beading on his jaundiced forehead.

"Do you know whether the boy has come in?" Madame Clappier asked. "Usually, when he comes in, as he sleeps above

---

possible implications of the suggestion when it is made to him.

us, I wake up."

"I don't know," Clappier replied—and went back to sleep shortly afterwards.

But the nightmare continued, except that the scene had changed.

Père Clappier found himself in his shirt-sleeves, bare-headed, with his hands tied behind his back, in a cart that was going along the Rue des Cures in Orléans, heading toward the Place du Martrol. Beside him was a priest, and behind the priest two gendarmes. As the cart emerged into the square, an immense murmur rose up, like the sound of an angry sea, and Père Clappier saw an ocean of human heads moving in all directions.

Then, raising his head, he perceived the two red stakes forming the arms of the guillotine....

This time, he did not have the strength to cry out.

Fortunately for him, there was a noise above his head, and the heavy footsteps of Hector, who had come back from the pavilion at the Sapinières bruised all over, with his clothes in tatters, woke the sleeper.

* * * * * *

I must be stupid! said Maître Clappier to himself at daybreak the following morning, as he combed in beard in front of a shard of a broken mirror. *To begin with, the dead don't come back, and secondly, the law thinks twice before cutting off the head of a man who has, as I do, a fortune of more than two million; and finally, there's no proof.*

"Where the devil did Hector go yesterday evening?" demanded the fat Mère Clappier, turning over indolently in her unbleached linen sheets. "It was at least three o'clock in the morning when he came in."

"He went hunting," Clappier replied. "Hasn't he got up?"

"I haven't heard anything up there yet."

"Well, let him sleep."

"Look, who's that coming in?"

Père Clappier went to the window and saw a peasant opening the gate to the poultry-yard. The peasant in question was none other than the Brocart.

The little poacher came in with a deliberate step and headed for the front door of the Meunerie.

"Aha!" Père Clappier shouted at him. "You've come to ask for mercy, wretch, haven't you?"

"Not at all!" the boy replied.

"Maupert's made a sworn statement...and you'll go to prison, I swear," Clappier went on.

"I don't know what you're talking about," the Brocart replied. "I've been given a letter for Monsieur Hector and I'm bringing it to him."

There was a noise above Clappier's head then. It was Hector, who leapt out of bed and opened the window.

"And who gave you a letter for me?" Hector asked.

"The old lady at the Sapinières."

Mère Clappier overheard these words. "Oh, I don't want him to marry the demoiselle!" she cried. "There'd be a terrible scandal in the neighborhood!"

"Shut up, woman!" said Clappier. "When they've had their say they'll shut up. The girl has a lot of écus! And écus, you see, always smell good, wherever they come from!"

VIII.

Père Clappier was evidently the richest landowner in the entire region. He had a dozen farms scattered over four communes surrounding the Meunerie, a hovel of which he was enormously fond, although no one had ever known why.

Near one of the farms, which was knows as the Saulayes,[14] which belonged territorially to the commune of Salbris, was a poor hut whose blackened roof, smoke-stained walls and sole window garnished with oiled paper, along with a quarter-acre

---

14. Another slightly unorthodox rendering of "The Willows."

of garden, testified to the poverty of its inhabitants.

That cottage, which was on a by-road that led from the Saulayes to Salbris, was the residence of Mère Malbèque, a poor old woman whose husband had died in prison and whom Maître Clappier had ruined.

Once, seven or eight years before, Père Malbèque, a cooper by trade, had had a little land: a meadow, a field, two acres of vines, and at home, as his wife put it when she talked about their former ease, they drank new wine out of silver goblets.

Unfortunately, Maître Clappier had bought the Saulayes, a fine large farm that he had decided to keep for himself. The edge of the cooper's meadow was adjacent to those of the farm; his field and vineyard were partly enclosed by the farm's lands. That was enough to prompt Maître Clappier to think about taking possession of all of it. He tried to buy it, but the cooper refused to sell; he had inherited it from his father and he was attached to it.

After that, Père Clappier whispered a few words into the ear of Maupert, who was still a bailiff, and Maupert said to him: "I'll take charge of it—in five years you'll have the lot."

Maupert kept his word.

The cooper was something of a hunter, like every true Solognot, and consequently a poacher, for he was ever ready to pick up his weapon.

One evening, when he was hunting in an oat-field near a mill, he was caught by a policeman, who laid a charge against him. The oat-field belonged to Maître Clappier. During the night, the mill burned down.

Maupert was moving things along.

When the tribunal at Romorantin sentenced the poacher to the maximum penalty and fine for hunting out of season, without a permit to carry a weapon at night—a total of one month in prison and a fine two hundred francs, Maupert alleged that the cooper had unintentionally set fire to the mill while lighting his pipe. Père Malbèque was sentenced to pay the price of the mill, and found himself compelled to sell his field or borrow money.

The peasant had so much difficulty letting go of his land, as he put it, that he preferred to borrow at ten or eleven per cent. Clappier found a front man who advanced a thousand francs to Père Malbèque, at a modest interest rate of seven per cent.

At the end of the year, in spite of determined effort, the cooper was unable to meet the interest payment. He was offered the money at twelve per cent. The following year, it was necessary to pay it back. The lender would not make any further arrangement; Malbèque was expropriated; the field and the meadow passed to him.

Then rage and chagrin took possession of the cooper; he neglected his work, took to hunting again, and trained his son, who was then ten or twelve years old, in the art. More court appearances followed, and ultimately, a condemnation to six months in prison. Père Clappier, called as a witness in that last trial, had made such forceful accusations against the cooper that he was given the maximum sentence.

This time, the vineyard went the way of the field and the meadow—but Maupert had miscalculated its dimensions; the debt to Maître Clappier was covered by the sale of the vineyard and the furniture. The house and garden remained intact.

Now, in the era in which the events of this story unfolded, the cooper had died in prison, and Mère Malbèque lived partly on charity and partly on the produce of her son's hunting. The Brocart had sworn a ferocious hatred against Clappier and Maupert. The latter, having become a gamekeeper, spent his life watching out for the Brocart, harassing him and pursuing him, but he was unlucky; he had not succeeded in catching him red-handed.

Mère Malbèque had gone home early on the evening when the Chambrion took the roebuck to the Sapinières, and had cooked her soup while waiting anxiously for her son—for she had met Maupert that morning, and Maupert had said to her: "You're going to have to sell your house, Mère; Monsieur Clappier wants it."

And while watching her soup cook, the poor old woman

wept, thinking of her former ease.

Suddenly, someone knocked rudely on the door, and as the door was only secured by a peg and a piece of string, it opened.

La Malbèque shuddered on seeing Maupert on the threshold.

"My good woman," said the gamekeeper, with a smile that would have made anyone tremble, "I've only come to warn you, and it's not my fault."

"What? What's happened?" she said, standing up and meeting the former usher's venomous gaze.

"I've caught the Brocart."

"That's not true," said the old woman, instinctively prudent. "My son hasn't been hunting."

"He killed a hare under the widows of the Meunerie."

"That's not true," repeated La Malbèque. "Have you caught him?"

"No, but I've seen him."

"You're mistaken—it wasn't him."

"Oh, I recognized his dog."

"His dog?" said La Malbèque, in a triumphant tone. "You're lying, Monsieur Maupert—look there."

Maupert cast a glance into a corner of the room and saw Gendarme's eyes sparkling like firebrands. At the same time, the dog growled dully.

"You'd better go away, Monsieur Maupert," said the old woman. "He's got sharp teeth."

Maupert put his hand on his rifle, which was slung over his shoulder. "If he budges," he said, "I'll put a handful of buckshot in his head."

"And by what right," cried the old woman, "would you come into my house to shoot my dog? To begin with, he's not a hunting-dog, he's a cattle-dog...."

"I'll only kill him if he bites me."

The dog was still growling.

"Peace, Gendarme, be quiet," said La Malbèque. "Get out, Monsieur Maupert, you can see that my son isn't here."

"But it's not him I've come to look for; I've come to seize...."

"Ah!" La Malbèque interjected, who had stated laughing in his face. "You're losing your mind, Monsieur Maupert—you're no longer a bailiff...."

"So I won't seize the furniture—just hunting equipment: snares and a decoy duck."

"There's none of that here. Look—if you find any, you'll be very clever, for there isn't any."

Maupert set about inspecting the house; he searched everywhere, but found nothing.

The dog was still growling.

"Quiet!" La Malbeque said to him. "Be quiet, Gendarme."

Maupert was still searching, and in order to do so more comfortably, had put his rifle down beside the fireplace. He went to the bed and searched the mattress.

"Do you know, Monsieur Maupert," said the old lady, calmly, "that only gendarmes have the right to do what you're doing? A private policeman has no power to come into people's homes like this."

"I don't care about that," said the former bailiff, cynically. "I'll take care of that in my sworn statement."

"You won't take care of anything, scoundrel!" said a voice from the threshold, where the door remained partly open. It was the Brocart.

The Brocart always went barefoot, even in the thorns and boar-thickets of the woods. He had, therefore, been able to approach without making the slightest noise. He had seen the rifle at a glance, and as Maupert turned round at his exclamation, he leapt upon the weapon and bounded backwards.

Then he shouted: "Go! Go, Gendarme!"

The dog leapt at Maupert's throat and bit him cruelly.

The Brocart, armed with the rifle, had run outside.

Maupert tried to fight and to strangle the dog, but the dog, intoxicated by fury, tore his shirt and bit his hands, arms and legs.

La Malbèque laughed—the nervous laughter of poor people to whom Heaven has finally granted revenge.

Maupert, mad with anger and pain, launched himself outside the cottage; the dog pursued him, continuing to bite.

As for the Brocart, he ran, the rifle over his shoulder, with a lightness that seemed to justify his nickname, and reached the farm of Les Saulayes.

Les Saulayes, as we have said, belonged to Père Clappier, but the farmer who leased it was an honest man who had a strong sense of justice. He was, moreover, a vigorous fellow between forty and fifty years of age, who could have knocked Maupert out with a single punch.

The Brocart found him laboring on his farm.

"Help me, Jean, help me!" he shouted to him. And he told him that Maupert had tried to assault his mother and kill his dog.

Jean took the rifle and said: "Don't worry—I'll only return the rifle to Père Clappier."

That was all the Brocart wanted.

Maupert, finally abandoned by the dog, arrived and tried to hurl himself on the Brocart, but Jean stopped him.

"You're an evil man, Maupert," he said, "and I won't let you beat a child."

"Give me my rifle."

"No," said the farmer. "I'll bring it to the Meunerie tomorrow."

"I'll have your lease revoked!"

"That will be difficult, as I pay in full and on time."

"I'll find some quibble...."

"That's your profession," said the farmer, calmly, "but the good Lord doesn't smite honest men." And Jean, the farmer of Les Saulayes, obstinately refused to give up the weapon.

Maupert left, disarmed, for the Meunerie, swearing to make sure that La Malbèque and her son died in prison, to poison their accursed dog and to ruin the farmer.

The Brocart thanked Jean for his intervention and went home.

His mother and he barricaded themselves in for supper. Then the child told her that the Chambrion had promised his protection, and would obtain employment for him with Monsieur de

Verne.

"He's a good lad, François Véru, the Chambrion," said La Malbèque said, "and he's the only man in the region who isn't afraid of the Clappiers, But will he be strong enough to ward off the new storm that's threatening us? After all, my boy, the dog bit that blackguard Maupert; he'll do anything and everything to ruin us."

"The Chambrion will defend us," the Bocart replied, confidently.

Mother and son went to bed when they had eaten, but before then, the young poacher opened the door and said to the dog: "Go fetch my gun!"

You will remember that, when the Brocart had seen Maupert and Monsieur Hector hot on his heels, he had thrown his rifle into a bush and sent his dog away. The dog was trained for that work; he slipped through the brambles and along the ditches like a beast laying down a scent and ran off without worrying about his master. Then, in the evening, if the latter ordered it, he went back to the spot where they had separated and found the rifle, which he picked up in his teeth by the middle of the barrel and brought it back, as if it were a partridge or some other item of prey.

Gendarme went to fetch the rifle. An hour later, he brought it back.

"Now," said the Brocart, "let Maupert come—we're ready." And he lay down beside his mother, and went to sleep.

But La Malbèque never closed her eyes. The poor woman could already see the gendarmes coming to arrest her son to take him to prison. She had good reason to fear Maupert's wrath.

At about two o'clock in the morning, footsteps became audible in the sunken road that went passed the cottage. La Malbèque began to tremble. The footsteps stopped at the door.

Then, shivering, the old woman woke her son.

Someone knocked.

"Who's there?" shouted the Brocart, leaping on his gun.

Gendarme began to growl—but a voice from outside replied:

"Don't be afraid; it's me."

The Brocart recognized the voice. "It's the Chambrion," he said.

"Are you alone?" asked La Malbèque.

"Yes, all alone—open up."

The Borcart unbolted the door; then, as the Chambrion came in, he went to stir the ashes of the fire, in which he found a brand that he picked up; and, blowing on it, he lit a fir-twig, by way of a candle.

"Oh, my poor François," said the old lady, "we've had such a fright."

"When was that, Mère?"

"This evening."

"Bah!" said the Chambrion. "To bring a charge of hunting, it's necessary to have caught the delinquent...and Maupert hasn't caught the Brocart."

"Oh, it's not that, François," La Malbèque said. "It's much worse."

"What is it, then?"

"Our dog bit Maupert." And La Malbèque told him what had happened earlier.

The Chambrion listened tranquilly. "Don't worry, Mère," he said, when she had finished.

"You're not afraid of Clappier, then?"

"It's him who'll soon be afraid of me," said the Chambrion mysteriously. La Malbèque looked at him in astonishment, but the Chambrion continued "You don't have anything to fear from Maupert tonight, for I'll stay here."

"Here?" said La Malbèque. "but where will you sleep, my boy?"

"In the barn where you once kept fodder for the cow."

"Alas," said the old woman, tearfully, "we no longer have a cow today."

"The time will come again, Mère."

"Never," the old woman sighed. "Clappier is our enemy."

The Chambrion went to the bed where Mère Malbèque was

enveloped in a scrap of blanket. "Mère," he said, "a day will come—and that day isn't far off—when the hand of God will weigh so heavily upon that man, who has reduced you and so many others to poverty, that he'll be even more wretched than you are."

"What do you mean?" said the old woman, with a gleam of somber hatred in her eyes.

"So wretched," the Chambrion went on, "that he'd probably give everything he has then to live for a long time in your cottage—for his days will be numbered."

The Chambrion suddenly lowered his voice, took the old woman by the hand and added: "On that day too, perhaps, a man who has marched thus far with his head held high, esteemed throughout the land, will curb his head and have need of the pity of others...no matter how paltry they are. Well, Mère Malbèque, if that day comes—and it will come, for God's justice must take its course—make me a promise."

"Speak, my boy," said the old woman, astonished.

"That you won't close your door to him; that you wont reject him; that you won't turn him away."

"But, that man...who is it?" asked the Brocart in his turn—for he had listened curiously to what the Chambrion was saying.

"You'll know tomorrow," said Fançois Véru, curtly. Then, after a pause, he added: "I have need of you, Brocart."

"What do I have to do?" asked the young poacher, in a tone of devotion.

"You have to go to the Meunerie."

"Oh, my God! But Maupert will beat me."

"No," said the Chambrion. "Maupert won't touch a hair on your head. If he threatens you, simply say to him: 'The Chambrion has told me that he'll break your back if you lay a finger on me.'"

"And you think, François...."

"I think," the Chambrion said, "that you'll go to the Meunerie with a fine passport."

"What's a passport?"

"I'll explain it to you," the Chambrion said. "Suppose that you were in the forest."

"All right."

"That you'd just killed a hare."

"It happens."

"And that Bauvais or Tremplin, the government's game-keepers, got their hands on you."

"Aagh!" said the child, with naïve dread.

"Well, suppose, as well, that you had a hunting permit...and that you were a shareholder in the government's wood."

"Oh la la!" said the Brocart, bewildered.

"You take out your papers, and the police salute you don't they?"

"And a bit more!" said the Brocart.

"Well, a passport, you see, is like a hunting permit for travelers."

"But I'm not a traveler."

"Yes you are, since you're going to the Meunerie. Whether one goes two kilometers or around the world, it's still traveling."

"That's true," said the child. "Well, where is this perm...I mean, passport?"

"It's this letter. And when you tell them where it comes from...."

"They won't do me any harm?"

"On the contrary. They'll offer you a glass of wine."

"You're joking, Chambrion," said the boy, with a hint of doubt. "Père Clappier never gives anyone a drink."

"Yes...once...." The Chambrion murmured, with a somber expression. "But believe me, a glass of wine from Père Clappier costs too much."

"Oh, if he's selling it, that's different," said the Brocart, who did not understand the Chambrion's terrible allusion.

"It costs one's honor," François Véru finished—and he went to bed.

* * * * * * *

The letter that the Chambrion had given to the Brocart and which the latter took to the Meunerie, announcing that it came from the Château des Sapinières, was signed by Madame Gertrude, addressed to Monsieur Hector, and was thus conceived:

Monsieur,

> *The step that you took yesterday with regard to Mademoiselle de Méreuil, my niece, is strange, to say the least. No man has ever conducted himself in that way. Before replying yes or no, it would be agreeable to me if you were to be introduced to me by your father, Monsieur Clappier, with whom I once had dealings.*
>
> *I have the honor of being, Monsieur, your most humble servant,*

Gertrude de R****

Père Clappier had gone up to Hector's room along with the Brocart—but Hector was so emotional as he took the famous letter from the Brocart's hand that he paid no attention to his father. The latter read the letter over his son's shoulder, Hector having lain down again.

"Well, well!" he said. "What happened to you yesterday? You've had a punch in the eye and your hand's crushed, as if someone had stepped on it."

"I fell as I was jumping the ditch in the park," Hector replied, embarrassed.

IX.

Père Clappier looked at his son from the corner of his eye. "So you've been to the Sapinières?"

"Of course!"

"And you've done something stupid," said Père Clappier, ironically.

"Not as stupid as all that, since you can see that they're calling me back. She's hooked, the girl."

Clappier shrugged his shoulders.

"Well, Papa," Hector went on. "You can see that it depends on you now."

"You think so."

"Oh, entirely. And if you go to the Sapinières...."

"Never!" replied Père Clappier, brusquely. And he left Hector's room.

Then the Brocart leaned closer to the younger Clappier's ear. "I know someone," he said, "who can make Père Clappier go to the demoiselle's house," he said.

"You?"

"Yes, me," said the Brocart. "But I'll keep what I know to myself. You're too unkind to poor folk, Monsieur Hector."

"And what if I pick up that riding crop over there?"

"What for?"

"To beat you. Perhaps you'll talk."

"That's a bad idea, Monsieur Hector."

"Really?" And Hector stood up in order to fetch his riding crop—but the Brocart did not flinch.

"Monsieur Hector," he said, "if you, or your father, or Maupert, have the misfortune to touch me, I know someone who'll avenge me."

"And who's that?" said Hector, frowning.

"The Chambrion."

That name produced an effect of terror on Hector. "Oh, the Chambrion will protect you!" he said, angrily.

"And you know that his fist is solid," the child added, calmly.

Hector did not pick up the crop.

"And you'd be wrong to put yourself at odds with him," the Brocart went on, "because he wants you to marry the demoiselle."

"And who told you that?"

"He did."

Hector seemed to reflect. "And you say," he said, "that you have a means of making my father go to the Sapinières?"

"Not me—the Chambrion. If you want to see him, he's waiting for you."

"Where?"

"Five hundred meters from here, on the edge of the ditch that forms the border between the Les Saulayes farm and the Meunerie's land."

"Well then, I'll go," said Hector, gripped by a sudden inspiration.

And he got dressed. As he was about to leave the room, the Brocart said to him: "Monsieur Hector, I had an argument with Maupert yesterday evening."

"And he beat you?"

"No, because Jean, the farmer at Les Saulayes, defended me."

"And you're afraid that he might beat you this morning."

"That depends on you," said the Brocart, confidently, "and you need me more than Maupert does."

"Well, I'll take you under my protection," said Clappier the younger. And he went out, followed by the Brocart.

In the courtyard, they met Maupert.

"Ah! Scoundrel! Wretch!" he said. "We're finally going to have a reckoning, you and I!"

"You won't be reckoning anything at all," Hector replied, who placed himself in front of the Brocart to protect him.

"And why's that?"

"Because I don't want you to," said the young man, coldly.

A window opened on the first floor of the Meunerie and Père Clappier appeared there. "Hey, Maupert!" he shouted. "Give that boy a god thrashing for me, and don't pay any attention to what my son says."

Maupert tried hurl himself upon the child, but Hector tripped him up and sent him sprawling into the duck-pond in the middle of the court-yard. Then he took the Brocart by the hand and drew him away.

Père Clappier watched them go, uttering a curse-and then a burst of laughter, as he saw Maupert get to his feet, covered in mud and wet dung.

"If that's how you make your son respect me," said the game-keeper, "it will hardly encourage me to devote myself to your interests."

"Why did you let him do it?" said Clappier, and closed the window.

"Sidore," said fat Mère Clappier, who had put on a dressing-gown and was disentangling her gray-tinted hair and adjusting her false teeth, which she carefully wrapped up every evening in a page from the newspaper *Le Loiret*, "I don't understand you any more, since yesterday evening."

"That's because you're not very bright," muttered the prop-erty-dealer.

"What?" said Mère Clappier. "You'll consent to this marriage?"

"That depends."

"But think of the scandal it will cause in the region...."

"I couldn't care less about that."

"Our cousins in Orléans, the Jousserands, the Providences and the Boumishels wouldn't want to see us again."

"That'll save us money, because they always come at least once a year."

"We can't fall out with the whole family, though."

"The family?" said the property-dealer, ironically. "What's that? What use is it, the family? Get away! They borrow money from you at five per cent and come to your house in a carriage, as if oats grew of their own accord in the ditches on government land."

Mère Clappier sighed and said no more.

Her husband started striding back and forth, muttering inconsequential words, prey to a certain agitation.

"Where has Hector gone then?" asked Mère Clappier, finally.

"To the Sapinières, no doubt."

"Personally," said the fat woman, "if this marriage takes

place, I'll leave the country...right away."

"That will depend," the property-dealer replied.

"On what?"

"You'll leave if I leave. The Code is definite in that regard: a wife has to reside with her husband."

Madame Clappier, née Jousserand, raised hr eyes to the heavens, remembering the romances of chivalry that had nourished her vaporous childhood, in which there was nothing but gallant knights and who rendered damsels the honor and glory of obedience. A few tears even moistened her red eyelids, and the spirit of revolt against conjugal tyranny was about to enter into her heart when Jeanette came in.

Jeanette was the only maidservant in the house; she did the cooking, made the beds, repaired the linen and baked the bread. "Madame," she said, "how much should one pay for hare-skins?"

That question brought Lucide back from the heavens; she found herself a housekeeper one again, an avaricious Orléanaise.

"Four sous," she said.

"The skin-dresser's only offering three."

"Let him go to the devil! The poulterer from La Moithe, who passes through every week, will pay four."

Jeanette went out, and Madame Clappier finished getting dressed.

During this exchange between his wife and the maidservant, the property-dealer had left the room and gone down into the courtyard.

Maupert, who had laid his shirt out in the sun to dry it, came to him.

"Tell me, Boss," he said. "Don't you want the Malbèques' house any longer?"

"No," said Clappier. "I'd have made a sheepfold of it once, but now I've built one at Les Saulayes, she can keep her house."

"Oh!" said Maupert, disappointed. "Yesterday, though, you didn't tell me that...."

"It's possible," the property dealer replied, distractedly, "that

I had other things on my mind."

"Oh!" said Maupert, again, who set about sketching arabesques with his toe in the greasy soil of the poultry yard. "That doesn't alter the fact that the house, in the very midst of the farms, is like a spying eye, always open."

"Well, what do you want me to do about it, since the old witch no longer owes me anything, and doesn't want to sell?"

"She didn't want to yesterday, but today...."

"Today will be just like yesterday."

"Oh, not at all," said Maupert. "I've had a god idea, Boss!"

"Let's hear it."

"Yesterday, the Brocartt's dog bit me."

"You should have shot it."

"I couldn't, since the Brocart had my rifle."

"Well, what do you propose to do?"

"Register a complaint with the imperial prosecutor—a complaint that you'll endorse. I'm a sworn policeman; there was a rebellion and a trap. With a little skill, we can get the Brocart into the hands of the correctional police...the expenses will end up ruining La Malbèque."

"Good. What then?"

"The law will order a sale, and we'll buy it."

"Well then, draft your complaint...."

"Oh, that's soon done," said the former bailiff. "I'll only need ten minutes." And he went into the kitchen, where there was a sort of greasy box on the mantelpiece, the last vestige of his former profession, in which he had everything required for writing.

He sat down in front of the board on which the bread dough was kneaded.

In the meantime, Père Clappier continued walking back and forth, and his monologue.

"It'll be necessary, in order to bring it off, for me to decide to go to the Sapinières. I'm not an emotional man, but the only time I went there after...the accident...it seemed to me that the ground I was walking on was burning my feet."

Maupert came back with his complaint well and truly drafted.

The former bailiff said that, having gone to the house of a poacher nicknamed the Brocart, but whose real name was Joseph Malbèque, in order to seize his poaching equipment, the aforesaid Brocart, having taken possession of his rifle, had taken aim with it and had set his dog on him; and that he, Maupert, a sworn policeman, had owed his salvation to the fortuitous passage of a cart along the road, which had intimidated the Brocart.

"Is that true?" asked Père Clappier, having read the complaint.

"Very nearly," said Maupert.

"Bah!" said Clappier. "With these people, it's always true." And he went into the kitchen and wrote the following at the bottom of the document drawn up by Maupert, which he signed:

> *I certify that the declaration of my private gamekeeper, Sieur Jean Maupert, is in complete conformity with the truth.*

"Now," he said, "are you going to put it in the post?"

"Oh no," said Maupert. "I'll take it to Romorantin myself. It's necessary to get things in motion quickly."

And he picked up his game-bag and rifle, and set forth.

In order to go from the Meunerie to Romorantin, which was no more than two leagues, it was necessary to go past Mère Malbèque's house.

The old woman and her son were sitting on the threshold; inside the cottage, the Chambrion was sitting by the fire, smoking his pipe. As for Hector, he had just left the Chambrion, but instead of going along the road he had gone by way of an oatfield in which partridges were singing. Maupert and he crossed paths without seeing one another, separated as they were by a high hedge.

Maupert greeted the Malbèques with an ironic expression. "Hey, Mère," he said, "you still don't want to sell your house to Père Clappier?"

"Go to the devil, wretch!" the old woman shouted, angrily.

"I'm not going as far as that, Mère."

"And where are you going?" asked the Brocart, in a mocking tone, feeling that he was shielded by the Chambrion's presence.

"I'm going to Romorntin to give you a recommendation."

"To whom?"

"To the imperial prosecutor," Maupert replied, who could not see the Chambrion.

The Brocart was afraid. Maupert saw that and continued: "Père Clappier has endorsed the complaint. Oh, you'll be taken care of, my lad. Perhaps you'll be able to go traveling. It wouldn't surprise me if they were to take you to Toulon[15]...."

And Maupert continued on his way, whistling, without having perceived the Chambrion.

"Oh!" cried Mere Malbèque, in despair. "There's no justice for poor folk, then?"

But the Chambrion came out of the cottage then and placed his hand on the poor woman's shoulder. "You're mistaken, Mère. There is one...and it's terrible, especially when it's slow."

"But they're going to put my poor boy in prison!" she cried.

"No, Mère, for they won't find him. I'll hide him."

"Oh, the gendarmes always find you in the end."

The Chambrion shook his head. "Listen to me, both of you," he said, "and look at that man." He pointed at Maupert, who was just disappearing around a bend in the road. "He's not carrying your condemnation, Brocart, but his master's...."

La Malbèque and her son looked at the Chambrion, who added: "I need the law to come here...and I'm content now that it will come." And as neither the mother or the son understood these mysterious words, he went on: "You know what you promised me yesterday, Mère."

"What was that, my boy?"

"Not to close your door one day on a poor man bowed down by shame...for that man will be me."

"You!" the mother and the son exclaimed, in unison. "Oh,

---

15. The location of a notorious *bagne*: a prison for convicts sentenced to hard labor.

you're mad, Chambrion. Aren't you honest?"

"Yes."

"A good worker with a good heart?"

"Yes, I think so."

"What, then, do you have to be ashamed of?"

"I was born under a baneful star," he murmured—and, not wishing to explain further, he said abruptly to the Brocart: "You mustn't stay here now. They might come to arrest you."

"Oh, my God!" said La Malbèque, shivering.

"Have no fear, Mère, they won't find him where I'll hide him."

"But they'll sentence him anyway."

"No," said the Chambrion, for he can only be pursued and tried on the basis of Maupert's and Monsieur Clappier's complaint, and they'll withdraw it within a week."

"May God hear you, my boy!"

The Chambrion picked up his rifle, which he always carried with him since the owners of the château had given him a hunting permit, and said to Brocart: "Follow me."

"Where are you taking me?" the Brocart asked.

"To the château first."

"And then?"

"Afterwards, we'll see. As for you, Mère, I'll give you some good advice. If you stay here, the Clappiers or Maupcrt, at least—might do you a bad turn. Come with us. The demoiselle has always been kind...."

"Oh, that's true—but we can't go to her," said La Malbèque, naively. "You know yourself, François, that her aunt, Madame Gertrude, doesn't want anyone to talk to her."

"Everything's changed now."

"Really? Why's that, my boy?"

"Because the demoiselle knows everything now."

"Even what happened to her parents?"

"Yes," said the Chambrion, with a somber expression.

Mère Malbèque picked up her begging-bowl and staff, and the clogs that she put on every Sunday—for she went barefoot on weekdays. While she was making those meager preparations, the Brocart broke his rifle—a true poacher's weapon—down into three pieces, which he then put inside his shirt.

"A day will come," the Chambrion said to him, "when you'll have a commission as a gamekeeper and a hunting permit, and you'll carry a double-barreled shotgun."

And all three of them took the road to the Sapinières.

* * * * * *

Meanwhile, Hector went back to the Meunerie.

What had the Chambrion said to him?

That might perhaps have been difficult to guess, but in the wake of their doubtless-mysterious conversation, it was as if the young man had undergone a complete metamorphosis.

When he arrived within view of the Meunerie, Père Clappier was in a neighboring field, where the day-laborers were busy laying drainage pipes. Hector went to him and said, in a disengaged and slightly impertinent tone: "We need to have a little talk, Father."

Clappier examined his son and thought his expression singular. He was so accustomed to having authority over everything that surrounded him, however, from his domestics and his farmer to his wife and son, that he replied dryly: "You've chosen a bad time: I don't have the leisure to chat."

"Ah!" said Hector. "Oh well, it'll do later." And he turned on his heel—but in his tone, his attitude and his curt and dismissive gesture, there was something so strange that Père Clappier was alarmed by it.

He called his son back. "Well," he said, "what do you want to say to me?"

Hector came back. "I wanted to talk to you about our business affairs, but since you don't have time...."

"What business affairs?" demanded Clappier, arrogantly. "I don't have any business dealings with you."

"We soon will have, I imagine."

"And why's that?" said the property-dealer, alarmed y his son's calm and disdainful attitude.

"If I marry the demoiselle."

"I don't have any business dealings with the demoiselle."

"Ah!"

That syllable was like a dagger-thrust that penetrated Clappier's heart. His face reddened, and there was a stinging sensation in his eyes, for it seemed to him, at that moment, that it was not a son but an examining magistrate standing before him.

"No," he repeated, in a tone that he attempted to render brutal, but was merely troubled, "I have no business dealings with the demoiselle,

"Oh! Pardon me..I thought...."

"I sold the Sapinières," Clapier continued, as his son fixed him with a cold, calm stare. "I sold them...I was paid...."

"Oh!" said Hector. "I believe so...and twice rather than once...."

With these words, which fell upon Clappier's head like the blow of a sledgehammer, Hector turned his back and went away.

For two minutes the stunned property dealer thought that the earth was about open beneath his feet. There was a strange ringing in his ears, and his eyes saw a kind of bloody mist before them. But the man was endowed with a harsh and savage energy; once the initial shock had passed, he stood up straight, grim and terrible, armed for the frightful battle that he glimpsed in the future. He ran after his son, took him by the arm, squeezed it as if to crush it, and stopped him dead.

"Explain yourself," he said.

At that moment, Clappier was fearful to behold.

"I don't have anything to explain," Hector replied. "I asked you whether you had any business outstanding with the demoiselle, and you said no. That's all. That's everything explained."

"You wanted to say something."

"No."

"Wretch! Dare you suspect your father?" cried Clappier,

losing his temper.

"Me? I don't suspect anything...I don't know anything."

"Who told you...that I was paid twice rather than once for the Sapinières?"

"Oh, you shan't know that," said Hector. "Everyone has his little secrets."

"And what if I want to know?"

"Look, Papa," said the young man, with a calmness that completed Clappier's alarm, "would you like me to give you some good advice?"

"I don't want advice from anyone!"

"You're mistaken."

"Well, what? What is it?" demanded the property-dealer, who felt overwhelmed by his son's calmness and self-confidence.

"You say that you have no business dealings with the Demoiselle des Sapinières?"

"No."

"Then you don't have any good reason for not going there. You'll introduce me there...and the marriage will take care of itself."

"All right, so be it—but you'll tell me...."

"Wait a minute," Hector continue. "I won't ask you for a marriage portion, because your money is so dear to your heart, but...."

"But?" said Clappier, quivering under his son's gaze.

"I don't want to give you the hundred acres of wood you asked for."

"And what if I refuse my consent? If I don't want to go to the château?"

"You'd be making a mistake," said Clappier the younger, coldly.

That calmness tipped the property dealer over the edge and caused him to lose his head. "But at least," he said, "you'll name the wretch who has dared to accuse your father?"

"When you've made the request, not before." This time, Hector went away for good, leaving his father flabbergasted.

For an hour, Père Clappier wandered through his fields in the vicinity of the Meunerie, like a body without a soul, prey to a sort of vertiginous terror—and he remembered the frightful dream he had had the night before.

X.

During that time, Hector went into the woods, his dog running in front of him, and while going through the undergrowth he said to himself: "I repeated what the Chambrion said to me word for word, but I'll be hanged if I understand any of it."

That reflection, which the younger Clappier made as he went through the woods, was quite accurate. Hector had been the unintelligent instrument of the Chambrion's secret plans; he had said what the Chambrion had told him to say, without understanding it—and the effect had been prodigious. Such, at least, was Hector's opinion, and he repeated it all along the path that separated the Meunerie from François Véru's house.

I've always had an idea, he thought, *while Maître Flambant, his gundog, ferreted in the undergrowth in quest of a woodcock, that my father didn't have a very clear conscience, and I wasn't mistaken, since he's already renounced his commission and consented to go and ask for the demoiselle for me. It's necessary to see whether there's more that can be done. If there's a means to blackmail Papa, that would be superb.*

As he was thinking along these lines, Flambant came to a halt before the projecting roots of a tree. Hector took three paces forward; a hare ran out, and was greeted by two precipitate gunshots.

"Got it! Got it! Fetch, Flambant!" Hector shouted.

"It's not worth the trouble, Monsieur Hector," said the Chambrion, emerging from the bushes. "Your hare is safe and sound—you missed."

"Oh, do you think so?" said the young man, disappointed.

"Well," the Chambrion murmured, in a sardonic tone, "one

can't succeed in everything—hunting heiresses and killing hares."

"That's true," said Hector.

"Well, have you seen your father?"

"Yes, and I left him a trifle disturbed, I can assure you."

"You told him...."

"Word for word, what you told me to say."

"And he's upset?"

"I thought he was going to faint."

"Then he'll consent to go to the Sapinières?"

"Of course! And he's renounced the hundred acres of woodland he wanted to swindle me out of. But tell me, François, you need to explain...."

"What?"

"What you meant by those words—that he got the price of the Sapinières twice rather than once."

"Monsieur Hector," said the Chambrion, "I'll tell you one thing, and that's that if you aren't clever, your father will roll you over. If you want to know, it's necessary that you stay with me, and that you don't see your father again this evening. For that reason, I propose we do a little hunting."

"And what if I don't go back to the Meunerie tonight?" said Hector. "What if I were to go and stay the night at our farm on the other side of the forest, Les Bauges?"

"That would be even better—and I promise you that tomorrow, when you go back, your father will go to the Sapinières to make the request."

"Well, that suits me," said Hector, "but tell me...."

"Listen: your father got the settlement for the Sapinières twice over."

"How?"

"When Monsieur de Méreuil came back from Paris he went to pay your father, who gave him a receipt for the settlement."

"Well?"

"When Monsieur de Méreuil committee suicide, people searched everywhere for the receipt and didn't find it. Monsieur de Méreuil had had his head turned by Mère Clappier, with regard to his wife. He galloped through the wood, went through the undergrowth, and didn't notice that a tree branch had snagged the bag he had slung over his shoulder. The receipt was in that bag. Père Clappier found it."

"Oh, I see," said Hector, who took the Chambrion at his word. "And he claimed the balance for a second time."

"Which was paid to him, Monsieur Hector."

"But how much was that settlement, François?" the younger Clappier asked.

"Two hundred thousand francs."

"Damn!" said Hector, with a coarse laugh. "He doesn't have a dead hand, my father, when it comes to theft." And he became very pensive.

The Chambrion's house appeared through the trees, through whose crowns a few rays of twilight were still filtering.

"We're going hunting, then?" asked Hector, emerging from his reverie.

"Which is to say," the Chambrion replied, "that I want to enable you to kill a roebuck, which you've probably never done—but it's not time yet, and we can have a bite to eat."

The Chambrion and Hector went into the cottage. Then the former lit a fire, set the table and placed a pitcher of wine and a piece of smoked lard on it. Then he put a piece of grease on the stove and said: "I'll cook you some eggs."

The Chambrion and his guest sat down at the table. Hector ate with an excellent appetite, while thinking about the demoiselle's écus and beauty.

At eight o'clock, the moon rose.

"It's time to go," said François Véru—and he covered his fire, picked up his rifle and passed a cord round Flambant's neck.

"The dog will slow us down," said Hector.

"We'll leave him with Jacomy, the charcoal-burner."

The charcoal-burner to whom François Véru was referring had a hut in the wood, to which he had bought the right of exploitation from the government. Hector and the Chambrion found him sitting on the edge of his charcoal-oven smoking his pipe.

"Here," Hector said to him. "Would you like to earn a ten-sou piece? Take my dog back to the Meunerie."

The charcoal-burner took the dog's leash and set forth, while the Chambrion and Hector headed toward the place in the forest known as the Mare aux Chevrettes, where we saw François Véru meet Horace de Verne on the previous evening..

The Chambrion placed Hector twenty meters from the pond, in a covert, and advised him not to smoke.

"Don't be in a hurry," he said. "They usually come in twos or threes, the buck first, then the doe, and finally the fawn. Aim at the buck, and if you kill him outright, take a shot at the doe, but leave the fawn alone if there is one."

"Aren't you going to stay with me?"

"No, I'm going to go a little bit further on."

"Oh—but you think the roe deer will come?"

"Perhaps right away, perhaps in an hour, perhaps later...but for sure; they come here every night." The Chambrion smiled. "It's a matter of patience, hunting! But this has more success than running dogs."

Hector took up his position and loaded his rifle.

"If you fire and miss your shot," the Chambrion said, "don't move, and reload your rifle. Others will come. You know that at night, it's always necessary to shoot at little high?"

"Yes."

"Well then, good luck...I'll come back to pick you up here."

The Chambrion went around the pond; then, instead of taking up a position, as he had said to Hector, he started running through the woods in the direction of the Sapinières, where, as we shall see, he was awaited with keen impatience....

* * * * * * *

What had happened at the Château des Sapinières since the previous night?

One could easily guess that on seeing Mademoiselle Denise de Méreuil out of bed. She was still pale and languid, but she smiled when she looked at Horace, kneeling before her chaise-longue, holding one of her hands in his.

Madame Gertrude was beside hem.

Denise had almost died, but, as the physician had suggested, a great joy had saved her.

"My child," Madame Gertrude had told her. "Monsieur le Vicomte Horace de Verne has done us the honor of asking for your hand in marriage, and I have granted it to him."

Those simple words had produced a violent reaction in Denise, and death, already preparing to take her, had retreated.

They had waited for morning to give the young woman an explanation. Then, when the nervous crisis had passed, they had told her everything.

Her parents had not committed suicide. Someone had murdered them, and the stain on Monsieur de Verne's memory was pure and simple slander.

In spite of her youth, Denise was a person of great intelligence and heart. "Where's the Chambrion?" she asked.

"He isn't at the château," Horace replied.

"Well, run after him, my friend. I don't want him to denounce the murderer before I've seen him."

"Perhaps it's already too late?" said Madame Gertrude.

"No," said Horace. "But is that possible, now? Isn't it necessary that the truth be brought to light?"

"Oh," Denise murmured, "You're not thinking about him, are you? So good, so noble, so devoted, and at whom people will henceforth point a finger and say: 'He's the murderer's son!'"

These words touched Horace. He set out in search of the Chambrion. But the Chambrion had gone, without telling anyone his plans. He had limited himself to having Madame Gertrude write the letter that we have seen addressed to the younger Clappier.

Horace had gone to the Chambrion's house; it was locked. He had searched the woods; he had even gone as far as Salbris, without any more success.

As he was coming back, he heard a whistle from a nearby bush, and recognized the Brocart's voice.

The Brocart was on his way to the Sapinières in the company of his mother, and the Chambrion was with them. As was his custom, the little poacher, instead of following the forest path hat went straight to the château, had made is mother take a false road through the woods. The Bocart's perennial preoccupation was not to meet any agent of authority in the forest, and La Malbèque, who, although she was not a poacher of game, went here and there to appropriate a little dead wood for the winter, was no less timorous with regard to the police.

Horace called to the Brocart, who came to him immediately.

"Hey, lad," he said. "Have you seen the Chambrion?"

"Sorry, Monsieur Hector—we've just left him."

"Where has he gone?"

At the moment when Horace had met the Brocart, it was almost dark.

"He left us to go do a little hunting."

"Do you know where?"

"Near the Mare aux Chevrettes."

"Well, I'll go there. I need to talk to him."

"With all due respect, Monsieur Horace," said the child, "Don't go there, if it would cause you the slightest inconvenience to run into the Clappier son."

"Ah!" said Monsieur de Verne shivering. "He's with him!"

"Yes, and also, as the gendarmes might come to arrest me at any moment...."

"What!" Horace interjected. "You say that the gendarmes are coming to arrest you?"

"Perhaps this evening, but tomorrow for sure...oh, don't look at me like that, Monsieur Horace. I haven't done anything bad... it's false testimony by Maupert, Clappier's gamekeeper. But the Chambrion told me that he'll sort it out. Besides, he'll hide me... and he also told me to go to the château with my mother, and he came to take me there."

What does all this signify? Horace thought, as he went to the Sapinières with La Malbèque and her son. *And why does the Chambrion want to bring Père Clappier to the château?*

On arrival at the Sapinières, Horace sent La Malbèque and her son to the servants' parlor, and then rejoined Denise and her aunt—and all three of them waited for the Chambrion, with a certain anxiety.

Finally, at about ten o'clock, he appeared.

He was sad and grave, like a man who has made a painful but unbreakable decision.

"You haven't denounced him yet, have you?" Denise exclaimed, on seeing him come in.

"No, Mademoiselle," said the Chambrion. "In any case, my testimony wouldn't prove anything...it's necessary that he betray himself."

"But we believe you," said the young woman.

"Oh, I know that."

"Then why deliver the wretch to the law?"

"Why?" said the Chambrion. "So that everyone can see perfectly well that you can marry Monsieur de Verne."

"Well," said Horace, "Denise is right, and her aunt shares our opinion. We'll leave the country, my poor François, go far away...and you won't see the name of your father besmirched."

"Yes," said the young woman, in her turn, taking the Chambrion's hand. "And you'll come with us, my good François. Are you not our friend?"

The Chambrion shook his head. "It's necessary that justice be done," he said.

"But you'll be dishonored."

"I shall have God on my side, Mademoiselle. I shall know that I have done my duty."

"Oh, my God!" murmured the young woman. "But have you thought, François, that your father might not be dead?"

The Chambrion shook his head again. "I've often feared that," he said, "but at present, I can only believe the contrary. He would have come back sooner or later. No, Mademoiselle, my father is dead...like yours...like your mother...like Monsieur Horace's father, and it's that man who has killed them all."

"But after all," said the young woman, "don't we have the right to forgive him?"

A cloud passed over the Chambrion's face. "No," he said, finally, "you don't have that right, for that man has many other crimes on his conscience." Vehemently, he added; "Oh, you don't know how many unfortunates he's ruined! Travel the countryside of our poor Sologne for ten leagues around, and pronounce that man's name—you'll hear groans and imprecations. He's caused the fathers of families to die in prison, he's had the poor widows' beds sold, and the orphans' cradles!"

"Well," said the young woman, "what if that man, in the presence of the punishment he has merited, were to repent?"

"Never! The man has a heart of bronze."

"What if he were to return what he has stolen? Oh, François, François," the young woman said, with an emotional vivacity, "I've jut had an idea...an inspiration from Heaven."

"Speak, Mademoiselle," said François Véru.

"If that man pays me back the two hundred thousand francs he stole from us. I'll distribute them around the vicinity before we leave, to all those he's ruined, and I'll also repair the damage he has done."

"At the foot of the scaffold, Mademoiselle, that man would still refuse to make restitution."

"François," said Mademoiselle de Méreuil, sadly, "why can't you leave me the hope of snatching a soul from Hell and a man from death?"

"Very well!" cried the Chambrion. "If you can bring that man to repentance, Mademoiselle, I'll show him mercy." He shook his head, though, and added: "But your efforts will be in vain."

"God is good," murmured the young woman.

The Chambrion abruptly left the room where Denise, Horace and Madame Gertrude were sitting. His head was on fire, and his legs were buckling under him. He went out into the park and sat at the foot of a tree, his head in his hands.

Suddenly, he heard a voice behind him—the soft and gentle voice of a child. It was the Brocart, who had followed him. The young poacher came toward him. "You're weeping?" he said, on seeing, in the moonlight, François' face bathed in tears.

"No, it's nothing."

"Oh, don't tell me that you're not in love with the demoiselle, my poor François," the child continued.

"Shut up! Shut up!" said the Chambrion. "Don't ever repeat that."

"Well, what of it?" the Brocart went on. "Is one master of one's own heart, after all? And aren't you an honest man? Is it your fault that you're only a poor peasant? I know full well that you can't be her husband...but you have every right to love her... without her knowing...."

The Chambrion passed his hand over his eyes. "Tomorrow, I'll no longer have that right," he said, "for I'll have hollowed out the most insurmountable of gulfs between us." And, taking the child in his arms, he said: "You mother will have bread for her old age; you'll have honest work, and you'll no longer be a poacher, but a gamekeeper. You'll owe me that, and if you're not an ingrate, you'll make me a promise."

"Oh, speak," said the child, "speak, my good Chambrion."

"Never tell a living soul that you've seen me weeping and have surprised the secret of my heart."

"I swear on my dead father," replied the young poacher, simply.

The Chambrion got to his feet. "Now," he said, "think about yourself. The gendarmes will come looking for you tomorrow."

"You promised to hide me."

"Yes."

"Where?"

"At my house."

"Oh, said Brocart, Maupert will guess that right away."

"Maupert won't guess anything. Leave it to me! I have a plan. Where's your dog?"

"Right here," said the Brocart, pointing to Gendarme, who

was standing motionless, with his tail lowered, behind him."

"Well, go and shut him up in the château's kennels...there are no longer any dogs there...and tell him to stay quiet."

Brocart obeyed, and came back to find the Chambrion. Then the latter picked him up and set him on his shoulders.

"What are you doing?" asked the child, astonished.

"I'm carrying you so that Gendarme won't set off to follow your trail when they let him out."

"Why?"

"Because, child that you are, the poor animal, in wanting to rejoin you, would inevitably betray you."

And the Chambrion set out, carrying the Brocart on his shoulders.

It was not until they were a quarter of a league from the park, near to the Mare aux Chevrettes, that François Véru set the child down on the ground. "Now," he told him, "you can walk."

"Where are we going?"

"You're going to my house. You'll find the key to the door under a stone by the well."

"Yes, I know where. But aren't you coming with me?"

"Not yet. I'm going to rejoin Monsieur Hector."

As he spoke, a rifle shot rang out.

"One dead," said the Chambrion.

"Bah!" said the Brocart, all of whose instincts were alert. "That's not bourgeois game—that's roe deer. Let's hope he'll have missed."

"Go to the house, don't light the fire, and go to bed," said the Chambrion. "I'll join you soon."

And he quit the Brocart and went down toward the Mare aux Chevrettes.

Monsieur Hector was cursing and swearing. He had fired at a roebuck at fifteen paces and missed.

"I think it was wounded," he said.

"Where did you shoot it?" asked the Chambrion.

"There, as it was lowering its head to drink."

"At that distance, the shot was almost a bullet. If you'd hit it, it would have stayed there. It's necessary to start again, Monsieur Hector."

"It's freezing cold."

"That's true—and now that you've fired, we won't see anything more until two o'clock in the morning. I advise you to go to bed, Monsieur Hector."

"At the Meunerie?"

"Oh, no—at Les Bauges farm, as we agreed. I'll take you there. We'll tell the farmer that we have a rendezvous tomorrow with hunters from Mothe-Beuvron at the pointed oak."

Hector and the Chambrion set out again.

"You know," said the younger Clappier, "I can't get those two hundred thousand francs out of my head?"

"Really?"

"For after all, if my father has stolen them from the demoiselle...."

"Well?"

"And I marry the demoiselle...it's as if he's stolen them from me."

"That's true."

"And I beg you to believe that I'm going to get them back from him."

"He'll send you packing."

"Well, I'll lodge a complaint."

"With whom?"

"The imperial prosecutor."

"But they'll put your father in prison."

"Well," said Hector, indifferently, "that's his business, not mine."

The Chambrion looked at Hector from the corner of his eyes and said: "But if you father's in prison, people will condemn you."

The younger Clappier replied calmly: "That's not the worse thing that could happen to me, Francois, you know."

"What do you mean, Monsieur Hector?"

"Follow my reasoning."

"I'm listening."

"My father will be condemned as a thief."

"All right."

"He'll be dead, in civil terms; he'll lose control of his wealth, and an administrator will be appointed."

"That's true."

"Well, that administrator will be me! And there I'll be—me, who never had a sou to my name—in control of all my father's funds."

"But it might kill your mother," said the Chambrion.

"Bah! Mother's solid...and then, there's the money, you see... that consoles everything."

"But you wouldn't recoil before the necessity of dragging your father before a tribunal?" said the Chambrion. "That's a serious dishonor!"

"Bah! Sins are personal. Then again, if there's too much outcry, I'll sell up here and go away, to Paris. There, you see, as long as you're rich, that's all that matters—no one asks any more of you."

That man is like his father, the Chambrion thought, whose heart revolted at those ignoble words, *and it's not the pity he inspires that will prevent me striking him down from now on.*

Without suspecting it, Hector Clappier might just have pronounced his father's death-sentence.

XI.

In domestic life as in business, Père Clappier was a hard and savage man. His son had frightened him at first, and for more than an hour it was as if he were under the influence of a mental prostration that made it impossible for him to think clearly—but that did not last long. Courage returned, and with courage the energy of evil that was, in him, developed to its ultimate extreme.

"I'll shove the words he permitted himself to say to me

back down his throat," he murmured, as he headed toward the Meunerie, "and I'll let him rot in his rags, for he won't get another sou out of me."

He almost expected to find Hector at the Meunerie, for the young man had gone around the house as he went away and his father had not seen him reach the edge of the woods. But Hector was not there; by that time, he had gone to meet the Chambrion. It was Mère Clappier who received the storm.

She was busy at that moment, like the good housekeeper she was, melting butter in a large brown stone jar, and had no inkling of what had happened.

"Where's Hector, then?" demanded the property-dealer.

"I thought he was with you," replied the stout Lucinde, née Jousserand.

"He's not here, then?"

"No, Master," said Jeannette, who came in carrying a pail of water. "He went hunting."

"Oh, the scoundrel!" said Clappier. "The wretch!"

"What has he done?" exclaimed Mère Clappier, trembling at her husband's sudden anger.

"He's lacked respect for his father—and that's your fault, woman, for you've brought him up badly, the idler, the good-for-nothing. He won't have a sou of my heritage, and I can certainly stop him marrying!"

Mère Clappier tried to speak, but the property-dealer went on: "I don't want him to set foot in here again!"

"And where do you expect him to go?"

"To the Devil, if it pleases him."

"But he's our son...and we've given him his status—what do you expect him to do?"

"He can become a carter, a shepherd or a soldier, as he wishes."

Mère Clappier had never seen her husband in such a state of irritation, but she thought that the best means of calming him down was to put on a show of agreeing with him. "If Hector's been disrespectful," she said, "he'll ask you to forgive him."

"I don't want to see him again! And if you dare to defend him, I'll kick you out along with him."

With these words, Père Clapier left the kitchen, and went up the Meunerie's wooden staircase. Soon, Mere Clappier and Jeanette heard a frightful racket. It was the property-dealer, who, having gone into his son's room, was throwing his clothes out of the window, along with a trunk, a rifle, a hunting-horn, an English saddle and a training harness.

All of that tumbled pell-mell on to the pavement of the court-yard, and the old man was heard to shout: "I don't want anything of his here—nothing at all! He can take his rags wherever he wants."

Mère Clappier and Jeannette looked at one another with a sort of terror. Fortunately, an event then occurred that forced Père Clappier to calm down temporarily.

Emerging from the sunken road that came from Salbris he saw a man mounted on a white mare, which was trotting gently, and he recognized one of his famers, who was known as Grand Jacques, whose farm was on the Vierzon road.

As it was getting close to Toussaint, Père Clapier, in spite of his anger, reasoned as follows: *Grand Jacques is a punctilious farmer; he's coming to pay me his rent.* Nothing calmed Père Clappier down like money. He therefore went downstairs and said to Jeannette: "Put everything I threw out of the window in a corner. It's necessary to wash one's dirty linen in private, and Grand Jacques is coming to pay the rent."

Five minutes later, Mère Clappier and the maidservant having got rid of the evidence the Maître's anger, Grand Jacques, on coming into the courtyard, found him smiling and good-humored.

The famer descended from his horse, tethered the animal to a ring fixed in the wall, and took off his otter-skin cap with the obsequiousness that poor people develop, in the country, with regard to those who own the land.

"You're punctual, my lad," said Père Clappier. "Come this way, and I'll give you your receipt."

"Excuse me, Maître," said Grand Jacques. "I'll pay you next week—that is to say, the Monday of Toussaint, when I come back from Orléans."

"Oh," said the property dealer. "I thought you were bringing me money."

"No, Maître. I've come to talk to you about a misfortune that has overtaken me."

"Oh," said Clappier, indifferently. "You've had a death in the family, perhaps...."

"No, Maître."

"Or your animals are sick...."

"No, Maître, worse than that. We've burned."

"Burned?" exclaimed Clappier, dominated by the sentiment of property. "You've burned. The Regrattières farm?"

"Not the farm, but the sheepfold. Nothing's left of it but the four walls."

"Well," said the property dealer, with an tranquil expression, "so much the worse for the company. The sheepfold and the buildings attached to it are insured for seventeen thousand francs."

"Double what they're worth," said Grand Jacques, "and for nine or ten thousand francs, I'll take care of it...."

"In that case," said Père Clappier, there's profit in burning. I'll put eight thousand francs in my pocket."

"It's just," the farmer said, timidly, "that I've been less prudent than you, Maître."

"You haven't insured your animals?"

"Alas, no. I've lost five cows, a pair of bullocks and thirty-four sheep. It's a loss that'll ruin me, Maître, if you don't help me out...with the money you'll get for the insurance."

"My boy," said Père Clappier, sententiously, "when one is punished because one has sinned, it's necessary not to complain. If you had insured your animals, the company would pay you; that's not my concern."

"In that case," said the poor man, "you have to give me time...."

"Time? For what?"

"Why, for the rent...."

"What!" said the property-dealer. "You can't pay it?"

"Alas, no. I was counting on selling my cows and my sheep."

"You can settle it with Maupert," said Clappier, and turned his back on the farmer.

When Clappier said to one of his farmers or tenants "You can settle it with Maupert," the unfortunate man knew that he would receive a visit from a bailiff a week later, and that his equipment, his crops and his carts would be sold, up to the value of the sum owed.

The farmer went away with death in his soul, with no suspicion that he had just provided a deflection for the property-dealer's anger.

"These brigands, these wretches," said Clappier, as he sat down at the table. "Not insuring their crops and their animals—which is to say, my guarantee. Oh, I'll make him sell everything, down to his last chicken, and he can get out; I don't want a man like that on my hands...."

But Père Clappier's anger did not prevent him from being anxious, and thinking from time to time about his son's mysterious words—and as the evening wore on, although his nerves relaxed and gradually calmed down, his mind was, as they say, working overtime, and he recalled Hector's mocking tone in marvelous detail.

Hector did not come home for supper. At ten o'clock Mère Clappier, having not seen him come in, began to get seriously anxious.

"Perhaps you beat him?" she said.

"No," said Clappier. "I didn't say anything at all. But don't worry—he'll lose nothing by waiting."

Maupert came back. He had returned from Romorantin.

His arrival brought some distraction to the property-dealer's unquiet mind. "What have you done?" he asked.

"I've seen the imperial prosecutor."

"And he didn't attach any importance to your complaint, did

he?"

"On the contrary. He summoned the brigadier of the gendarmerie."

"Aha!" said Clappier, smiling.

"And he issued an arrest warrant." Maupert added. "It's necessary to tell you, mind, that I laid it on a bit thick. You know that there was a robbery in Salbris last month."

"Yes, and no one knows who the thief was."

"I let it be understood that it might be the Brocart...."

Clappier looked at his gamekeeper, and started to laugh. "I would have thought that it was more likely to be you," he said.

Maupert took the joke quite well, and joined in with his master, beginning to laugh himself.

At that moment, Jeannette opened the door that led to the dining-room and the kitchen. "Look," she said. "Here's Jacomy, who's brought back Flambant, Monsieur Hector's dog."

Clappier got up, and saw the dog, which was being freed from its leash. "Was it lost?" he asked the woodcutter. "Did you find him in the woods?"

"No, Maître," Jacomy replied. "Monsieur Hector told me to bring him back."

"Why hasn't he kept it with him?" asked Madame Clappier, astonished.

"Because it's a pointer, no good for ambushes."

"So he's gone night-hunting."

"Yes, with the Chambrion, François Véru."

At that moment, if the Biblical *Mene Mene Tekel Upharsin* had suddenly been displayed in letters of fire on one of the walls of the during-room, Père Clappier would certainly not have experienced a more terrible sensation.

The Chambrion!

That name was a revelation for him.

It was the Chambrion who had told Hector that he had collected his money twice.

And Père Clappier's memory suddenly made an abrupt return to the past.

He remembered that during the night of the crime, he had seen that child holding his unfortunate father's hand, and that he had not suspected....

The Chambrion knew everything!

* * * * * * *

It was a terrible night that Père Clappier spent, waiting anxiously for his son to return. He would grab him by the throat, he would question him...and he would find out exactly how far the Chambrion had taken him into his confidence.

But Hector did not come back.

Then a thousand forgotten circumstances came back to his mind.

He remembered that the Chambrion never came to the Meunerie; that he avoided crossing paths with him, scarcely recognizing his presence—him, Clappier, before whom everyone bowed, if not out of respect, at least out of terror.

Ah! he said to himself, finally. *That man knows my secret; that man knows that I'm a murderer...but he's kept quiet for fifteen years. Why would he talk today?*

Clappier certainly did not go to sleep, as he had the previous night, but he dreamed while awake, and the dream that he had with his eyes open had the assize court for a theater and the scaffold for a denouement. At first he went to bed, but he could not sleep and got up. Finally, at dawn, after having wandered around the garden, the courtyard and the acacia nursery, feverish and tormented, he made an important resolution.

That resolution was to go into danger with his head held high—which is to say, to go to the Chambrion's house.

I'll buy the man off, he said to himself. *Today is no time to play the skinflint.*

And he left, still hoping to meet his son on the way—but he arrived at the clearing where François Véru's house stood without having seen Hector.

On the other hand, the Chambrion, with his sleeves rolled

up, was calmly hooping a barrel in front of his door, singing. He was perfectly tranquil, and gave the appearance of a good worker who begins his day early under God's gaze.

On seeing Père Clappier, he took of his cap and said to him: "I know why you've come, Maître."

"Oh!" said Père Clappier, stopping dead and feeling his heart flutter in his breast. "You know...why...."

"Monsieur Hector didn't come back to the Meunerie last night."

"That's true," said Père Clappier, staring in a strange fashion at the Chambrion's placid and smiling face.

"Perhaps that's partly my fault," François Véru continued, "but these young men, you know, when they get an idea in their heads...."

"Ah," said Clappier's to whom the Chambrion's calmness rendered a certain confidence. "And what has he got into his head?"

"He came here yesterday morning. He wanted to kill a roe deer, and asked me to show him where to lie in ambush."

Père Clappier took another step forward, and, on seeing François Véru's insouciant attitude, was further reassured.

"Ah! He wanted to kill a roe deer?"

"Yes, to offer it to the Demoiselle des Sapinières.

Clappier received that name head on, and did not flinch.

"Because," the Chambrion continued, "he's smittten with the Demoiselle des Sapinières, and is absolutely determined to marry her."

The Chambrion's tone was so tranquil that Père Clappier said to himself: *Either that man's stronger than I am, or he knows nothing at all.* "Well," he said, "what do you think about that, Chambrion."

"Personally," replied the Chambrion, "I think there's no reason, just because the demoiselle's mother behaved badly and her father killed himself, why she shouldn't find a husband, and if Monsieur Hector wants her, I'm sure that you have enough écus to arrange it." The Chambrion expressed himself with a certain indifference.

Clappier was completely wrong-footed. "But where's Hector now?" he said.

"Oh, I forgot to tell you that he missed a superb roebuck last night."

"And then?"

"Then he went to stay the night at your farm, whose farmer has two good bassets. He'll go hunting this morning, for sure." François added: "And it also appears that you and he had words yesterday—he told me that."

"What did he say?" Clappier demanded, urgently, all his anxieties returning.

"Perhaps that's partly my fault too," the Chambrion replied, with a naïve smile on his lips. "Can you imagine that yesterday morning, when he came to ask me to take him to the roe deer, he said to me: 'Would you believe that my father doesn't want to go to the Sapinières? He doesn't owe money to the demoiselle, though, nor she to him. He's been paid for the château.'"

"Ah!" said Clappier, the blood congealing in his veins. "He said that."

"Yes," said the Chambrion, "and I, who had always heard it said that Monsieur de Méreuil had paid too dear for the Sapinières, said to him without meaning any harm: 'Oh, doubtless your father was paid, twice rather than once.'"

While the Chambrion was speaking, Père Clappier tried to probe the depths of his soul with his gaze, but François Véru remained impassive.

"Then," he concluded, "it appears that Monsieur Hector took the words the wrong way, and that he repeated them to you, and that you were annoyed."

"Well," said Père Clappier, "one would get annoyed for less."

"You mustn't hold it against him," the Chambrion said. "It's entirely my fault, Monsieur Clappier."

"And you say that he's at the farm."

"Yes."

"Well, I'll go there," said Clappier, resumed his hard and

arrogant tone. And he drew away, satisfied with the Chambrion's explanation.

"Oh," he said, "I've had a real fright...that boy doesn't know anything. All the same, he'll pay me back...I'll unleash Maupert on him one day."

* * * * * * *

The Chambrion watched Père Clappier draw away; then a silent smile came to his lips.

He's had a scare, he said to himself. *The time's not far off when he'll betray himself.*

While the property-dealer was talking to him, the Chambrion had remained in front of the door of his house, which was closed, and the idea of going into it had never occurred to Père Clappier.

When the latter had gone, the Chambrion opened the door and went into his cabin. Hector was sitting quietly by the fireside, and he had heard the conversation between his father and the Chambrion without understanding it.

"Well," he said to him, "what was all that about?"

"Monsieur Hector," said the Chambrion, "do you still have your heart set on those two hundred thousand francs?"

"Still," said Hector, "and if I marry the demoiselle, he'll give them back."

"Well, I know a means of getting him to hand them over. Do you have anything to write with?"

"Yes—I have a pencil in my wallet."

"Then write what I dictate to you." And the Chambrion dictated to Hector, who wrote:

My dear father,

> *For all your cunning, you're as simple as a child. Go see the Chambrion right away. He knows everything, and by paying him the price, and not haggling, you can get yourself out of it.*

"Good," said the Chambrion, when Hector had signed the letter. "You can rest easy now."

"You mean stay here?"

"Oh no," the Chambrion replied. "Pick up your rifle and go find the farmer's bassets; your affairs will go more smoothly than if you were there."

"You think so?" said Hector, who had great confidence in the Chambrion since the result he had obtained the day before.

"I'm sure of it," said François. "You can see that everything I've said to you has been realized. And do you know where your father has gone?"

"To the farm, I believe."

"No—he took the path to the Sapinières. He's gone to make the request."

"Really? Are you sure?"

"You'll see."

"But what are you going to do with that letter I've just written?" Hector asked.

"Don't worry about that—that's my business."

Hector Clappier, as we have seen, although he was endowed with evil instincts, was not very intelligent. He had ended up considering the Chambrion as a being superior to him, and he took him at his word. He therefore left him the letter he had just written, picked up his rifle, and took the false road that went down to the pond in order to get back to the forest path that led to the farm where he had spent the night.

Then the Chambrion raised his head and whistled.

Immediately, the trap-door to the loft opened and the Brocart, who had been hiding there, and whose presence Monsieur Hector had not suspected, showed his alert face.

"Listen carefully, my boy," the Chambrion said to him.

"Go on, Chambrion."

"You stay where you are—you have enough to eat and drink, don't you?"

"Undoubtedly."

"I'll come back. I don't know exactly when...perhaps this

evening, perhaps in an hour...perhaps not until tomorrow. If you hear anyone coming, don't budge."

"That's fine," said the child. "You know that I'll do as you say."

The Chambrion went out.

A few minutes later he was on his way to the Sapinières, and went past Maître Clappier like a shadow. The latter did not see him, separated as they were by thick bushes.

XII.

Père Clappier had stopped a hundred and fifty meters away from the Chambrion's house.

A great captain, halting on high ground before a battle in order to finalize his plan of attack, could not have been calmer or more earnest than the property-dealer was at that solemn moment.

He had two paths before him: two of those forest paths that wind around thickets and pass straight under the crowns of the trees. One led to the farm where Hector had spent the night; the other went down to the Mare aux Chevrettes, alongside the pond, and then climbed up again toward the park of the Château des Sapinières.

Père Clappier stopped in that location, and seemed to reflect. Then, suddenly, talking to himself, he said: "Come on! The time has come to finish with all these superstitions, which are only fit for children, at best. I don't believe in God, and the only man who could accuse me is dead. Why hesitate, then, to go to the château?"

After that, he set out again, slowly at first, examining the various species of trees, their growth and their value, and observing that the demoiselle's woods had been carefully maintained.

Aunt Gertrude is a clever woman, he said to himself. *She's almost doubled the value of the Sapinières; I'd be stupid, after all, not to get my hands on all this—for Hector's an imbecile, and will do whatever I want....*

And while he walked, the property-dealer started calculating Mademoiselle de Mérueil's fortune.

There were three hundred acres of arable land, eight hundred acres of woods, a hundred and fifty of meadows, and a reserve around the château that might well be worth a hundred thousand francs. In addition, the worthy man remembered that once, when Monsieur de Méreuil had become his customer, he had obtained information about his fortune, and that a notary in Paris had written to tell him that the Baron owned two houses in Paris, which produced and annual income of twenty-seven thousand livres.

They don't spend anything at the Sapinières, he said to himself, *and in fifteen years the fortune must have increased by a third. The girl can't have much less than forty-eight thousand francs a year. That's a nice touch!*

And while devoting himself to these suppositions and approximate calculations, Clappier lengthened his stride and headed straight for the Sapinières, like a wild boar, having spent the night in the oat-fields, heading back to its lair in the morning.

He arrived at the gate of the park and rang the bell; a gardener working in a nearby path hastened to open up.

"I'm Monsieur Clappier, my boy," said the property-dealer.

The gardened bowed, with the fearful respect that the property-dealer inspired throughout the region. Then he opened the gate, without asking for any further explanation.

Clappier went straight to the perron like a general entering a conquered city. At the top of the perron there was a domestic in petty livery. The domestic bowed with no less respect than the gardener.

"Is it possible to see Madame Gertude?" Clappier asked.

"Madame Gertrude is very ill, Monsieur," the domestic replied, "and is confined to bed, but Mademoiselle is doubtless expecting your visit."

"Ah!" said Clappier, with a satisfied expression.

"Mademoiselle," the valet continued, "has instructed that Monsieur be taken into the drawing-room."

All this is working out marvelously, Clappier thought. *I'll get a better bargain from the niece than the aunt.* And he followed the valet, who opened two double doors in front of him.

The drawing-room of the Sapinières had conserved the same furniture as fifteen years before. Above the settee, facing the fireplace and perfectly lit, was a portrait of the Baron de Méreuil, and that portrait was a striking likeness. At the sight of it, Clappier felt a slight frisson and his heart skipped a beat, because the dead man seemed to be looking at him—but he quickly pulled himself together, turned his eyes away from the portrait of his victim and looked the other way.

Facing the Baron's portrait was another, that of a woman. It was Madame de Méreuil. That was another bad moment for Clappier to pass through, but he was well-tempered, and to stiffen himself against emotion he drew nearer to the frame and started examining it, as a connoisseur.

The portrait bore the date 1840, and although he had never seen Madame de Méreuil alive, Clappier could not be mistaken. It was definitely the unfortunate woman that had been found strangled in her bed.

Clappier translated that further emotion into this atrocious reflection:

It's annoying, all the same, to die so young!

As if hazard had wanted to make him a liar, however, there was a noise behind the property dealer, who turned round and uttered an exclamation.

The door of the drawing-room had just opened, and a woman who was the living image of the portrait, a woman dressed in black, her long blonde hair pinned back, came in and bowed to Père Clappier, who felt a few drops of sweat form on his forehead and moisten his temples.

"Excuse me, Monsieur," Denise said to him—for it was her—"for keeping you waiting. It's very early and I wasn't dressed, for I spent part of the night with my aunt, who is ill."

Oof! thought Clappier, breathing again. *It's the daughter...but she resembles her mother so perfectly that I thought momentarily that the dead returned.* He added mentally, to give himself courage: *The dead are well and truly dead...don't be stupid!* And he returned the young woman's bow.

The latter offered him a seat, and seemed to be waiting for him to state the purpose of his visit. Clappier was unaccustomed to society; in a drawing-room, words failed him. Not knowing how to begin the conversation, he said to Denise, with the brutality of a peasant: "You're in mourning, then, Mademoiselle?"

Denise replied, with a sad gravity: "I'm wearing mourning for my father and mother, Monsieur."

"What!" Clappier exclaimed. "After fifteen years?"

"I had put it away, Monsieur, but my father appeared to me last night and instructed me to put it on again."

That reply stunned Père Clappier, who felt a chill run down his spine.

"What's that you're saying?" he said, with an abruptness that failed to conceal his emotion.

"The truth, Monsieur. "Last night, in a dream, I saw my father again...."

"Oh, I a dream...that's different...one calls that a nightmare... you must have been sleeping on your left side."

"However, Monsieur," the young woman said, "my father told me to expect your visit, and I expected it."

"That's mischievous," murmured Clappier, laughing in order to overcome the strange emotion that had caught him by the throat. "Your aunt wrote to me yesterday...."

"Really?" said the young woman, with an ingenuousness that threw Clappier completely off his stride. "I have no idea what my aunt can have said to you, Monsieur, but I know what my father confided to me."

"Your father...confided...something to you? And it...concerns me?" stammered the property-dealer, invaded by a vague terror.

"A frightful secret, Monsieur," said Denise, sadly."

"My dear demoiselle," the property-dealer replied, rising to his feet, "I believe that you're not entirely in your right mind."

But Denise, with a gesture that had a singular authority, nailed him to the spot.

"Yes, Monsieur," the young woman went on. "Last night, my father rose from the grave to reveal something frightful to me. My father did not commit suicide, as everyone thinks."

Clappier felt dizzy.

"He was murdered," Denise concluded.

Clappier uttered a horse exclamation. That cry, which might have been attributed to astonishment, was one of anguish and terror.

The young woman continued: "And he told me the name of his murderer."

At first, Père Clappier nearly fell over, but the excess of his emotion saved him; he stiffened; his clenched throat recovered its ordinary voice—that acerbic and harshly mocking voice.

"Mademoiselle," he said, "I don't believe in dreams, in dead men who return, and all that nonsense. But I believe in...."

Clappier stopped, and met Mademoiselle de Méreuil's gaze brazenly.

"What will you do, Monsieur?" she asked him, softly.

"I'll make you a very simple reply: if your father was murdered, it's necessary to address yourself to the law, and not to me. I'm not the imperial prosecutor."

"Monsieur," Denise went on, still calm and sad, "what if your name were combined with other names in my father's story?"

Clappier shrugged his shoulders. "I don't believe in dreams!" he repeated, with the brutality of a peasant.

"So be it," said Denise. "But you won't refuse to hear me out."

Clappier made a gesture, which meant: *If I knew how to get out of it, I wouldn't listen.*

Denise continued: "My father was murdered one night, on returning from your house."

"Why, that's true," said Clappier, recovering his audacity and courage. "I remember that, not being able to make the payment that he had to make to me, he'd come to ask me for a delay."

Denise looked at the property-dealer calmly. "Monsieur Clappier," she said, "you don't believe in ghosts or in dreams...."

"Indeed not!"

"But perhaps you believe in Providence."

"Pooh!" said the property-dealer. "That's...."

"In the Providence that pardons repentance...and which is inflexible to those who disregard it."

"My dear Demoiselle," Clappier sniggered, "I didn't come here to listen to a sermon. I go on Sunday to hear the curé of Salbris preach. That's quite enough."

And for a second time, he tried to leave. But Denise did not take her eyes off him, and the young woman's gaze weighed upon him so heavily that he did ot have the strength to beat a retreat.

"I believe, on the contrary," she went on, "that my father paid you, that evening, two hundred thousand francs."

"Never!" said the property-dealer, in a strangle voice.

"Are you perfectly sure?"

"Where's the receipt, if your father paid me?" cried Clappier, deciding to take the offensive.

"Monsieur," the young woman continued, "it appears that the receipt was stolen by the man who murdered my father."

"Thunder!" exclaimed Clappier, rendered furious by terror. "It only remains for me to tell me that it was me who murdered your father!"

"I don't say that," Denise replied, "but in the name of the Providence that you have perhaps misunderstood, Monsieur, I've come to beg you...."

"To beg me to what?" he said, straightening up, with his eyes ablaze.

"To return the two hundred thousand francs to me, with which I shall do a little good...to repair the evil that you have caused—and at that price, Monsieur," she concluded, "there are secrets that I shall keep in the depths of my heart, and which will die with me...."

Having struck the blow, Denise waited—but the noble child did not know the man, and did not know that one might do better bargaining for his head than his money. He vomited a frightful blasphemy, and cried: "You want to steal two hundred thousand francs from me with your nonsense! Back! Vagabond.... Adventuress.... Back! I'm not in a house, I'm in a den of cutthroats!"

And he pushed Denise away—who put her hand together, still imploring him—and went out like a hurricane.

Then a door opened and a man came in, pale, sad and solemn. It was the Chambrion.

"Mademoiselle," he said, "as you see, the man is condemned!" And he made as if to leave.

"Where are you going?" Denise asked, shivering.

"I'm going to bring forward God's justice," he replied.

On the threshold of the drawing-room he turned round, directed a long and dolorous glance at the young woman, and stifled a sob.

The Chambrion had just made a vow: that he would never see her again.

But God decided otherwise.

* * * * * * *

Père Clappier went straight along the avenue, like a wounded old boar, knocking down two or three domestics as he went and uttering horrible blasphemies.

The Chambrion saw him disappear through the gate. Then he went down into the courtyard of the château and went to open the door of the kennel in which the Brocart had locked his dog Gendarme the previous evening.

Gendarme did not follow anyone except the Brocart. He came out of the kennel howling, but he looked at the Chambrion and made as if to go away. Then the latter drew nearer, caressed him, and let him sniff his shirt. It was the Bocart's shirt.

The dog smelled his master's odor, and when the Chambrion

went away, he followed him.

The Chambrion went through the park by the shortest route, threw himself into the woods and ran as fat as he could to the hut of Jacomy the woodcutter. He knew where the key was—in a corner of the garden, under a plank. He took the key and opened the door. The dog, who was missing his master, went in and searched everywhere.

Then François closed the door again swiftly, put the key in his pocket and set forth.

As he went in the direction of the Meunerie, he met Jacomy—the man who had taken the younger Clappier's dog back the previous night. Jacomy was running toward him, in alarm.

"What's happened?" the Chambrion asked him.

"Oh," said the charcoal-burner, "it's surely another one of Père Clappier's blows. That brigand will have us all in the straw."

"What has he done?" asked the Chambrion, calmly.

"I've just gone past the Meunerie."

"So?"

"I saw two gendarmes talking to Maupert."

"An utter rogue, that one," said François. "What were they saying?"

"They were talking about arresting poor little Brocart."

"Ah!" said the Chambrion.

"Then I took to my heels as fast as I could and ran to warn the Brocart."

"You're a good man, Jacomy," said the Chambrion, "but don't worry—the Brocart and his mother aren't at home."

"Where are they?"

"I've hidden them."

"Oh, you're a good lad too, François," said the charcoal-burner.

"Do you think so?"

"Of that's what everyone thinks around here."

"Then if I tell you something, you'll believe me?"

"Will I believe you! Everyone knows that you never lie."

"Well, listen to me," said the Chambrion. "Before long, Père

Clappier won't do any more harm to anyone."

"What do you mean?"

"You'll know later, but for today, it's necessary to do as I say."

"I'll do whatever you want, Chambrion."

François Véru took the letter that he had had young Clappier write that morning out of his pocket. "Go to the Meunerie, ask to speak to the Père, and give him this letter, saying that Monsieur Hector gave it to you."

"I'm damned if I understand any of this!" said the charcoal-burner.

"You soon will," said the Chambrion, sadly. And he went back into the forest.

XIII.

Night was approaching—a foggy night, of which there are a great many in Sologne, where the vapors of the ponds rise into the atmosphere in the evenings, and obscure it.

François Véru walked along pensively.

This morning, he thought, *I condemned Hector Clappier in condemning his father—but have I the right to do that? Didn't the demoiselle say no? Children aren't responsible for their parents' crimes, and if lightning has to strike them, it's God who should do it. That's why I want to wait a little longer. I've made the sacrifice of my own honor, but just because it pleases me to accept that shame, do I really have the right to inflict it on someone else before attempting one last proof?*

It was while thinking in this manner that he arrived home.

The Brocart had not left his hiding-place. He was still up in the loft, under a thick layer of faggots and branches.

When he heard the sound of the door opening, the child looked through a crack in the ceiling.

"Can I come down?" he asked.

"Yes."

"There's no danger?"

"None."

The Brocart climbed down briskly—but he was struck by the Chambrion's terrible and solemn expression. "My God!" he said. "What's the matter?"

"The time is nigh," Francois replied, lighting a lamp.

Then he sat down at the table that was in a corner of the hut. On that table there was paper, ink and quills. The Chambrion wrote rapidly, sealed his letter and handed it to the Brocart.

"Here," he said. "It's the passport I promised you."

"What?" said the child, taking the letter tremulously.

"You're going to go to Romorantin..."

"Me?" exclaimed the Brocart. "But that's where the gendarmes...."

"First of all, the Chambrion said, "the gendarmes are here, not in Romorantin."

"Here?" said the Brocart, terrified.

"In the neighborhood, at least, looking for you. But as the road to Romorantin is in the opposite direction, they won't find you. In any case, if they do find you...."

"What?" asked the Brocart, shivering.

"Show them the address on this letter."

The child cast his eyes over the letter, and an exclamation escaped him. "To...the imperial prosecutor!"

"Yes."

"But why?" said the Bocart, in a distraught voice.

"To denounce a crime."

"A crime, you say?" the child murmured. "Ah...I think I can guess...." The Brocart looked at François Véru with a kind of terror. "It's Père Clappier you're denouncing," he said.

"Perhaps."

"But then...Monsieur Hector...."

The Chambrion interrupted him with a gesture. "Listen carefully," he said.

"Speak."

"Follow the forest path facing this window...."

"All right."

"And stop at the signpost of the eight roads."

"And then?"

"Wait for me to give you a signal."

"What signal?"

"You see this lamp?"

"Yes."

"It's here on the table. Well, when I put it on the window-sill, you set off."

"For Romorantin?"

"Yes."

"And if you don't give me the signal?"

"It's because I'll have got what I want...and you can come back here, at daybreak. Go."

The Brocart obeyed the Chambrion passively. He left, and François Véru remained alone.

Anxious and troubled, he wandered around his house, sometimes opening the door and listening.

"Oh, he'll come," he said. "He'll come!"

There was a noise outside. The Chambrion shuddered—but it was not Père Clappier who came in. It was Mère Malbeque. She was anxious about her son.

"Go away, Mère," the Chambrion told her, "and don't worry about your son."

"Where is he?" the old woman demanded."

"In hiding—I told you."

"But the gendarmes are looking for him."

"The gendarmes will soon have better things to do. Go away."

And the Chambrion sent La Malbèque away without any further explanation.

Then he continued waiting.

Finally, precipitate footsteps resounded in the distance.

"Ah! This time, it's him!" exclaimed the Chambrion—and he ran the door, and plunged an ardent eye into the darkness.

* * * * * * *

Meanwhile, on leaving the Château des Sapinières, Clappier, beside himself, furious and terrified by turns, had gone back to the Meunerie.

Mère Clappier was weeping. She had had no news of her dear Hector.

Clappier thrust her away when she came to him, talking about her son. Somber and grim, his sparse hair prickling, he went to shut himself up in his room. He spent the rest of the day there, without wanting to see anyone, and it was only there that he began to reassemble his confused ideas.

"No," he repeated, "the dead don't come back...and I don't believe in dreams. And yet, that girl told the truth. She knows. Who told her, then?"

And the interrogation he made of himself as full of terror. Who, then, knew that Père Clappier was a murderer and a thief?

Who, then, could send him to the scaffold?

His forehead was bathed with sweat; his temples were hammering; he had a bloody mist before his eyes.

Suddenly, he heard a voice in the courtyard, which said: "It's Monsieur Hector who sent me."

He went to the window and saw Jacomy, the charcoal-burner, who had brought the letter that the Chambrion had given to him.

Clappier ran downstairs and took possession of the letter, which he opened with a horrible constriction in his heart.

Suddenly, the Chambrion's name flared before his eyes, and a frightful blasphemy escaped his clenched throat.

"Hector's right!" he cried. "I'm an imbecile!"

And Père Clappier pushed past Jacomy, whom he found in front of him, and ran out of the courtyard.

He was bare-headed, but gave it no thought. He ran straight ahead, jumping the ditches and galloping across the fields as if he had found the legs he had had at twenty.

He went straight to the Chambrion's house, leaving shreds of the eternal black frock-coat that he wore in all seasons in the forest undergrowth, tearing his hands on thorns, sometimes stumbling, getting up again and setting off again at a run.

When he arrived at the Chambrion's house the clearing was deserted, and the door had closed again.

Clappier knocked.

"Come in," said a voice from inside.

XIV.

Clappier went in with the brutality of a mortally-wounded wild animal.

The Chambrion was alone by the fireside, placidly smoking his pipe.

Clappier slammed the door shut behind him. "Bonsoir," he said.

"Bonsoir, Monsieur Clappier," François replied, phlegmatically.

"Are you alone?" asked the property-dealer, parading a sly glance around him.

"As you can see."

Clappier was emboldened. "You weren't expecting me to come so late, were you?" he said.

"It's true," the Chambrion replied, "that you don't come to see me very often."

"I come when I have business to do."

"Oh," said the Chambrion, calmly. "You have business to do with me?"

"Perhaps...yes and no...."

"That's not an answer, Monsieur Clappier."

Clappier shrugged his shoulders. "I can see that you were expecting me," he said.

"That's possible."

From then on, for Clappier, one thing was definite—which is, to make use of a Parisian expression, that the Chambrion wanted to blackmail him. And he went on the defensive.

But the Chambrion did not seem to be in any hurry to resume the conversation.

"So, you were expecting me?" Clappier repeated.

"Don't we have an old account to settle?"

"Oh, you think so?"

"You have," said the Chambrion, "a mortgage of forty-five louis—which is to say, nine hundred francs—on this house."

"No," said Clappier. "You father paid me."

"However," François Véru observed, "the mortgage still exists."

"That's forgetfulness on my part. I'll have it torn up."

The Chambrion laughed. "You'd be wrong," he said.

"Why?" said the property-dealer.

"Because my father can't have paid you."

"But...I assure you...."

"With what, then, did he pay you?"

"With what...?" Clappier stammered. "With...well, with his savings...."

The Chambrion laughed again. "You're very kind to make use of that word," he said. "Do you know, Monsieur Claoppier, that I was ten years old when my father died."

"So what?"

"At that age," the Chambrion continued, "one begins to reason...to take account...to remember...."

And of what do you take account?" asked Clappier.

"Of the straitened circumstances that my father was in when he died."

"And what do you... remember?"

"That you came here one night...."

Clappier made an abrupt movement.

"The night when Monsieur and Madame de Méreuil died...so mysteriously," the Chambrion continued."

"I don't recall whether it was that night," said Clappier, abruptly.

"Then your memory is letting you down."

"That's permissible, at my age," said Clappier, "but after all, what connection is there between my visit here...."

"You know as well as I do," the Chambrion interjected.

"Me! Oh, not at al!"

François Véru looked at Père Clappier coldly. "Then why are you here?" he said.

Clappier wiped away a few drops of sweat that had formed on his brow. "Let's put our cards on the table," he said.

"I'd like that," said François Véru.

"You've spoken to the demoiselle," Clappier said.

"Yes."

"What did you tell her?"

"That my father murdered hers."

Clappier recoiled at that word, but François Véru said to him, ironically: "It's not worth the trouble of being astonished by that, since you settled his debt on the sole condition that he committed the crime."

"And you dared to tell the demoiselle...."

"I told her," said the Chambrion, "that I knew the man who had commissioned the murder."

"But you didn't name me, at least!" cried the property-dealer.

"Oh, that's what you'd like to know, isn't it?" sniggered the Chambrion. "But we need to reach an understanding first."

"Which is to say that you want money."

"Well, didn't you say it yourself? Let's put our cards on the table."

"That's true," sighed Clappier. "How much do you want?"

"Oh, that's worth a great deal," said François. "For, if I don't say anything, you'll be Monsieur Clappier, as before."

"And if you talk, what will happen?"

"The law will stick its nose into your affairs."

"Pooh!" said Clappier, trying to recover some confidence. "It requires evidence for that."

"What I've seen...what I've heard..."

"That's not enough!"

"Bah!" said the Chambrion.

"You were only ten years old," said Clappier. "You were dreaming...no one will believe you."

If that's the case," replied the Chambrion, calmly, "why are you here?"

"Why?" stammered Clappier. "Because I'd rather have a bad business deal than a fair trial."

"So be it," said the Chambrion. "Let's negotiate."

"I'll make you secure from need. You can go to Paris...no one will hear mention of you again."

"Oh, you want me to leave the region?" the Chambrion replied.

"Yes, I'd prefer that."

"Well, what will you give me?"

Clappier blew into his cheeks and his eyes rounded. "Would you like ten thousand francs?" he said. "It's a pretty penny, eh, for a man like you? With that, you could open a little shop."

The Chambrion looked at the old man scornfully. "I believe you're joking," he said. "You won't buy my silence, it seems...."

"Come on!" said Clappier, adopting a hearty manner. "I'm a good man, fundamentally, and I can make a sacrifice. I'll make it fifteen, and we'll say no more. Look, I have a check-book from the Banque d'Orléans...I'll give you one. You can go to Salbris, take the train that leaves at one o'clock in the morning and go...." But as the Chambrion did not move, he said, anxiously. "Come on—is that it?"

Then the Chambrion resumed his indifferent and scornful attitude. "Tell me, Monsieur Clappier," he said, "hasn't the demoiselle also asked you for money?"

Clappier shivered. "Oh—you know that!"

The Chambrion nodded his head.

"And how do you know it?"

"I was at the Sapinières this morning when you came, hidden in the next room...."

"And you heard everything, did you?"

"Everything."

Oh! thought Clappier, angrily. *He's got me.*

The Chambrion went on: "The demoiselle asked you for two hundred thousand francs."

"She's mad!" said Clappier, disdainfully.

"The stolen two hundred thousand francs...." The Chambrion continued.

"You're lying—it's not true."

"Then why," said François Véru, tranquilly, "are you offering money to me?"

Clappier did not have time to reply, because someone knocked on the door rudely.

Who's there?" sked the Chambrion.

"It's me," replied a voice from outside, "Hector, who's been beating the bushes all day and doesn't want to go home empty-handed."

"Don't open the door!" said Clappier, in a whisper.

"On the contrary," replied the Chambrion. "You're son will only know what we want him to know." And he opened the door.

Hector came in and saw his father.

"What!" he said. "Papa's here!"

"Yes," said Clapier, in a surly tone, "and I'm doing some business...leave us alone."

"Oh, no," said Hector, "The opportunity to obtain a explanation is too good, and I want to take advantage of it."

"An explanation? Of what?" said the property-dealer, arrogantly.

"With regard to the demoiselle...to thc two hundred thousand francs...and your crooked dealings...."

"Later, later!"

"No, right away," Hector insisted.

"I don't have to tell you anything," said Clappier, angrily.

"That's where you're mistaken," Hector replied. "I'm your son and I bear your name...."

The elder Clappier was red with fury. "I believe you're threatening me!" he said.

The Chambrion came to his aid. "I have to talk to your father," he said to Hector, "but since you're here, I'll have a word with you."

"Me?" said Hector.

"Yes."

"But you've nothing to discuss with my son!" cried Clappier.

"Indeed I have," the Chambrion said, tranquilly. "I want to make him a millionaire...."

At that word, Hector seemed suddenly dazzled, and Père Clappier wondered whether the Chambrion had suddenly gone mad.

But neither Hector's shocked expression, as the word "millionaire" rang in his ears as a trumpet blast rings in the ear of an old regimental horse long reduced to pulling a cart, nor Père Clappier's amazement disturbed the Chambrion, who continued to address Hector.

"Do you know the proverb that says: Don't look a gift horse in the mouth?"

"Certainly," said Hector, "and it's a good proverb, that one."

"Well," the Chambrion went on, "wasn't it only yesterday that your father demanded a commission from you for marrying you to the demoiselle?"

Hector laughed insolently. "You know full well that my father's always demanding."

"Yes," said François Véru," but in the end, you'd have given it to him, wouldn't you?"

"Of course."

What? thought Père Clappier, who had started pacing up and down, and was giving signs of great anxiety. *What is he getting at?*

The Chambrion went on: "Well, if I give you a fortune, then...."

"What!" Hector exclaimed. "You're going to marry me to the demoiselle?"

Clappier stopped dead, in mid-stride.

"No, Monsieur Hector," said the Chambrion. "The demoiselle's not for you—but I'm offering you a fortune."

"But where will you get it?"

"That's my business."

"You're offering me a fortune—you!"

"Yes, me."

"But where will you get it?"

"He's mad," growled Père Clappier, resuming his march.

"I'll give you a fortune," the Chambrion continued, "but I want ten per cent."

This time, incredulity took possession of Hector. "Why are you making fun of me, François?" he said. "I'm not in the mood to laugh today."

"Bah!" replied the Chambrion. "You'll no longer be sad, once you've killed a roebuck. But believe me, Monsieur Hector, I'm not laughing. Come on, will you give me ten per cent? I want two hundred thousand francs if it's two million."

"But after all," said Hector, nonplussed by the Chambrion's serious expression, "Where will you get the money?"

"Yes," said Père Clappier. "Where will you get the money?"

"What does it matter? Answer me—yes or no."

"Yes, of course," said Hector. "I'm not risking anything."

"Then I need you to sign something."

"How do you mean?"

François Véru took the young man by the arm and, to the increasing amazement of Père Clappier, led him to the table where, a little while ago, he had written the letter that Brocart had taken away.

"Here" he said. "There's a piece of paper. Write this for me: *On the day when I come into possession of a fortune of at least two million francs, I will pay to François Véru, alias the Chambrion....*"

Hector was still hesitating over picking up the pen. As for Père Clappier; he had let himself fall on to a stool, dumbfounded.

"Write, then, Monsieur Hector," insisted the Chambrion, in a voice that suddenly acquired authority over the young man.

And Hector wrote.

"They're both mad," murmured Clappier, who thought that he was dreaming.

The Chambrion picked up Hector's acknowledgement, folded it up and put it in his pocket. "And now," he said, "since you have such a strong desire to shoot a roe deer from ambush, go down to the Mare aux Chevrettes. Take up a position behind the big beech-tree near the bush...and wait!"

"Damn it!" said Hector, intoxicated by the Chambrion's promises, "this is hardly the time to go set an ambush."

"On the contrary," François replied. "It's the time when the roe deer come to drink...so leave us in peace."

"You talk to me about millions, and you want...."

"I want," said the Chambrion, coldly, "to be left alone with your father, and to occupy myself with him."

Père Clappier started, and said abruptly, almost fearfully: "This business has nothing to do with me."

"One never knows," murmured François. "Get going, Monsieur Hector. I'll call you when I've finished with Monsieur Clappier."

Hector, a trifle bewildered, picked up his rifle, which he had set down beside the fireplace. "All right," he said, "I'm going—but you'll call me?"

"Yes, I promise."

Hector headed for the door. Then, as he was crossing the threshold, he murmured: "Well, people say that that fortune comes while sleeping...now it seems that it also comes while hunting...."

And he took the path to the Mare aux Chevrettes.

* * * * * * *

The moon had just risen, resplendent over the white vapor of the pond, its light passing through the forest and projecting its slightly fantastic light over everything. Hector Clappier was neither a poet nor a dreamer; he did not believe in ghosts and had never interrogated turning tables. Nevertheless, what the Chambrion had just said to him was so extraordinary that he wondered whether he might not be the victim of some dream and might really be in his bed at the Meunerie, prey to a nightmare.

The moonlight, which, at a distance, made the birch-trees resemble white phantoms, completed his illusion.

The autumn leaves crackled lugubriously under his feet. It seemed to him that there were vague murmurs in the air.

However, having stopped abruptly halfway down the slope that led down to the Mare aux Chevrettes, he turned round and saw the light in the Chambrion's house shining above him.

Am I stupid! I'm not asleep, I'm wide awake! But it's strange how the prospect of being a millionaire has that effect on me.

He continued on his way, and fell back into his reverie.

But where the devil will he get the money to give me? he wondered, as he arrived beside the bush that the Chambrion had indicated to him as the ambush position.

He crouched down in the bush, sitting on a cut tree-trunk, set his loaded rifle between his knees, having stuck a piece of white paper at the end of the barrel, and, with his eyes fixed on the pool that he had just come halfway around, he waited....

The night was calm, the moon still shining on the dormant waters of the Mare aux Chevrettes, and after having looked at the edge—which is to say, at the strip of grass that surrounded it—Hector allowed himself to be fascinated by the radiation of the water and returned to his reverie.

Half asleep and half awake, plunged in a singular torpor, the hunter thought he could hear the clink of gold coins. It was the dream of fortune that was beginning.

That dream took on strange proportions. Hector saw himself in the midst of immense terrains, bordered by vast woods. He was on horseback, galloping and galloping; the woods gradually drew away into the distance and the fields ahead of him were magnified.

At the same time, a deformed dwarf perched on his saddle-bow said to him: "All this is yours!"

And the fields succeeded one another, and farms and houses loomed up in their midst.

And the deformed dwarf was still repeating: "All this is yours!"

Finally, the horse stopped on the edge of the vast woods. Then the dwarf shoved the rider, who fell rudely to the ground.

Hector opened his eyes.

"Good!" he said. "I'd fallen asleep." And he suddenly returned to a sense of reality, forgot the promised millions and thought about the roe deer that could not be long delayed in coming to drink.

But the reflection of the moon exerted the influence of its radiation again, and the chill of the night gradually numbed the hunter. The hallucination gripped him again, and, bizarrely, he found himself back at the point where he had left it, exactly as one finds the turned-back corner of the page of an interrupted novel the following day.

He was on the ground at the edge of the woods. The horse that had been galloping a little while before had disappeared, but the deformed dwarf was still beside Hector.

"Come on," the dwarf said, taking him by the hand.

"Where are you taking me?"

"To where you live."

"And where do I live?"

"You'll see, you'll see...." And the dwarf started to laugh, and Hector felt himself drawn along, and started running at a fantastic speed.

The wood became thicker and darker the further they advanced.

Finally, a square house, with narrow barred windows and blackened walls, with an appearance of desolate bleakness, appeared in the middle of a clearing."

"There it is!" sniggered the dwarf.

A door opened, and Hector went in.

The dwarf disappeared in his turn.

Then Hector Clappier found himself in a large courtyard, in the middle of which procession was filing, It was a procession of monks, in white habits, chanting hymns. The procession passed close by, and each monk looked at Hector compassionately.

Finally, when the last one had made him a small, sad and

amicable gesture, the younger Clappier felt himself dragged away by an irresistible force, and he followed the procession.

The monks made a tour of the courtyard, and then entered the chapel of the convent, and each one went to a stall that appeared to be reserved for him.

Hector was astonished to see that one of the stalls bore his name.

He went into it and knelt down.

The monks celebrated mass; afterwards, they left the chapel and went to their cells.

Hector was still following them.

The cells opened into a long, narrow corridor; every door was surmounted by a placard bearing a name.

The younger Clappier read: *Père Hector.*

And, still driven by the mysterious and irresistible force, he went into the cell.

There, he saw black bread, a jug full of water and a discipline hanging on the wall.

Then the dwarf reappeared, and his mocking laughter resounded. "This is where you live," said the deformed being. "This is it!"

Hector uttered a cry, and woke up again.

The moon was still shining; the night was cold and dark.

"How stupid it is to sleep like that!" he murmured. "I'll wager that the roe deer have been to drink."

As he pronounced those words in a faint voice, there was a noise on the far side off the pond: the sound of rapid running and rustling foliage. Then a black form appeared, bounding through the undergrowth in somersaults.

There's the roe deer! thought Hector, who was entirely awake,

And he put the butt of his rifle to his shoulder and took aim....

XV.

After Hector's departure, the Chambrion had closed the door and returned to Clappier.

Clappier, still seated, had recovered all his composure. He even had a smile on his lips, full of bitter irony.

"Just us, now," the Chambrion said to him. "We're alone, Monsieur Clappier."

Clappier looked at him coldly. "François," he said, "I believe I was mistaken just now."

"Mistaken about what, Monsieur Clappier?"

"In offering you money."

"And why is that, Monsieur Clappier?"

"Because you're raving mad," replied Clappier, phlegmatically, "and the deposition of a madman is nothing to fear."

"Oh, really?" said the Chambrion.

"My God, yes," said Clappier. "And now, let's agree that I haven't said anything."

"As you wish."

"And bonsoir—I'm going."

Clappier got to his feet with those words—but the Chambrion stopped him.

"All right," he said. "You haven't offered me anything. But listen to me."

"Why?"

"I have some plans."

"Oh?"

"And I want to tell you about them."

"All right," said Clappier, "but hurry...and, as I'm a good man, I'd like to believe that you aren't mad...so I'll get back my offers."

"Go on, then."

"Except," Clappier hastened to say, "let's settle it right away."

"Are you pressed for time?" said François Véru.

"Yes, for I don't want to be here all night."

"In that case," said the Chambrion, calmly, "we'll leave together."

"What?" said Clappier, almost taking a step back.

"Yes," the Chambrion continued, "when you mentioned Paris, you gave me an idea."

"What idea?"

"The idea of taking you there; you can come with me."

"Me?"

"When we've finished, of course. Paris, as you said just now, is a fine place, Monsieur Clappier."

"I have nothing do in Paris, myself."

"Oh well, you can live there in idleness, on a nice pension that Monsieur Hector will give you."

This time, there was no *almost* about it; it was a backward step that Père Clappier took. "What? What do you mean?" he said, in a strangle voice.

The Chambrion continued: "Yes, Monsieur Hector will give you a pension. You've brought him up badly, that boy, Monsieur Clappier, but he's not fundamentally wicked, he's only bad, and when he has your wealth, he'll make better use of it than you."

"My wealth!" cried Clappier. "He'll have my wealth."

"Yes."

"Ha ha ha!" laughed Père Clappier. "But I'm not dead yet."

"He'll have it while you're alive," said the Chambrion, coldly.

This time, Clappier recalled again, fixing the Chambrion with a wild state, and cried: "Oh, but I was right! The boy's mad!"

"Bah! You think so?"

"He needs to be locked up!" howled Clappier. "He's raving mad!" And he retreated further.

The Chambrion had the tranquil expression of a man in full possession of his reason. "You're mistaken, Monsieur Clappier," he said. "I'm very well."

Clappier had a sudden access of fury. "My wealth!" he cried. "And who, then, will give him my wealth?"

"Me," said the Chambrion.

Fear took hold of Père Clappier, who backed up against the wall and assumed a defensive stance. "Ah!" he said, his teeth chattering. "I believe they're going to murder me!"

The Chambrion made no move toward him; he merely continued. "Did the demoiselle not ask you for two hundred thousand francs this morning?" he said.

Clappier's fear was succeeded by a kind of delirium.

"The demoiselle is mad," he said. "As mad as you are!"

But the Chambrion added: "You were wrong to refuse, Monsieur Clappier."

Clappier, beside himself, continued laughing.

"You were wrong," the Chambrion went on, "because I shall be more demanding." Then he took a step toward Clappier, and shook his arm. "The demoiselle would have taken pity on your white hair. I shan't have any pity, myself, and if I spare you the court of assizes, it's because you'll obey me in handing over all your wealth to your son."

"Never!" howled Clappier.

"Because," the Chambrion continued, "you'll be leaving the region, where you have done so much harm, and you'll never see it again!"

Clappier still had delirium in his eyes. "He's mad! He's mad!" he murmured, looking at the Chambrion.

"Be careful!" the latter continued. "This is a solemn moment, Monsieur Clappier; it's necessary to do as I wish...."

"I shan't do anything!" cried Clappier. "you can denounce me; no one will believe you!"

"But what if I had evidence?" said the Chambrion.

"You have none...you can't have any!"

"Be careful, Monsieur Clappier," said the Chambrion, again.

Clappier had a further access of fury, and shook his fists. "Denounce me, then, imbecile!" he shouted. "Denounce me! Can a man like me be dragged to the court of assizes? Am I not a great landowner?"

The Chambrion shrugged his shoulders.

"For the last time," said Clappier, "do you want fifteen thousand francs?

"For the last time," the Chambrion replied, "will you accept my conditions?"

"Ah!" said Clapier, shrugging his shoulders. "I'm too simple, in truth, to worry about such a madman." And he took a step toward the door.

Then, as solemn and sad as a judge pronouncing sentence, the Chambrion picked up the lamp that was on the table, and went to place it on the window-sill.

Clappier watched him, and said, swiftly: "What are you doing?"

"I'm sending a signal," François Véru replied.

"To whom?"

"To a man who's waiting, hidden in the woods."

"And that man...?" demanded Clappier, with a sudden emotion.

"That man," said the Chambrion, "is now on the road to Romorantin, and within two hours, the law will be at your door."

"But I tell you that you have no evidence!" protested Clappier.

"But what if I have?"

"It's impossible. I didn't say anything to your father, and nothing can prove that I did."

"Monsieur de Méreuil's satchel might be discovered," said the Chambrion.

"The satchel, you say?"

"A satchel stained with blood, containing a stack of gold coins."

"But all that proves nothing!" howled Père Clappier.

"And with that stack of gold coins, a receipt for forty-five louis," the Chambrion concluded.

Père Clappier uttered a screech.

"And that satchel, which you believed to be lost," said the Chambrion, "I can show you!"

François Véru went to the fireplace then, and, as he had seen his unfortunate father do fourteen years before, he set about loosening a flagstone in the fireplace with his knife.

Clappier watched him, wild-eyed.

When the stone was lifted up, he saw a hole, and in that hole was an object that the Chambrion took out.

It was the satchel.

"Oh! Wretch!" cried Clappier—and he launched himself forward to grab it—but François Véru pushed him back.

"You can't use force on me, Monsieur Clappier," he said. "I could kill you with a single blow."

"Give me that satchel!" howled Clappier.

"What would be the point?"

"I'll give you what you want!"

"It's too late."

Those words brought a further screech from Père Clappier. "Too late, you say! Too late!"

"Yes."

"Why is it too late? Answer me? Answer me?" said the old man, half-crazed.

"Because my man is on his way to Romorantin."

"Well, I'll run after him...I'll catch up with him...I'll get the denunciation back from him. I'll kill him if he resists."

The Chambrion shrugged his shoulders. "He has better legs than yours," he said. "He's a young man."

Those words lit up Clappier's intelligence. "Ah!" he said. "I too have a young man for running! My son!"

"That's true," said the Chambrion, sarcastically.

"My son will run after him. He's armed."

"Your son's out hunting," said François Véru, "and he's not thinking about you at all."

Clappier, drunk with rage and madness, hurled himself upon the Chambrion again. "Give me my satchel!" he howled. "Give it to me!"

Again, the Chambrion pushed him away. "It's too late," he repeated. "You've pronounced your own condemnation."

"Oh, my son!" protested Clappier. "My son! He won't allow his father to be dishonored!"

He hurled himself outside—and the Chambrion, who had

followed him to the threshold, saw him go down the slope at a run toward the Mare aux Chevrettes.

"Fool!" he said. "The Brocart has good legs. He's taken a shortcut...and he's already halfway there...."

As he was about to go back into his house, he heard the distant sound of small bells. The highway passed through the woods a hundred meters away, behind his house.

"One would think that were a post-chaise!" he murmured. "That's rare today, though, now that there's the railway. And he listened.

At the same time, a red light shone in the distance, and the Chambrion looked at it curiously.

The sound of bells became more distinct, and was then mingled with the crack of a whip; then the red light grew larger and came nearer rapidly. It was the beacon-light of a post-chaise.

And as the post-chaise went past the forest path at right angles to the Chambrion's house, it stopped.

At the same time, someone called out to him in the distance: "François! François!" The Chambrion recognized Horace de Verne's voice, and, utterly astonished, he ran toward the post-chaise.

The chaise was harnessed to three vigorous Percheron horses.

By the light of the lantern, François perceived Horace, Denise and Madame Gertrude inside

"We're leaving," Horace told him.

"You're leaving!" stammered the Chambrion.

Denise showed her charming and melancholy face. "Yes," she said, "we're going to Paris, with my aunt, and we're taking...."

"Me!" exclaimed the Chambrion, taking a step backwards.

"You, my good François," Denise continued, "and you're no longer leaving us. We're rich—Horace has just come into an inheritance. We'll give two hundred thousand francs of our money to repair the harm that that man has done...."

"And you can leave him in peace," said Horace.

The Chambrion shook his head.

"For I don't want you to be dishonored, my good François,"

Denise exclaimed, squeezing his hands.

"Come on," said Horace. "Go pack your clothes...and come back quickly."

But the Chambrion shook his head. "It's too late, Monsieur Horace," he said. "It's too late, Mademoiselle."

"Why is that?" said the young woman.

"Because my complaint is on its way. The Brocart has left for Romorantin."

Horace began to laugh. "You're mistaken," he said.

At the same time, something moved on the seat of the carriage, and an alert and cheerful face entered the beam of light projected by the headlight.

"Brocart!" exclaimed François Véru."

"Yes," said Horace. "The Brocart ran into us, and we forbade him to go any further.

"Oh, Monsieur Horace," said the Chambrion, "that's a bad thing you did there."

"Bad, you say? Why?"

"It's bad," the Chambrion replied, "because you don't have the right to show mercy to Père Clappier."

"Since when," exclaimed Denise, "don't victims have the right to forgive their executioners?"

"Oh, have you never seen that man roaming the region, raising murmurs of hatred as he passes by, imprecations or rage and moans of agony?"

"Since we'll repair the evil he's done..."

"And that which he might yet do?" cried the Chambrion, for whom the time for pity had passed....

Denise and Horace trembled.

"Don't you know," François Véru continued, "that that man has been the scourge, the ruin and desolation of the entire region for thirty years? That child, who goes along the road half-naked, has been ruined by him; that poor old woman, spending her final days begging for bread has been made a widow and a vagabond by him; and that young woman, who had painfully amassed the price of her fiancé's exoneration, has she not been spoiled by him?

The Chambrion's words had a bitter and robust eloquence as he continued: "Stamp a foot anywhere in the four corners of the land of Sologne, and voices will rise up from the earth, and vengeful shades, which will demand the punishment of that man!"

And as the Chambrion spoke, two gunshots rang out in the woods, in the direction of the Mare aux Chevrettes.

At the same time, a faint voice cried: "Help! Help!"

Then another voice uttered piercing screams: cries of terror and desolation.

Troubled by those cries, agitated by a somber presentiment, Horace, the Brocart and the Chambrion ran in the direction of the pond, guided by the cries of anguish....

* * * * * * *

In the moonlight, they saw a strange group.

Hector Clappier, mad with grief, was wringing his hands, calling loudly for his father.

His father was lying on the ground, bleeding, and made no reply.

Hector had mistaken his father, running toward him, for a roe deer, and had put two shots in the middle of his breast.

Père Clappier was no longer calling for help. Père Clappier was no longer making any sound at all.

Père Clappier was dead.

The Chambrion took off his hat before the cadaver, and said to Horace, his voice sad and solemn. "As you see, humans wish to forgive—but God is inexorable.

Epilogue

The traveler who departs from Mothe-Beuvron, when the highway is firm enough to reach Salbris, if he disdains the railway and goes tranquilly through the woods, will now perceive a large gap in the forest, and, in the middle of that gap, large brand new buildings.

It is a model farm of the largest dimensions, where numerous families have been living and working for about four years. The feverish ponds in the vicinity have been drained, the woods of little value cleared and converted into arable land. The neighboring hamlets are no longer poor, and everyone has work.

And if, struck by the fortunate air and prosperous physiognomy of that area, the traveler asks to whom that metamorphosis is due, and shepherd sitting on the edge of a ditch, and woodcutter or any laborer that he asks will reply: "We had a great deal of poverty once in this feverish and unhealthy Sologne, and there was a rich man who took pleasure in oppressing us—but today there is a man as rich as the other and as good as the other was wicked, and that man has become everyone's benefactor."

And if the traveler asks the name of that man, the reply will be given to him in the form of a soubriquet: the Chambrion.

Yes, the Chambrion has become rich, and has devoted his life to repairing the harm done by Père Clappier, all of whose fortune he now possesses.

The involuntary parricide Hector, after having gone mad, has gradually recovered his reason, but the bloody shade of his father pursued him incessantly, and he has gone into a convent built in the middle of the woods of Morvan, in lower Burgundy. Hector is today a Frère de la Pierre-qui-vive, which is the name of that community.[16] Thus has been realized the bizarre and terrible dream that he had on the edge of the Mare aux Chevrettes a few minutes before shooting his father.

On entering religion, Frère Hector bequeathed all of his fortune to the Chambrion.

As for Mère Clappier, she died of a catastrophic apoplexy on the day of her husband's burial.

---

16. The Benedictine Abbaye de la Pierre-qui-vive, named after a local rocking-stone, situated in woods north of Morvan still exists; it was funded in 1850 by Jean-Baptiste Muard.

* * * * * * *

Sometimes, on Sundays in spring, at the exit from mass, the peasants grouped around an elm planted beside the church rise to their feet respectfully and bow to a charming couple who pass by with smiles on their lips and joy in their eyes.

It is Horace and Denise, who did not leave the area, and lead by the hand a rosy-cheeked and blonde-haired child, who, perceiving the Chambrion in the midst of his protégés, runs to him and holds out his arms.

The Chambrion presses the child to his heart, and sometimes wipes away a tear as he contemplates the young mother.

Old Mère Malbeque is dead, but the Chambrion does not want to marry and has adopted the Brocart; he has sent him to Grignon[17] to complete his agricultural studies, and will leave him half of his wealth.

The other half is for the child of Horace and Denise.

---

17. *i.e.*, to the celebrated École nationale supérieure d'Agronomic de Grignan.

THE FAIRY

A CHRISTMAS STORY

I. The Three Gold Coins

In my grandfather's château....

Don't believe, my young friends, that my ancestor was a great lord. He was a poor soldier, esteemed by everyone because he was brave, and whom I loved myself, with veneration and respect, because he was good. His château was old and poor, like him; its decoration was sparse, and its cracked walls were somewhat reminiscent the threadbare cloaks full of holes in which Spanish beggars—the proudest and noblest in the world—drape themselves so arrogantly.

Fortunately, God, who always reestablishes equilibrium, had hidden some of those holes beneath the festoons of a climbing vine and green ivy; he had encircled it with a meadow, through which a babbling brook ran, had given it the blue sky for a roof and the mountains of the Alps for a majestic horizon.

In my grandfather's château there was a vast hall, in which a large fire blazed in winter. In the corner of that hearth, sitting in old leather armchairs with gilded nails, an old man and a child were to be found every evening. The old man had a young mind, an excellent memory and a facile verve; he told fine stories of times past, full of noble actions, great heroic deeds, and humble traits of virtue.

The child listened with profound gratitude.

That old man was my grandfather; that child was me.

The evening usually extended from seven to ten o'clock.

At ten o'clock, my grandfather asked for his cane and his candlestick, and went to bed.

I sometimes stayed by the fireside for another half-hour, dreaming, as one does at twelve, with my eyes fixed on the bizarre pictures formed by the blaze, which underwent incessant metamorphoses, sometimes into a palaces and often into cottages, occasionally throwing forth little a blue flame that I imagined to be a good fairy, impertinent and smiling, whose indecisive and wild reflection would take delight in throwing a fantastic gleam upon the old tapestries with discolored characters that extended over the walls.

One evening, my young friends—it was Christmas Eve— it was exceedingly cold, I can assure you; snow covered the meadow, the wind was moaning in the chimneys and making the fir-trees shiver, and my grandfather, who had many old wounds and rheumatism, had asked that his big bed with serge curtains be warmed.

There was a clock in the big hall. The clock had chimed eleven, and yet I was still beside the fire, all alone, dreaming delightfully and building many castles in Spain—for I had in my hand three tawny yellow shiny disks, whose tremulous gleam I considered in the firelight with an indescribable joy, because they were three gold coins.

My grandfather had just given them to me, saying: "Last year, at this time, I gave you toys; this year I prefer to let you make your own choice. You can go to town tomorrow with Pierre and buy whatever you want. Think hard."

My grandfather doubtless had a hidden motive in doing that.

I was, therefore, reflecting, and like the good La Fontaine's milkmaid, I was hesitating between buying a farm and acquiring a palace...all for sixty francs!

At first I settled on a rifle: a real rifle with which I could shoot rabbits in the warrens and water-fowl in the ditches; then I thought that I had one of those already, and wondered whether I would do better to opt for fishing equipment and furnish myself with hooks, lines and nets.

Then again, from nets I passed on to a boat: a beautiful new boat, panted green and yellow, which would surely do marvelous service in the river that passed five hundred meters from the château.

Then, finally—and I certainly should have begun with that—I remembered on display a library of beautiful books bound in gilt-trimmed morocco, containing a host of things much more beautiful than their binding.

The rifle, the nets and the boat struggled hard for a minute against that fourth and more serious fantasy, but, in the end, the books won, and my choice would have been definitively made, if....

If I had not suddenly see one of the logs in the fire throw out a little blue flame.

That flame grew, little by little, soon lighting up the entire hearth, and then the room.

I closed my eyes, dazzled, and when I opened them again, the flame had disappeared—but in its place, before me, I saw a beautiful young woman, the sight of whom drew a cry of admiration from me.

If you want to imagine her exactly, my friends, look at your older sister, your sister of fifteen or sixteen, whose eyes are thoughtful and whose mouth is slightly earnest; or, better still, imagine the portrait of your mother, painted at eighteen, who was doubtless already anticipating the petty chagrins and anxieties that you would cause her, and whose forehead was beginning to be veiled by a pensive melancholy, when her lips still had a fresh and open smile—the naïve and joyful smile of youth.

She had blonde hair, large blue eyes, thoughtful and very soft, little pink and diaphanous hands, which one would gladly have kissed, respectfully, for an entire day. She was dressed in white, like the angels of paradise, and her head bore a crown of cornflowers and daisies that perfumed the air around her.

She came toward me, smiling, scarcely touching the parquet with her tiny feet, and placed her white hand on my shoulder.

"I'm the Christmas fairy," she said to me, "and I bring children toys much more beautiful than those they can buy."

I looked at her in astonishment.

"Because I'm a fairy," she went on, "I'm able to know everything. I saw your hesitation, and I came to advise you. Would you like to come with me?"

"Oh, yes!" I said, enthusiastically.

"We're going to midnight mass. Come on."

I picked up my mantle and cap, and I followed her. We went through the corridors without making a sound, and arrived at the front door, which opened without creaking, and Lord Ebony, the big black dog that mounted guard by night, let us pass without a murmur.

As I've said, there was already a thick mantle of snow on the ground; the trees were so heavily laden with it that they resembled the forests of crystallized sugar that confectioners display on New Year's Day. It was no longer cold, though, because the fairy seemed to spread a gentle warmth around her, and the wind, doubtless at the sight of her, eased and took refuge in the dark forests that serve as its shelter on fine days.

The snow gradually hardened beneath our footsteps, and the moon lit our route.

The village was half a league away, but we were going at a rapid pace and we soon reached the first houses—humble cottages covered with thatch, built with dry stones cemented with clay, sheltering poor laborers who scarcely earned enough during the summer to have bread to eat in the winter.

"It's not yet time for mass," the little Chritmas fairy said to me, still holding me by the hand. "Let's go into Père Jean's house for a little while; I can see light through the worm-eaten planks of his door."

Père Jean was an old soldier who had served under my grandfather and who only had one leg. He was poor and had nothing to live on but his trade and the work done by his daughter, a beautiful virtuous girl full of courage, whom God had sent him, like Oedipus' Antigone or Fingal's Malvina, to shore up his old age with her sturdy youth.

Père Jean wove baskets with rushes from the river and reseated the crude chairs of the village. His daughter worked in the fields.

We went into the cabin, the fairy being invisible to its inhabitants, of course. The fairy was only manifest to me.

Père Jean was lying down, moaning dolorously. Winter was a harsh season for him; the stump of his leg made him suffer horribly; his wounds often reopened, and it was often impossible for him to work for entire months.

That day was the twentieth that Père Jean had spent in his bed.

"Look, and think hard," the fairy breathed in my ear.

I did, indeed, look—and I saw that there was nothing on the table but a pot of frozen water instead of wine, nothing in the fireplace but meager twigs, nothing in the bread-bin but a small quantity of black bread. I still had my three gold coins in my hand. I considered them furtively by the light of the hearth; I saw an effigy of Napoléon shining on one, and I put it in the hand of the old soldier, who wept effusively and called me his son.

"Come on," said the Christmas fairy, drawing me away.

We went out. It was still not yet time for mass, and near the church there was another cottage, similarly lit.

"Knock and go in," the fairy said to me.

The cottage belonged to a widow named Marthe, a poor woman whose husband, a chamois-hunter, had been killed in a ravine the preceding year, leaving her with five children, a tiny field and a house that now seemed large and empty.

The village laborers, taking pity on the widow's distress, had agreed to take turns cultivating her field, but the year had been bad, the potatoes had failed and the hemp was poor.

Marthe was sitting by her meager fire, surrounded by her young children, who had put on their poor Sunday clothes in order to attend the birth of the infant Jesus. In the meantime, they were devouring a black wheat galette, and the dear children of the god Lord offered some to me—and as, when they came to the château, they shared my games and my bread and jam, I accepted my share of their coarse cake.

"They won't have any Christmas toys," the little fairy whispered to me very softly.

I opened my hand and considered my second gold coin. It bore the imprint of King Louis XVI—Louis XVI, who had initially been called Louis the Desired before being given the name of the Martyr King. I remembered the many acts of noble charity about which my grandfather, who had had the honor of being among the officers of his household, had told me during our winter evenings...and I let my Louis XVI fall into the apron worn by Rose, the youngest of the widow's children.

"Come to the church," the fairy set to me.

"I still have one gold coin," I murmured.

"Come nevertheless," she said, with a smile.

We went into the church, where all of the candles were burning, and where the altar was dressed with its finest and whitest cloth. Instead of letting me sit down on the old seigneurial bench where I usually sat, the fairy took me to the sacristy, where the curé was getting ready to put on the gilded chasuble that was used on solemn occasions.

He was a good old priest who put the gospel into practice, the providence of the poor, the father of orphans, the mainstay of widows, the consoler of all. He had baptized me, taught me the first pages of the catechism and given me my first instruction in Latin.

"Ask him," the fairy whispered to me, "why, on Chistmas Eve, he has a worn soutane."

I went to him.

"My good Monsieur le Curé," I said to him, "didn't my good father give you a little money last month, telling you that it was for a new soutane?"

"Yes, my friend," the pastor replied, naively, "but the next day, Marguerite Dubois—you know, little Marguerite—married Pierre the shepherd. Well, my child, Marguerite had no dress new enough to be married in, and I thought that, old as it was, my soutane might perhaps last until next Easter."

For the third time I opened my hand and examined my third and last gold coin. It bore the effigy of King Charles X.

A few days earlier, I had seen grandfather go pale on reading an issue of the *Quotidienne*, and then shed hot and silent tears as he let it fall to the ground. And when I asked him, in alarm, why he was weeping, he had replied: "I'm weeping for my old king, who has just died in exile."

Charles X had died on foreign soil.

"Monsieur le Curé," I said, then, taking on a coaxing voice, "you know that every year, on Saint Charles's Day, Papa had the custom of coming to mass in his best suit. This year, we shall have a mass for the dead instead of a celebration mass, and Papa would be very displeased if you celebrated that funeral ceremony in an old soutane. Here's twenty francs that I'll lend you; if that's not enough, I'll ask my mother for some money, and you can give it back to me later, when your poor folk have everything the need."

The old priest took me in his arms and said to me, emotionally; "May God bless you, my child, as I bless you myself."

I turned around, very proudly, to search with my gaze for the kindly eye of the little Christmas fairy...but the fairy had disappeared.

II. Armand

A year later, to the day, I was at school.

I had said farewell to the pleasant evenings at the château, to my grandfather's beautiful stories, to the indulgent lessons of the old curé, and I missed all that, placed as I was in the presence of stern and indifferent masters who stimulated my idleness with impositions.

We came back from Christmas mass, celebrated in the college chapel, and went sadly up to our dormitory, where cold beds awaited us.

On my bed, I found a small purse. In that purse were three gold coins—my grandfather's annual three gold coins.

Oh! I thought, turning them over in my fingers, thoughtfully. *I'm so far away from the village! And then, Père Jean is dead, perhaps Monsieur le Curé's soutane isn't worn out yet...and Papa will give Christmas presents to the widow Marthe's children this year. What shall I d with my three gold coins, then? What shall I buy? A rifle? I have one. A boat? I have one of those too. Books? I now have more of them than I want...and not every amusing ones, either.*

I was still turning my purse over in my fingers.

"Little fairy," I murmured, finally, "little Christmas fairy, where are you? Don't you want to come and advise me?"

I had scarcely finished when the little fairy was before me.

As she had the previous year, she took me by the hand, rendering me invisible to my fellows, took me out of the dormitory and led me to the study-room, where I perceived Armand, my best friend, leaning over his desk and writing, at that late hour of the night.

He was a sad and grave young man, sadder than his age warranted—he was fourteen. He rarely enjoyed himself and never laughed, but he was studious, and his comrades, doubtless impressed by his pale and somewhat lofty forehead, liked and respected him.

Armand was the son of one of my father's old friends. His father had been killed on the ramparts of Constantine while leading his regiment in an attack.

Armand was taller, stronger and wiser than me. He knew that our fathers had been friends, and he had continued that friendship by becoming my protector. Thanks to him, I had avoided what in schoolboy terminology is called "ragging"—the harsh ordeals that await new pupils.

The little Christmas fairy put a finger over her mouth to bid me to keep silent and let me behind him. Then, showing me the letter that Armand was writing, she said to me: "Read!"

I leaned forward, holding my breath, and read:

My dear little sister,

> *I have a heavy heart today, for it's Christmas, and the children have all that day's fine presents. Alas, I have none to send you, my poor angel. You know that our mother has had great difficulty, since Papa died in the service of France, paying my fees, and she has not been able to send me any money this year. Poor little sister, my heart breaks when I think that I won't be able to give you one of those pretty gifts that brothers give their sisters. But be patient—one day I'll be an officer, like our father, and then, little sister, I'll have money....*

I did not have the strength to read any more, and I took Armand in my arms. He turned round, amazed, and blushed.

"Here," I said. "The day will come when we'll both be officers and we'll be able to share again; take half my present to send to your little sister...."

And while Armand shed a proud tear, the little fairy took my hand, squeezed it gently, planted a charming kiss on my forehead, and fled.

III. The Fairy's Name

Many Christmas Eves had passed, and I had not seen the little fairy again—but every year, I remembered the joy I experienced in consoling a proud and noble misfortune.

My poor grandfather had been sleeping his final slumber for a long time, in the shadow of the cypresses in my village; I had become a man, and I lived in that great city with black sky and burning pavements, which we call Paris.

People had treated me harshly; the cares of life had hollowed out more than one imperceptible wrinkle in my forehead, and I had passed through the solemn moment that separates one forever from adolescence, and is called the twentieth year.

It was Christmas Eve again. It was cold, it was raining, and the wind was making the flames of the street lights shiver lugubriously.

I was going along the boulevard with a furrowed brow, wrapped in my cloak, with one hand in my pocket, no longer tormenting my poor grandfather's napoléons with my feverish fingers, but a little of the gold that men sold me, at the price of my long late nights and my labor.

In the middle of the boulevard, there was a splendidly-illuminated house, from which the sound of joyful and frenetic laughter reached me. It was one of those fashionable restaurants that opened all night from Christmas to the end of the carnival. Among the voices that were resounding inside I thought I recognized a few, and I got ready to go in.

On the threshold of the door was a beggar-woman in rags, holding a child, blue with the cold, in her shivering arms, who was soaked by the rain.

"Pity, for the love of God, Monsieur!" the woman murmured. "I'm very hungry, and my child is frozen."

I hesitated momentarily; for a second I was tempted to change the poor woman's distress into joy. But as I said, people had treated me harshly, they had wounded my heart with their lips and feet, and my bruised youth had been crumpled, and my heart closed.

I passed by, abruptly, without heeding the beggar-woman; I went upstairs, guided by the laughter; I arrived in a drawing-room where there was a magnificently-laid table—and I recognized around it my old friends, young men crumpled like me, having suffered like me, and who needed to forget.

I took my place with them; quivering, I extended my glass beneath the floods of Aï wine that were flowing; I drank and I laughed, feverishly, all night—and when, in the morning, the first light of dawn came to pale our candlelight, when we went out, tottering and exhausted...the beggar-woman was no longer there.

I remembered then her dull and tortured voice, the thin hand that she had extended to me with an imploring gaze...and remorse gripped me by the throat, and I fled, all alone, through the streets, striding through the black mud, my head bared in order that the kisses of the rain might calm the delirium of my brow a little.

I arrived home.

My fire was still burning; my lamp had just gone out; my dog was sleeping in a corner—the peaceful slumber of fidelity.

One the hearthstone, by the indecisive light of the last fire-brand, I saw a white form, bent down—or, rather, kneeling down—in an attitude of grief. I heard labored breathing, punctuated by sobs; shivering, I asked who was there.

The white form rose slowly to her feet, and I recognized the Christmas fairy—no longer the beautiful and serene fairy that had appeared to me twice, but a young woman with a sad and weary gaze, full of tears, with a pale forehead and the discolored lips of a phantom.

"Christmas fairy," I cried, "is that you?"

"I'm no longer the Christmas fairy," she replied, weeping. "You've just killed me, wretch! And I want to tell you my true name before I die."

Then I saw her dissolve, gradually, into a blue-tinted flame, like the one that had once given birth to her. At first, that flame illuminated the hearth, and then diminished, tremulously, into a luminous fringe over the final firebrand, and was abruptly extinguished.

And then I heard a heart-rending voice, imprinted with a death-rattle, which pierced the silence surrounding me, and cried out to me: "I am no more; I was your youth!"

Children, who read this story, with an ever-open hand; give without cease and without wearying of it; youth only departs when the heart is closed.

A FATAL LEGEND

One evening in the autumn of 1831 people were taking tea and chatting by the fireside in the home of the young Baronne de Damfrein.

Madame de Damfrein was a widow, twenty-one years old, still in mourning, but quite ready to marry again after two years of rigor devoted to weeping for her first husband. Moreover, her choice was already made; on quitting her lugubrious garments. Madame de Damfrein was to Marry Monsieur Roger de Kérouare, a former officer in the Garde Royale.

After the Baron de Damfrein's death, the Comte de Loiseray, his father-in-law, had come to chaperone the young widow during her mourning, and since then, after the first six months having been spent in complete solitude, the Baronne had reopened her drawing-room to a few friends of her husband and her father, a small number of intelligent women and an even smaller number of young people—some of those to whom the new regime had closed all doors and who, breaking their swords or ripping up their togas, would become the original stock of that idle and brilliant youth that would call itself "gilded youth" for the next eighteen years.

Among that number was Vicomte Roger de Kérouare. Handsome, bearing a slight scar on his forehead—a glorious souvenir of his brave conduct during the days of July—young and witty, he had everything logically required to turn the head of a woman of twenty widowed of a husband who had been over fifty.

Roger was an only son, rich and beloved. The Baronne was beautiful, free and similarly adored. It was a love-match rather than a marriage of convenience.

The contract was to be signed and the marriage concluded a week after the expiration of the Baronne's mourning—and it was twenty-two and a half months since Monsieur de Damfrein had died.

In the meantime, the future spouses saw one another every day. Roger de Kérouare arrived every evening at nine o'clock, sat down beside the widow to the left of the large fireplace, and they both abandoned themselves without inhibitions to the charming conversation to which love lends a mantle while it is tempered by respect and rigid laws of society.

At ten o'clock, Monsieur de Loiseray and the dowager Madame de Langerin, the Baronne's aunt, would conclude their game of chess; the scattered groups in the drawing-room would draw together, and soon formed a circle around Madame de Damfrein, whose private conversation they had initially respected, for the sake of discretion. Then they chatted.

Often, one of the Baronne's guests took center stage and related an anecdote—and everyone would perform in turn, with the utmost grace.

That evening, the role of storyteller fell to Roger.

"There's a rather strange tradition accredited on the banks of the Loire," he said, "which concerns my family. It claims that if a Kérouare, who is an elder or only son, fails to marry before the age of twenty-five, he will die the following year; in the former case, the fief will pass to his younger brothers; in the later, the name will become extinct."

"And on what is that tradition based?" someone asked.

"On the legend that I shall relate to you."

Roger de Kérouare leaned on the mantelpiece and began, in the midst of a religious silence, the Legend of St. Paul's Protégé.

* * * * * * *

There was once, in the era of the crusades, a chatelaine named Yseult de Kérouare.

The aforesaid chatelaine had married very young and had worn the long veils of widowhood since the age of twenty-two. The Sire de Kérouare had died five years after the wedding, leaving a sole heir placed under the influential patronage of St. Paul.

Now, in the epoch when my story begins, Paul de Kérouare was nineteen years old and his mother thirty-seven. Paul was a charming cavalier, a trifle frail and a trifle timid, with large blue eyes, curly blond hair, a peach-like down on his cheeks and a feminine waist and hands. When he rode over the plain, the great ladies of the region, hidden behind the arched windows of their manses, regretted the twenty years that they no longer had, envied the twenty years that he had not yet had, and would have dearly wished to be widows if the hourglass of their oratory had not whispered to them that the wings of time had creased their white foreheads with a few slight wrinkles.

When he wandered behind the willows of the Loire, like a melancholy guardian angel in search of the poor mortal confined to his care, and whom Satan had led astray, the genteel washer-women in their velvet corsets, the boatwomen with their braided hair and the young peasant-women with rosy cheeks scything hemp by the bank felt their young hearts beat faster, and thought that it as a great pity that he was not a humble vassal instead of a rich lord. But alas, the noble ladies, the washerwomen, the boatwomen and the peasant-women were wasting their time in sighing.

A league from the Manoir de Kérouare there was another manor, similarly leaning its gray and mossy towers over the Loire, and, just as the former manor sheltered a blond seraphim, it had for a chatelaine a young woman of fifteen years, pale and brunette, with dark eyes as shiny as glow-worms, and alabaster skin compared with which the marble of the archipelago was gray and poorly veined. That young woman lived with her aged father, and had no husband as yet.

Husbands were very scarce in that epoch, for two reasons—firstly, because His Majesty the King of France, when he went to fight in the Holy Land, had taken with him the flower of his fine nobility; and secondly, because in order to marry an heiress like Marguerite de Kerven it was necessary to be a noble Comte, or at least a valiant Chevalier with a escutcheon pure of any bar of bastardy, with numerous vassals and a manse surrounded by deep ditches and thick walls.

So, while awaiting a husband, the young Comtesse de Kerven went out every day, followed by a squire, at a hack gallop, through the hills, heaths and heather, unleashing her gyrfalcons or throwing her large greyhounds a silk scarf, which they brought back faithfully after contesting in agility and speed to reach it.

As really happened in those days, and as still happens in today's romances, the Sire de Kérouare, out riding, and the Comtesse de Kerven, out galloping, encountered one another one day and blushed so deeply that they bowed to one another silently, not daring to speak.

The following day, hazard, that great master, did its work so well that they met one another again in the same place; the day after, the palfrey of the one and the destrier of the other grazed the same grass beside the same path behind a hedge of flowering hawthorn—and that was repeated from the dawns to the sunsets that followed—except that it is very difficult to affirm that hazard had conserved its role in that naïve comedy.

In brief, those two young hearts, which felt attracted to one another, gradually understood that the amity of man and woman is nothing other than love; and as Paul de Kérouare was rich and noble, the young Comtesse affirmed that her father would not hesitate for a moment to give him her hand, if he cared to ask for it.

Paul, as I have said, was slightly timid, and he judged it prudent to let his mother take care of the negotiations. He therefore went to find the chatelaine and, not without blushing and paling by turns, confessed his penchant for the Comte de

Kerven's daughter.

The noble chatelaine had regretted many times that she was no longer a marriageable damsel; her beauty had resisted the insults of time, and her mourning-dress suited her marvelously. The ladies of the region even claimed that she only continued to wear it out of pure coquetry, and that the Sire de Kérouare, her husband, had a tomb in her heart as solidly enclosed as the one in which his body was sealed beneath the black marble of the mortuary chapel.

Now, although she had never thought seriously about taking a new husband, the noble lady was somewhat vain regarding her beauty, and thought that her son had grown up a little too rapidly, seeming to want to push her by the shoulders toward that antechamber of ripe age that poets, being exceedingly courteous individuals, have nicknamed second youth.

Thus, great was her amazement when the young man with the golden hair, whom it pleased her to treat as a child, came to talk to her gravely about his marriage plans. That amazement was succeeded by anger; the chatelaine could not hide it from herself that, in the eyes of the malicious crowd, her son's nineteen years mounted a rude assault on the mature glare of her beauty. What would happen, then, when she had beside her a daughter-in-law of fifteen, fresh and pink, who would not take long to populate her manor with blond and cheerful children, who would give her, with a respect full of irony, the ugly-sounding name of grandmother?

In that epoch of chivalric courtesy and religious respect for the family, a son would rather have died a thousand times than disobey his mother. Madame de Kérouare had, therefore, only to reply to her son that she refused such an alliance—but that refusal would have caused him a great deal of pain, and she was a mother in spite of her coquetry.

She therefore reflected that, sooner or later, it would be necessary to go along that road, and that her obstinacy would alienate her child's heart, without shielding her from a young and beautiful daughter-in-law.

Like the intelligent woman she was, the chatelaine went to visit the Comte de Kervel and, when she returned, told her son that he could marry Marguerite, but in a few years' time, when he had won his knight's spurs on the battlefield and proved that he was not unworthy of his blood.

The good lady was so eloquent, and spoke so well about the great deeds of the Kérouare family, and the laurels to be won under the hot sun of Palestine, that the enthused Paul replied that he was ready to do anything to obtain Marguerite, and that, in order to be worthy of her hand, he felt the courage to attack Jerusalem, its forts and redoubts, on his own.

And immediately, the young Sire de Kérouare summoned his vassals and men-at-arms, had his warhorse saddled, kissed his fiancée's hand, received his mother's blessing on bended knee, and set forth, lance held high and his heart filled with masculine ardor.

As for the chatelaine, reassured by the absence of that importunate witness to her thirty-seven years, she abandoned her mourning-dress and, six months later, married a knight of a noble and ancient family, of martial appearance but very poor. In consequence, when he came to live in the Manoir de Kérouare, he brought nothing but his armor, his ragged clothing and a huge appetite. The knight in question was twenty-seven.

* * * * * * *

The adventurous young man disembarked, with his men-at-arms, on Egyptian soil three months after his departure from Kérouare, and took the road to the crusaders' camp, commanded by the King of France, Louis VII.

Paul de Kérouare proved everywhere that his blood was noble and boiling; the ardent desert sun bronzed his face and made his beard grow; his slender white hands were hardened by handling a battle-ax, and in three years the blond seraphim of the banks of the Loire metamorphosed into a robust and valiant knight.

Marguerite de Kerven would have been proud of him; if the

Lady de Kérouare had envisaged that tall stature, that bronzed face, that thick beard, she would have applauded herself more than ever for having sent away that living proof of her forty years.

Paul de Kérouare had been fighting for three years when the king, recalled to France by his conjugal dispute with Eléonore d'Aquitaine, who was eager to barter his fleur-de-lys-ornamented crown for that of Henry of England, reassembled his knights and faithful followers and lifted the siege of Damascus, which he had been blockading for six months, in order to re-embark and return to Europe. He left behind a rearguard, however, charged with keeping the Saracens at bay, and Paul de Kérouare was among the barons and knights who stayed behind.

The crusaders had been subjected to many setbacks; the plague had decimated them; it was even worse when the king had gone. After a year, there were scarcely three hundred left, and in a final battle that they sustained with the obstinacy of despair, fifty of them were captured by the Saracens. Paul de Kéroare was among them.

The knight was taken to Tunis and sold in the slave-market. He was bought by a rich Muslim whose residence was beside the sea, and who employed him in cultivating his gardens.

Paul spent his brief hours of rest on the shore, and raised his eyes toward the mute horizon where only enemy sails were to be seen. When he thought about his manor, his mother and his fiancée, he wept. He wept because the image of the beautiful young woman was as vivid in his heart as on the day of his departure, because he would probably never see her again, nor the roof of his forefathers, nor the chatelaine de Kérouare—everything, in brief, that made life sweet and good: family and fatherland. And every day, when he resumed his rude labor, he felt weaker and more discouraged, and that terrible homesickness, complicated by lovesickness and slavery, undermined him dully and led him toward the tomb.

Finally, one day, in stifling heat, allowing himself to fall exhausted on the burning sand, he believed that he was about to die, and, remembering his young and beautiful years, and Marguerite, who was doubtless still waiting for him, he murmured: "Oh, to see her for just one hour, I would give all of those that might perhaps remain to me, and my eternal salvation with them."

Scarcely had he uttered those fateful words when a mocking voice replied: "So be it, Master—I accept, and I shall be your good prince; I'll grant you one entire day, from sunrise to sunset."

Paul de Kérouare shuddered, and, on turning round, saw a little old man sitting on the sand and contemplating him with a mocking gaze.

"Yes, Messire," he continued, "if you want to promise me your share of paradise on the word of a gentleman, you shall see Marguerite de Kerven and your mother for a full day."

"Who are you, then?" asked the astonished knight.

"My good friend," said the old man, "God gives me the name of fallen angel, and men call me Satan, but my real name is Lucifer, although I did not obtain it by baptism."

"The Devil!" Paul murmured, terrified. "Oh, I would never sign such a pact!"

"As you please—but you're going to die in a few hours."

"To die! Without seeing her again!"

"Why not?"

The knight hesitated momentarily; for a moment, Hell appeared before him with its livid flames, its sparkling laughter, its blasphemies and the crack of the metal-tipped whips that tear the bruised flesh of the damned. After all that, however, he believed that he saw a white and diaphanous robe floating in the mist; it seemed to him that the air was impregnated with the penetrating perfume that a young woman exhales as she runs though green fields amid the flowers of spring. A vague sound brought, like a sigh, the name of Marguerite to his ears—and, holding out his hand to Satan, he said: "I accept."

"Knight's honor?"

"Of course."

"Then, Master," the Devil cried, with a sinister laugh, "be satisfied, for you belong to me for eternity."

And immediately, Lucifer took the knight in his arms; his human vestments fell away; his old man's face disappeared; his eyes blazed; his wings grew and deployed—and the accursed angel took flight and launched himself through the air, carrying his victim.

For an hour that seemed to him to be a century, Paul felt himself drawn through a whirlwind of smoke, respiring the Devil's sulfurous breath, seeing nothing and hearing nothing except the sinister laughter of his terrible guide.

Then, suddenly, he felt a violent shock, as if Satan had dropped him from a height on to a rock, as an eagle might do with a lamb held in its claws. He opened his eyes, and was very astonished to find himself on the bank of the Loire, equidistant between Kérouare and Kerven.

The sun had not yet risen; dawn was sliding its silvery rays over the horizon; the birds were waking up in the crowns of the trees, the flowers bowing their dew-laden heads in the breath of the morning breeze; a light mist, similar to a veil of gauze, was floating over the waters of the river.

It was a magnificent spring day that the damned man was about to enjoy, as one enjoys one's last gold coin. And the Devil, it is necessary to admit, had shown himself to be generous, for he could have only granted his prey a dismal, damp and frosty day, instead of a spring day full of sunlight, flowers and perfumes.

* * * * * * *

In widowhood as in liberty, one has difficulty getting used to what follows. Lady de Kérouare, when her honeymoon was over, perceived that her new husband had more than one fault not mentioned in the parchments that had been scribbled during her marriage, and among those faults, she soon placed in the first rank, and by experience, a very determined desire to be the master.

The late Sire de Kérouare had been a worthy knight, but the rumor had gone around, during his life, that in his manor he quit the halberd and the lance for the skirt and distaff. Madame de Kérouare had, therefore, always been the unique arbiter of her own will; so, when the young knight to whom she had just enchained herself for the rest of her life abandoned the lover's smile for a husband's cold gravity, the noble chatelaine bucked like a stallion on to whose virgin back a bold cavalier has just launched himself. Alas, it was too late, and the yoke had been so well forged, so solidly applied, that she had bowed her head and dropped the conjugal scepter—the emblem of authority.

Her spouse dissipated a part of the patrimony of the Kérouares, heaped taxes and rents upon the vassals, and then left one day for a tournament, in which he was killed by the thrust of a lance.

Madame de Kérouare was free again—but this time, she judged it prudent to keep her widow's independence, and began to wish ardently for the young knight's return. During her long hours of suffering, she had called out to him so many times, and during her nights of insomnia she had so often thought that she saw him lift up the heavy curtains of her bed, like a phantom, and reproach her for his death, that the unhappy woman, returned to the sentiment of maternal love, prayed night and day in her oratory, invoked all the saints in paradise, for God to return her son to her.

In the meantime, her beauty was unalterable, and the forty-third year was about to sound for her without the slightest wrinkle tarnishing the purity of her forehead, without her eyes losing their gleam and their fascinating gaze....

The old Comte de Kerven was dead; she had brought Marguerite to live with her, called her daughter, and no longer feared her as a rival. Kneeling, every evening, on the stone floor of the chapel, the two women implored Heaven and begged for the young crusader's return.

Finally, one night, when her eyes red with tears, the poor chatelaine, her hands joined in her oratory, addressed a mother's prayer to the Virgin, a great light burst forth around her, and a celestial warrior, having nothing about his body but half a cloak, appeared standing before her prie-Dieu; it was St. Paul.

"Woman," he said the chatelaine, "God has sent me to tell you that he will allow you to see your son again, but only on one condition."

"Oh!" she cried. "Let me see him for just an hour, just one, that I might press him to my heart, that I might intoxicate myself with his gaze...and the take my life!"

"No," said St. Paul, "it is what remains of your beauty that God wants in exchange—the fatal beauty that sent your son away."

"Oh, Monseigneur," murmured the mother, "whiten my hair, curb my back, hollow out my cheeks and wrinkle my hands, but return my son to me...."

"It shall be done as you desire," said the saint. "You shall see him again tomorrow, at sunrise."

And as he finished, the chatelaine felt an icy frisson run through her body, freeze her blood and turn her heart upside-down.

"Look," said the Apostle then, presenting her with a steel mirror, which his celestial aureole illuminated.

The chatelaine darted a glance at her image, and did not recognize herself. She had white hair, her body was doubled over, her pearly teeth no longer existed, and her face, so white and so pure before, was as shiny and yellow as old parchment.

St. Paul opened the window, and as the saints have wings as soon as they enter paradise, he flew away, taking an eastward direction, in which he had to go, on God's orders, to seek out Paul de Kérouare and bring him to his mother.

On the way, however, not far from the manor, he saw Satan cleaving the air with his wing-beats, holding his victim in his claws....

That unexpected encounter knocked the Devil over, and he dropped the knight, who fell heavily to the ground—where he would have fractured his skull had the saint, his patron, not deadened his fall.

Then the Apostle, insulting Beelzebub, demanded to know what this meant, and how he had dared to carry out orders that God had given to St. Paul.

The Devil, however, recovered from his upset, replied: "It's neither for you nor for God, Master, that I'm performing this task, but on my own account, for the young man has sold me his soul."

And Satan, sitting down on a small cloud that was floating nearby, recounted what had passed between himself and Paul de Kérouare, and what bargain he had sealed.

The saint shivered, for Satan was perfectly within his rights—but immediately, a luminous idea occurred to him.

"Satan," he said, showing him the knight, still stunned from his fall and rubbing his eyes, "would you care to make a wager?"

"Two, Master, if you like."

"Look—that knight is exactly halfway between his mother's château and that of his mistress. Where will he go?"

"To his mistress, by my horns! He hasn't enough virtue to sacrifice profane love to filial love."

"Well then, abstain from advising him and I'll do the same. If he takes the road to Kerven, I won't dispute either his life or his soul with you—but if, on the contrary, he takes the path to Kérouare, you'll surrender both to me."

"Oh," Satan sniggered, "have no fear!"

"Do you accept the wager?"

"Of course, for it's won in advance."

And Hell and Paradise, represented by Satan and St. Paul, waited, motionless on the two clouds they were sitting astride, for the poor knight to decide the bet and lose or save his soul.

The Devil sniggered with the arrogantly modest smile of triumph; St, Paul waited anxiously....

But suddenly, the knight's hesitation disappeared, and, turning his back on Kerven, he headed toward Kérouare with a rapid stride.

The Apostle uttered a cry of joy.

The accursed angel bit his lips, made a frightful grimace and resumed his flight, drunk with rage ad shame—but he had experienced too many setbacks since his creation to allow himself to be defeated by such a minor loss; he stopped abruptly, waited until St. Paul had disappeared among the clouds, and then launched himself in the direction of Kérouare like lightning, entering by way of a chimney and going to hide in a panel of the woodwork, from which he could see the chatelaine on her knees in her oratory, waiting for the saint's promise to be fulfilled.

* * * * * * *

As Paul got closer to the manor, he felt his heart quiver and hammer in his breast, and at the same time, a hot sweat beaded on his brow.

At the sight of those beloved places, those flowery meadows, those green trees, those hedges populated with songbirds, and the melancholy towers forming the enclosure of his manor, a host of memories disturbed his mind, coming to remind him of his happy childhood, his dreamy adolescence and his fresh amour....

As he arrived at the drawbridge, the sun rose and gilded the spire of the belfry.

The poor exile crossed the threshold at a run, although he was very weary, passed through a host of varlets and soldiers, who did not recognize him in his rags, climbed the large stone staircase and ran through the corridors, shouting: "Mother! Mother!"

To that shout responded another shout, uttered by a quavering voice, and a little old woman came running as fast as her debilitated legs could carry her, her arms open sand tears in hr eyes.

She was no longer the beautiful chatelaine, alas....

But Paul threw himself into the arms that were held out to him, tenderly kissed the snowy tresses that he had left as black as ebony, covered the wrinkled hands that gripped him with caresses, and thought that he would die of joy....

The mother and the son embraced one another for a long time, and then Paul cried: "And Marguerite, Mother? Where is she? Does she still love me?"

"Marguerite is here," replied the old woman, coughing. "She's waiting, my child, and I'll take you to her bedside."

"Here?" said the knight. "Oh, thank...."

But his face suddenly darkened; a livid pallor spread over his face. "Come quickly," he said, "for I only have one day to give both of you...."

"What do you mean?" exclaimed the chatelaine.

"I mean," Paul murmured, dully, "that I've sold my soul in order to hug you—you and her—to my heart one last time, and that this evening, at sunset, Satan will come to take it, for I'm damned."

"Damned?" exclaimed the poor mother, with a stifled cry, collapsing like a pine-tree uprooted by a hurricane. "Damned!"

But Paul paid no heed, and continued running through the corridors to find Marguerite—and the chatelaine, thunderstruck by that revelation, remained motionless, inert, almost mad.

It was then that Satan, who had quit his hiding-place and as standing in the shadows, showed himself to her and said: "There's a simple means of redeeming your son's soul."

The old woman recoiled in terror, but Satan went on: "If you wish, your son won't be damned."

"If I wish?" she cried. "Oh, what do I have to do to soften God's wrath?"

"This," said the fallen angel, gravely, "has nothing to do with the Eternal Father, but the Devil, which is me. Your son's soul belongs to me, and that's your fault. Give me yours and I'll return his. I'll lose by the exchange for yours is already three-quarters mine, but I'm a good fellow and I take pity on good mothers."

A smile of joy passed over the chatelaine's wrinkled face. "Oh, I accept," she said. "Take my soul, Satan; I'll suffer less in thinking that my son is saved!"

"Is that settled?"

"Yes," said the chatelaine.

"Then sign this contract." And the Devil put a pen and parchment in front of the old woman, which exhaled a frightful odor of burning.

The poor mother signed, and Satan said to her: "Go rejoin your son; you may live until sunset. Then I'll come to look for you."

With those words, Satan bowed tranquilly, put the parchment in his pocket, and rubbed his hands, saying: "There! I haven't wasted my day, and for one soul lost, I've gained another."

The chatelaine found her son at Marguerite's feet, kissing her hands deliriously and getting drunk on a joy that he thought everlasting.

The mother keeping silent about her sublime devotion, the son almost forgetting the fatal hour, the young woman ignorant of everything, the day passed in that fashion: hands in hands, eyes looking into eyes, hearts beating with a common pulsation....

But at the moment when the sun, having declined rapidly, arrived at the ultimate limit of the horizon, the knight and the old woman both shivered and fixed a hectic gaze on the majestic star, ready to bury itself in a magnificent shroud of orange- and red-tinted mists...

And holding their breath, motionless, frozen, they followed the degradation of the light in the heavens, as if their last sigh were about to be exhaled as soon as the last ray of light died away....

At that moment, the Devil appeared.

"Knight," he said, "your soul no longer belongs to me, but your mother has sold hers." In a strident voice he continued: "Woman, the sun has set; you have to go with me...."

But as the poor woman was already tottering at the approach of the wind of death, another voice, more strident and more terrible than that of the accursed angel, was heard.

"Satan!" it shouted. "This soul does not belong to you, for that of Paul de Kérouare did not belong to you when you made that woman sign the redemption of her son at the price of her eternal damnation. The woman shall live, and not go with you!" The voice was that of St. Paul, who had just appeared on the threshold. "Woman," he added, turning to the chatelaine, "God pardons your sin in favor of your maternal love, but in order that no other will imitate you, he condemns all of your posterity who, destined to perpetuate your name, do not marry before the age of twenty-five, to die within the following year."

The Devil fled, howling with rage, and the saint returned to take his place at the foot of Jehovah's throne.

As for Paul, he married the beautiful Marguerite de Kerven the next day, on his twenty-fifth birthday.

* * * * * * *

"And that is doubtless why I am here," the narrator concluded, "occupied in telling you this true story."

"And I hope," said Madame de Damfrein, when Roger had finished, "that the prediction of the legend has never been fulfilled?"

"To tell the truth," the young man replied, whether by pure hazard or the will of Heaven, the tradition has been justified twice."

"Get away!" said someone, with a murmur of incredulity.

"The first time, it was at Marignan, that fabulous battle which was dubbed the Combat of Giants, and before which François I, according to chivalric memory, prepared himself by sleeping, fully armed, on the barrel of a cannon. Laurent de Kérouare, aged two months fewer than twenty-six years and still a bachelor, was killed, struck by six arquebus bullets.

"The second time, it was at the terrible affair at Fontenoy. René de Kérouare, a lieutenant in the musketeers, received a cannonball full in the chest, and was carried away dead by his terrified horse. He was twenty-five years and eight months old. Fortunately, each of them had a younger brother condemned to celibacy, and the deaths obliged them to marry in order to perpetuate the name."

"Well then," said the dowager Lady de Langevin, how old are you, Monsieur de Kérouare?"

"Twenty five years less two months."

"It's very fortunate," replied Monsieur de Loiseray, "that the Baronne's mourning expires in six weeks, for if your twenty-fifth year found you a bachelor and the fatal tradition were accomplished, you wouldn't even have a brother to continue the family."

"Indeed," said Roger. "I'm an only son." And he darted a tender and respectful glance at the widow.

"Bah!" said various people. "Fairy tales, all that!"

"You can make fun of me if you wish," said Madame de Damfrein, laughing, "but I believe in traditions."

The most incredulous contented themselves with smiling, and everyone retired.

Madame de Damfrein went to her room anxious, did not sleep at all that night, and was agitated by a thousand crazy fears.

The next morning, at eight o'clock, her chambermaid came in silently, and, finding her awake, told her that Monsieur de Kérouare was asking to see her.

"At this hour" cried the Baronne. "What's wrong? My God, what's wrong?"

She put on a dressing-gown, put slippers on her feet, put a mantlet over her shoulders, and said: "Show Monsieur de Kérouaire into my boudoir: I'll be in shortly.

Roger de Kérouaire was in traveling costume, with a riding-crop in his hand and an anxious from on his face.

"My God!" cried Madame de Damnfrein, when she came in. "What's the matter, Roger, and where are you going?"

"What's the matter?" he said, kissing her hand. "The anxiety of mystery. Where am I going? To Kérouare."

"Is your father...?"

"Ill? No; he's very well."

"Your aunt...?"

"In perfect health."

"What is it, then? Explain."

"Impossible—I know absolutely nothing myself. Yesterday, when I got home, I found Antoine, my father's old domestic, who gave me this note. Read it."

The Baronne took it, and read:

My son,

Put everything aside, interrupt all your plans, mount a fast horse and come here.

Comte de Kérouare.

"But your domestic must have told you...," said the Baronne.

"Antoine knows absolutely nothing. My father has been receiving many letters for several days; he is visiting his neighbors urgently, and seems increasingly agitated, but has not said a word."

"My God!" the widow murmured.

"Dear soul," Roger replied, "have no fear. Whatever my father's wishes are, my life is yours, and for always."

"Your life, Roger? Look, in two months, you'll be twenty-five, and if we're not married, then...."

"Good," said the young man. "Do you believe my legend?"

"Well, yes, I believe it. I had a presentiment of everything that is happening, for I didn't sleep last night."

"Silly!" said Roger. "In any case, it only takes two days to go to Kérouare, as many to come back, and I have plenty of time. My sharpest pain is that separation."

"Write to me when you arrive."

"Before I take my boots off—don't worry."

The future spouses made their tender adieux, full of regrets and hopes. Then Roger mounted up, and took the road to Angers, at a gallop.

* * * * * * *

Roger de Kérouare to Madame la Baronne de
Damfrein
Kéraoure ..... 1831.

Dear Angel,

I've arrived. I've found Kérouare just as I left it in
June of last year, except that the trees in the park, de-
prived of their leaves, are creaking lugubriously under
the effort of the autumn wind; the swallows have gone,
the meadows are burned by frost, and the banks of the
Loire are heart-breakingly sad.

I found my father leaning, as is his custom, against
the mantelpiece of the large fireplace in the drawing-
room—formerly the armory. My aunt, Mademoiselle
de Kérouare, was huddled in her armchair beside the
fire, her dog Azor at her feet and her triple-layered lace
bonnet on her head. She was rereading, for at least the
third time, the late Crébillon fils' *Le Sopha*. My father
was silent and severe, with his eagle's nose and his
short-cropped white hair. He offered me his hand, silently, indicated an armchair to me, and sent away the
domestics who had introduced me, in accordance with
the old French custom, pronouncing my title and my
name.

In the meantime, I couldn't help examining the
family portraits that are hanging on the walls of the
drawing-room, and perhaps I never felt as much respect for those grave and mute individuals—a historical pageant recalling in their costumes all the reigns,
from the halberds and helmets of the crusaders to the
gold-embroidered red uniforms of the king's musketeers.

When the three of us were alone, my father sat down and sad: "Roger, you're brave, I know."

"That's a very feeble merit when one's name is Kérouare," I said.

"Since the July catastrophe returned you to civilian status a year ago, have you changed your principles?"

"Oh, Father, I didn't expect such an insult or suspicion!"

"That's good," he said. "In that case, the time has come to take up your sword again."

"What do you mean, Father?"

"That *Madame*[18] has been in the Vendée for three days, that I am one of the leaders of the uprising that will take place in the West, and that we're leaving this evening."

"Very well," I replied. "I'm ready."

Then the Comte de Kérouare asked me for your news, talked to me about our impending marriage, and when, in spite of myself, I recalled the popular legend that has weighed upon our family for five centuries, he said: "Bah! You have two months ahead of you, and we'll only need one to open the gates of Paris to His Majesty."

It's now two o'clock; we shall mount up at nightfall, and reach the Vendée at the gallop.

Adieu, dear angel—or, rather, *au revoir*. I'll write to you when I can. It's a perilous enterprise on which we're about to gamble our heads and the salvation of our cause, but when one has love in one's heart and

---

18. The reference us to the Duchesse de Berry, who provoked the rising in the Vendée that was intended to win back the French throne for the Bourbons; the deposed Charles X had taken refuge in Scotland, but was said to have agreed to surrender his right to the throne he had abdicated to his young grandson, the Duc de Bordeaux, whom the legitimists called "Henri V." The Duchesse de Berry was his mother, who would have ruled as regent had the insurrection been successful, but it was soon put down.

one takes up the sword for one's king, death retreats and victory takes its place.

I am covering this letter with kisses.

Roger.

* * * * * * *

Roger de Kérouare to Madame la Baronne de Damfrein .... Vendée, November 1831.

It is exhausted by fatigue, with my hand on my rifle, the stormy sky for a ceiling, a forest for wallpaper and a haversack for a writing-desk that I am writing to you, dear angel. It's painful to say, but in our first encounter, we have been smashed and overwhelmed by force of numbers. We're battling like lions; my father and I are safe and sound. I'm putting my entire soul into your heart, and I'm pronouncing your name in a whisper, telling myself that perhaps I shall see you soon.

Adieu,

Roger.

* * * * * * *

A month had gone by since the receipt of that letter, and Roger had reached his twenty-fifth year.

Madame de Damfrein, after having put away her widow's weeds and awaiting her fiancé, began to yield to crazy terrors. Apart from the continual danger that he was in, she thought incessantly about that fatal legend.

Every day she devoured the issue of the *Quotidienne* that gave the number of the dead and their names. Roger's was nowhere to be found; then she began to breathe again. In the evening, her terrors returned, until the following day, when she read an almost-identical line: "After prodigies of valor, Monsieur le Comte de Kérouare and his son have withdrawn safe and sound."

Finally, one evening, someone announced:

"Monsieur de Kérouare."

The Baronne uttered a cry of joy, and turned to the door.

Instead of Roger, however, she saw an old man, grave and austere, dressed in black, who came to her and silently kissed her hand, while he held out a handkerchief spattered with blood, and a gold ring encasing a fine pearl.

At the sight of that ring—the one she had given to Roger—the poor woman uttered a cry of despair, and fell in a faint on to the parquet.

When she came round, the Comte was at her bedside.

"Madame," he said, "Roger died a brave gentleman, and if the sight of a greater dolor can soften another, I say to you: Look at this old man; he has seen his king depart into exile, his son fall at his right-hand side, and he will descend alone into the tomb of the Kérouares, which will close forever on them and on him, for he has no scion...."

And the old gentleman, finally broken by grief, hid his head in his hands and wept.

The legend had completed its work.

The Comte died within the year—and Madame de Damfrein, after having wept for Roger for a time, ended up marrying again.

It is only a father's dolor that is mortal.

THE DEVIL'S MANSE

"What a pity it is, Monsieur le Comte, to have been traveling thus for a fortnight in the midst of such beautiful hunting country, without having cut loose and taken to the woods once."

"My dear Bouquin, the war makes imperious demands; when we have beaten the Imperials soundly enough to be able to dictate the terms of a peace-treaty to them, we'll request a leave and come back to Pouzanges, where the deer and wild boar are abundant enough in the vicinity to keep our retinues breathless for an entire year."

"That's well said and well thought, Monsieur le Comte," Bouquin replied, in a surly tone, "but it really wasn't worth the trouble of bringing our dogs eight hundred leagues to drag them along in chains day and night with their tails down behind a campaign-wagon. Since I arrived, that's all we've done. Every time we go under cover we pass through a thicket and emerge into a ten-league plain were the beast would be permanently in view; everywhere we perceive the stump of a horn, the antler of a ten-pointer, the tail of an ibex....the dogs howl, my trumpet dances all alone on my shoulder, I have fanfares, tally-hos and view-halloos in my ears...and nothing! We continue to march at the head of these stupid dragoons, who shrug their shoulders like the ignorant and profane individuals they are, at the sight of our best Vendean dogs and our most beautiful Saintonges."

And Bouquin—who, as our readers will have guessed, was an old huntsman full of fire and cynegetic courage, in spite of his sixty winters elapsed at the recent festival of the great Saint

Hubert—having delivered that tirade in a fit of bad temper, retreated into majestic silence, and darted a glance molded by supreme disdain at the company of dragoons that was riding behind its commander, the Comte de Main-Hardye, Captain of Dragoons and Commandant of a rearguard of cavalry that was going through the steppes and immense forests of Bohemia to rejoin the main body of a French army under the orders of the Maréchal de Belle-Isle, camped outside Prague.

The Comte was a young man of twenty-eight or thirty, a handsome fellow, brave to the point of temerity, adventurous to the extent of folly, and endowed, to a supreme degree, with the noble passion for hunting that was already, although it was only 1750, beginning to die out in many gentlemen, although admirably situated, whom war and—more often—the intrigues of the court took away from their estates almost every year. The Comte hunted regularly every day during the six months of annual leave that he requested from the king, and during the other six he did his best to join in, once or twice a week, whether at Saint-Germain and Compiègne with His Majesty's great hunts, or at Chantilly, with the Prince de Condé, or Sceaux, with Monsieur de Duc.

Three months ago, an order from the king had arrived in the middle of an all-out pursuit with the Gentleman of Boscage, and that order had been to rejoin his regiment, forming part of an army operating in Bohemia, in concert with Prussia, against Austria and Russia combined. Like the true gentleman he was, the Comte had taken off his hunting-garments immediately in order to don his uniform, replaced his knife with a sword, and had hung up his horn and knife over the fireplace in his drawing room, condemning them, not without regret, to a repose whose duration he was unable to anticipate.

"Bouquin, my friend," he had said, as he put his foot in the stirrup, to his old huntsman, whose head was bowed and his eyes dejected, wondering how long the Boscage would remain silent, devoid of the magnificent bass voices of the great white dogs and burning fervor, "it's possible that I won't be back for a year, but it's also possible that I'll be back within a month. Take good care of my pack; let them loose in the woods of Jarry every Sunday and in the thickets of Pouzanges every Wednesday, and shoot rabbits in the Parc de Bienvenue with my basset hounds, and take good care never to force the ten-pointers. In addition, I recommend you, for the health of your ears, to respect my hunting-knife at all costs, and only to permit my neighbors rare campaigns on my lands. I don't want them to be depopulated."

And having given these instructions, the Comte had left for his regiment.

He had arrived on the eve of a battle and two days before a siege; then, the battle having been won and the besieged town taken by storm, he had been left in garrison in a small frontier village in eastern Prussia—a village of no importance to him, but from which the enemy would have gained a gained a significant advantage by recapturing it. The Maréchal de Belle-Isle had confided its defense to him and had gone to lay siege to Prague.

For a week, the Comte de Main-Hardye had maintained his guard, making his soldiers observe a strict discipline, giving them orders, expecting to be attacked at any moment by a company of Imperial infantry that was on campaign less than ten leagues away—but on orders from above, the company had withdrawn a further ten leagues, and then an idea had occurred to the Comte: *What if I were to go hunting?*

The village and the surrounding countryside were admirably situated. Dense woods, young thickets, sonorous valleys, uniform stony plains, numerous pools, ponds and streams where the dogs could drink...nothing was lacking. Animals were abundant. Roe deer were mere small fry, for, apart from red deer and wild boar there were also wolves, elk and bears aplenty. That luxury of game was due to two causes: firstly, the excellent situation of the region; and secondly, the total absence of hunters in the vicinity. That advantage had its inconvenience, for the simple reason that every coin has two sides; the complete absence of hunters naturally implied a total dearth of hounds.

Without a pack, how could one hunt?

The Comte had struck a vein; having had one idea, it was easy for him to have a second, and he did. *What if I were to summon my dogs here?* he thought. *It's a long trot, but they could make it, with a few forced marches, in eighteen days. It might well be that I'll spend the winter here, and in that case, serving the king will be easy for me. If, on the other hand, I change garrison, I'll be unlucky if I don't end up in hunting country. In Bohemia, one can hunt anywhere.*

With that, Monsieur de Main-Hardye summoned his manservant and dictated the following letter:

> *My dear Bouquin, on receipt of my letter, you will procure a cart as wide as a street, put fifteen of my best Vendean dogs into it, twenty-five of my largest Sain-tonges, and my dog-groom Letaillis, and you will hitch it up to two good Limousin horses. After which, you will install yourself on the seat with my manservant, who will bring you this letter, and set forth for Germany. When the horses are weary you'll renew them. If my steward is short of money, sell a hundred hectares of land right away—as long we keep the woods, that's all we need. Bring me my horn and my hunting-knife.*

When this letter was written and the manservant had set off at a gallop, the Comte had said to himself:

While awaiting Bouquin, I'll procure myself a pointer and shake up the hares and partridges in the vicinity.

He had begun the following day. In spite of all his efforts, he had not been able to find a pointer, but he had replaced it with an enormous sheep-dog with an infernal nose and legs, tenacious and intelligent, well up to the job. On the very first day, the mastiff had killed him a hare. In the evening it gave voice three times in a thicket; the Comte had assumed that it was another hare, but saw a hind emerge, which he shot dead with a single bullet.

The next day, the dog had flushed out an elk, which met the same fate. The Comte acquired a taste for that kind of hunting, and thought that when his pack arrived, he would be the happiest officer in France and Germany.

The pack finally arrived. Bouquin, easily transported, had shown incredible diligence and left along his route the equivalent value of the Château de Bienvenue in broken horses. Alas, however, good and bad look often follow one another. Bouquin arrived in the evening, and the next morning, the Comte had just put his foot in the stirrup to go hunting, when a courier from the Maréchal de Belle-Isle had arrived with an order thus conceived:

> On receipt of this message, mount up and undertake a
> forced march. The king's service.

"Bouquin," said the Comte, sadly, "couple the dogs and start walking. We'll hunt another day." Then he turned to his lieutenant, who was about to go hunting with him, and said: "Sound the call to arms, and have the company mount up!"

So, instead of going hunting, the Comte departed with his men and marched for a fortnight, with Bouquin and his pack trailing behind. It was at the end of the fourteenth day that Bouquin risked embarking on the dialogue with which our story began.

The Comte experienced a surge of bad temper on listening to Bouquin, whose abrupt eloquence awoke so sharply all his appetites as a hunter of merit, but as, before being a hunter, he was a gentleman and a loyal servant of the king, he stifled his egotistical instincts and strove to adopt an insouciant expression. So he made no reply to Bouquin, contenting himself with uttering a philosophical "Heu!" which the breeze carried away, but which Bouquin caught on the wing and which drew from him the following mental reflection:

The hunters are going forth! Where are we bound?

Four hours later, the Comte and his men arrived at the

Maréchal's camp.

Monsieur de Belle-Isle was waiting for the Comte impatiently. "Finally!" he said, on seeing him.

The Comte was only in command of a small company. His men, in consequence, could only led very modest assistance if there were to be an attack the next day, and he was astonished by the sigh of relief that the Maréchal uttered when he went into his tent.

"Monsieur le Comte," said the Maréchal, having sent away his aides-de-camp and made sure that they were quite alone, "I know that you're as brave as Bayard and the most adventurous gentleman in France."

"Your lordship is too kind."

"I have an almost-impossible mission to propose to you; you would be risking your life therein, and I regard it myself, as a virtual suicide mission."

"Damn!" said the Comte, smiling.

"It's a matter of passing, all alone, through thirty thousand Russians and two hundred thousand Austrians to carry letters from the King to the Sultan."

"Give me the letters," said the Comte, simply.

"I warn you that you'll be running a thousand dangers, the least of which could cost you your head."

"Monseigneur," said Monsieur de Main-Harye, with superb self-composure, "If I might add a word, exhausted as I am and as hungry as Ugolin, if it were necessary, for my honor, for me to dispense with shaking the dust from my boots and mount up again without swallowing a single mouthful, I'd do it."

The Maréchal smiled—a smile that was worth a royal eulogy.

"Are these letters very important?" asked the Comte.

"So important," the Maréchal replied, "that if you don't arrive, we might lose a couple of provinces."

"Then it's necessary that I arrive at any price—and I shall!"

"Are you sure of that?"

"I believe so. You're going to grant me a month's leave."

"Why?"

"Wait. Then, put at my disposal three Austrian prisoners, who will carry three letters: one to Goritz, the second to the vicinity of Vienna, the third to Pest in Hungary. The first is for Baron von Hollingen, Colonel of the Goritz garrison; the second for Graf von Hochoenbrun, a courtier is great favor at the count of Vienna; the third is for the Ban Rodstock, a Hungarian nobleman. I knew all three in Paris and I have taken two of them to my home in the Vendée, where they spent an autumn hunting. They are three meritorious and passionate hunters, who would go to catch a hare under a bell-tower if it were necessary."

"What do you expect to come of it?"

"This: you give me a leave; I take advantage of it to go hunting on these gentlemen's estates. Once at Pest, I'll only have fifty leagues to go to reach the Ottoman possessions. I'll get there—don't worry. On my way, no one will stop me. I'll be going, as a hunter to the home of a senior officer in the Imperial Army; I'll be alone, with my huntsman and kennel-groom. I won't inspire any suspicion."

"And thus," said the amazed Maréchal, "you'll get to Constantinople....."

"As a hunter, Monsieur le Marcéchal."

"That's prodigious!" aid Monsieur de Belle-Isle. "It only remains for you to procure, immediately, dogs and huntsmen."

"I have all that, Monsieur le Maréchal."

"And where did you get them?"

"From my château in the Vendée. I summoned my huntsman and my pack."

The Maréchal was stunned. Monsieur de Main-Hardye contented himself with smiling with the proud modesty of a superior man who finds the admiration he excites quite natural, and then asked when he had to leave.

"Tomorrow morning."

The Comte returned to Bouquin with his leave in his hand, and said to him: "We're going hunting tomorrow; take the road to Goritz immediately and flush me out a red deer ten leagues from here. An Austrian who'll be liberated for that express purpose, will serve as your guide."

Bouquin nearly died of joy. The Comte then wrote the following circular to his three old friends, only changing the name of the recipient and the address on each exemplar:

> My dear...., the King of France, in consideration of the fact that I have been deprived of hunting for the last three months, solely for his service, has deigned to grant me a month's leave. I am, therefore, no longer a Captain of Dragoons but a simple disciple of St. Hubert, who asks you, by horn and cries, for a safe conduct in order to reach you, and to hunt your boar and elk in peace, until his leave expires. Yours, Comte de Main-Hardye.
>
> P.S. I am setting out straight away; I expect to encounter your safe conduct halfway.

* * * * * * *

The next day, at daybreak, the Comte was on horseback. Bouquin's dogs had left during the night, along with the messengers. The Comte, who had the King's letters sown into the lining of his hunting-jacket, left in his turn, escorted only by his manservant.

French troops held the terrain on the road to Goritz for a radius of twenty leagues. Monsieur de Main-Hardye therefore had no anxieties during the first two days. He arrived at the meeting-point for the hunt at ten o'clock, fund Bouquin, who offered him a choice between a red deer and an elk, opted for the elk, and let loose the hounds. The dogs, idle for a long time, launched forward with an unparalleled ardor. At five o'clock in the evening the elk was cornered without a single snag.

The Comte completed the kill, spotted a nearby village and said to Bouquin: "For today we'll sleep here. You'll depart at half past two in the morning and go to the woods five leagues further on."

Bouquin bowed without any further response. The Comte, his huntsman, his manservant and his kennel-groom ate supper at the same table in a wretched inn, and then went to bed in a hay-loft.

The next day, Monsieur de Main-Hardye killed a boar and gained another five leagues.

"Where shall I beat the woods tomorrow?" asked Bouquin.

"Ten leagues further on."

"Hmm!" said the huntsman, admiringly. "Are we going far, and for a long time, like that?"

"To begin with, we're going to Goritz."

"And then?"

"Then to Vienna."

"And afterwards?"

"After that, to Pest—and then we'll go on to Constantinople."

Bouquin, who had got up from the table, supported himself on his chair in order not to fall over. "Monsieur le Comte is mad!" he murmured, in a tone of commiseration.

"Not at all," said the Comte, "but I've always had a yen to see for myself whether the Turks are passable hunters."

Bouquin shrugged his shoulders. "Since Monsieur le Comte intends to travel," he said, with a kind of sardonic humor, "why don't we go all the way to China?"

"I might decide to do that," the Comte replied, phlegmatically. "I'll give your proposal some thought, Bouquin."

"Monsieur le Comte will doubtless find relays of dogs *en route*," Bouquin continued, with mocking humility.

"Don't we have ours?"

"If they hunt for such a long time, we'll need to put them in a carriage before long."

"We'll rest for one day in four."

"They won't last the course...."

"If that happens," said the Comte, coldly, "people will say that Main-Hardye has poor dogs and a poor huntsman."

Bouquin bit his lip in anger. "They'll get there," he said, "if I have to carry them."

On the third day, Monsieur de Main-Hardye hunted a deer and covered thirty leagues. On the fourth, he called a halt and the pack rested—but as he wanted to take advantage of his leave, he took his rifle and went to sleep three leagues further on than his men, shooting partridges and snipe on the way. That worked out all the better because his shelter was a woodcutter's hut, where, without his game, he would only have had rancid sauerkraut to eat.

On the fifth day, while he was on the track of an elk, he ran into an Austrian advance post. At first they wanted to arrest him, but he showed them his ticket of leave, named Baron von Hollingenn to whose home he was going, and was released by the officer in command of the detachment. That evening, Monsieur de Main-Hardye judged it prudent to go to a small town to seek shelter, mistrusting the woodcutters and peasants who had so far been his hosts.

The Comte finally found himself within the bounds of mountainous Bohemia. Until then he had only been traversing plains, forests and imperceptible hills; now he was facing a chain of somber mountains, wooded from base to summit, pierced by narrow, profound valleys with numerous caverns where bears and thieves lodged pell-mell.

A gentleman less brave than Monsieur de Main-Hardye, at the description he had been given in the last town where he lodged of the country he was about to pass through, would have been, if not frightened, at least made to reflect on the appropriate measures to take to avoid any unfortunate encounter. There were at that time, in the hills and vales, enough irregular and vagabond soldiers, known as Znapans, of whose morality we will paint an accurate picture if we say that the French word *chenapan*[19] is directly derived from their name.

There were, as we said, enough Znapans on campaign for it to be easy, with a thousand florins, to hire two hundred of them as an escort, but Monsieur de Main-Hardye was never afraid,

---

19. English has no such derivative; the nearest equivalent would be something like "scoundrel."

and he contented himself with saying to Bouquin: "Since we're going into bear country, I only want to hunt bears from now on. As I don't want anything to happen to you, though, I'll beat the woods with you."

At three o'clock in the morning, the Comte set out again and went into a valley surrounded on all sides by high mountains. That valley, known in the region as the Red Valley, had its own petty fantastic legend, like all the corners of worthy and naïve Germany. Its legend, like all the others, had the Devil as its eternal pivot, and dated from the Middle Ages.

* * * * * * *

This is the legend, in brief:

Satan, who had always liked to relax, had long coveted the domains and the schloss of a nobleman who, during the crusades, gripped by a desire to return home, had sold his soul to Hell in order to satisfy that desire. Satan had transported him to his schloss in less than one night, and had promised to let him live for a long time yet, but the nobleman seemed to abuse that latitude considerably, living beyond the age of a hundred and twenty.

Every year the Devil appeared to him and said: "How are you?"

"Not so good," replied the crafty castellan, couching and spitting like a dying man. "You won't have to wait much longer, Your Majesty; I'm fading...."

The Devil went away, came back after a year, and found the nobleman in the same state of health as twelve months before.

Satan was patient for ninety years, as people lived that long in those days; at a hundred he became impatient; at a hundred and ten he became furious, and when the hundred and twentieth sounded, he could no longer hold back. He presented himself to the castellan that evening. The nobleman was in bed, a torch on the side-table and a Bible in his hand.

Satan quivered. "What are you reading?" he asked.

"The Bible, Sire. I had a visit this morning."

"Oh? From whom?"

"From Saint Peter, who said to me: 'If you can live another year and learn a hundred and twenty-one pages of the Bible by heart, present yourself at the gate of Paradise as soon as you're dead, call for me in a low voice, and recite the hundred and twenty-one pages. If you don't make a single mistake, I'll raise the bar surreptitiously, and the Devil will be cheated."

"Ah!" said Satan, pale with ager.

"As you see, Sire," said the castellan, humbly. "I'm studying. I already know the first sixty. Would you like to hear me repeat them?" And he handed the Bible to Satan.

But Satan thrust it away, and, furiously, picked up the torch and applied it to the bed-curtains. The bed caught fire, the Devil fled, and the castellan, who was too old to be sprightly, burned, along with his Bible. His frightened soul fled toward Hell, but a voice called to him on the way. The soul turned round and saw the great apostle, the eternal concierge of Paradise.

"Come on," he said, "recite the sixty pages you know for me; I'll let you off the rest."

The castellan made two or three slight mistakes, but the indulgent apostle coughed at the appropriate moments and pretended not to notice them. The castellan went into Paradise.

"I haven't come off too badly," said Satan. "What I wanted was the schloss. I've snuffed him out properly; it belongs to me and I'll be able to reside there occasionally."

Since then, the woodcutters claim that at midnight on Saturday, the cracked walls of the manse can be seen through the clearings ablaze, whence it has acquire the name of the Red Castle, and that lasciviously-entwined shadows pass back and forth behind the windows, from which bursts of strident laughter and the muffled strains of an orchestra can be heard.

The castle was haunted. No one had gone near it since; woodcutters made the sign of the cross on seeing it, and shepherds shivered if they caught a glimpse, above the fir trees, of the pointed spires of it towers. The valley was accursed and abandoned to the bears....

* * * * * * *

It was in that very valley that, after eight hours of walking, the Comte de Main-Hardye was assailed by a violent storm and separated from the hunt—which is to say, from his three servants and his dogs—on emerging from a dense thicket. The noise of the thunder had drowned out the horn and the raucous voices of his dogs.

The Comte took refuge under a tree, where he and his horse sheltered as best they could, and waited for the storm to pass, sounding his horn every quarter of an hour to rally the hunt. No horn replied to his, and the storm lasted until dusk.

Impatiently, the Comte set forth again with the last rainfall, and plunged deeper and deeper into the Red Valley, whose wild aspect became sinister by night. Monsieur de Main-Hardye was hungry, soaked to the skin and chilled to the marrow. He kept going for a few more hours in darkness, through the woods, still hoping to encounter a woodcutter's hut, but not perceiving any.

"Damn it!" he swore, exasperatedly. "Since I'm in the Devil's valley, the Devil might have the courtesy to offer me hospitality."

He had scarcely finished the remark when, on going round a bend in the valley, he perceived a dark ad imposing mass in the distance, striped with luminous streaks, and recognized the Devil's Manse, illuminated from the attics to the kitchens.

It was Saturday, and midnight was approaching.

"Oho!" said the Comte. "There's a sabbat tonight, and I'll find a numerous company."

And without manifesting any astonishment, he urged his horse forward, which recovered its courage and deposited him, twenty minutes later, at the castle gate.

The Comte sounded a fanfare; the drawbridge was lowered. He went into the courtyard, but could not see anyone. He marched toward the perron, climbed it, and arrived in the vestibule. The perron and the vestibule were deserted. He went up the main staircase, in red marble, went into a vast hall with red walls, and then another, and another....

They were all red, all illuminated, as if for a fête, but no one was there.

In the last room into which he penetrated the Comte found a table with two place-settings.

"My word," he said, "I'm dying of hunger, and the Master of the House wouldn't want me to wait for him. I'll get stuck into that venison pâté and that bear-ham."

And the Comte sat down at the table, boldly. The Comte was hungry, as we said; moreover, he was one of those rare strong-minded individuals who does not take the trouble to delve into a mystery where there are better things to do first. He was hungry....

The venison pâté disappeared almost entirely. Them, the pâté was followed, almost without interruption, by a woodcock salmi and a partridge bisque, a few meager pickles, half a jar of Oriental jam and a few Hungarian pastries. He washed it all down with a Johannisberg of a rather good vintage, a red Muscat whose origin the Comte could not determine, and a few drops of Aï—a scrupulous and delicate attention on the part of the unknown host who was serving wines from his native country to an exile.

"My God!" exclaimed the Comte, laughing. "This closely resembles the late Monsieur Perrault's tale of the Beauty and the Beast; the lodgings and the table are splendid, the host remains invisible, and he'll only show himself, I'll wager, in the depths of the gardens in the form of a female monster that I'll only have to marry to convert into a seductive princess clad in silk and cashmere!"

We would not dare affirm that that remark of the Comte's resembled a challenge, or that he had any intention of provoking the appearance of his host, but if that was the case, his effort was wasted, for the host did not appear.

When he had finished his supper, the Comte sat back philosophically in his armchair and said to himself, quietly: "All that's lacking is a drop of coffee."

"If Monsieur le Comte would care to pass into the drawing room," replied a voice, "he will find coffee and Oriental pipes."

The Comte raised his head swiftly, and looked around, his eyes searching for the owner of the voice that he had just heard, but he could not see anyone. However, a door had just opened at the back of the dining-room, allowing the sight of a splendidly decorated drawing room, with a bright and crackling fire, next to which a pile of cushions had been placed and a table set up on which there was hot mocha and a chibouk with an amber stem, full of latakia. The Comte crouched down, without too much stiffness, on the cushions, lit the chibouk, and started philosophizing about the bizarreries of life in general and the existence of the schloss in particular. The schloss, above all, which he found so comfortable in all respects, and yet deserted, at least in appearance, seemed curious enough to warrant examination.

When he had drunk the coffee and discarded the extinct ashes of his chibouk in the fireplace, the Comte got to his feet, picked up a torch and said to himself: *Since there's no one here who can show me the castle in detail and serve as my cicerone, I'll show it to myself, and get my bearings as best I can.*

And with that, he set off, commencing his inspection with the drawing room in which he found himself. It was a huge room, its walls clad in dark green damask, with golden rods on the ceiling, arabesques and moldings in a tasteful style. Louis XV furniture, in silk and gold, displayed its sofas and round-backs armchairs around the walls. A few costly paintings, a few masterly bronzes, a miniature and a pastel were distributed here and there; two gilded copper tritons supported the fire-irons; on a table set up in the middle of the room, books magazines and alums were distributed pell-mell, including the moral tales of Monsieur de Marmontel[20] and the latest issue of the *Mercure de France.*

---

20. *Contes moraux*, by Jean-François Marmontel, published individually in the *Mercure de France* and collected in 1791.

It appears, the Comte thought, *that my host is a lover of arts and letters.*

After examining every detail of the drawing room, the Comte opened a door and found himself in a charming blue and white boudoir, cluttered with lacquer and porcelain vases, rare flowers and miniature trees grown at great expense, delightful bagatelles randomly scattered on dressers and sideboards—in a word, the thousand ruinous trivia with which a woman likes to surround herself.

I'm definitely in the home of an enchantress, the Comte said to himself.

And he went into another room. This one was completely different from the preceding one. It was a cabinet of natural history, an arsenal, a cynegetic museum—anything one might wish.

Two wolves, marvelously stuffed and mounted, were sitting on their tails at either side of the door, seemingly fixing the nocturnal visitor who had penetrated into their lair with their enamel eyes. An elk, a reed deer, several hinds, a black bear and an infinite number of wildfowl, pheasants and partridges cluttered the room.

The walls were hung with furs; marvelously adapted to those furs were curious panoplies arranged according to their historical era. Here there were the bows and quivers of the ancients; beneath them, a Medieval pike; a little lower down, an arquebus with a fuse, a wheel-lock rifle, a flintlock musket and a primitive double-barreled shotgun. Further on were Oriental weapons, marvelous daggers, pistols encrusted with nacre, hunting-knives with carved sheaths. Further still there was a complete collection of horns, clarions, hunting-trumpets and Swiss horns. All of that was supported by the antlers of red deer and elk, and buffalo horns. Piled on a table were several books on venery, almost all exceedingly rare and very curious.

Good, thought the Comte. *It appears that the enchantress has a hunter for a husband; if he cares to show himself we can hunt together.*

"Tomorrow," a voice replied.

The Comte shivered, and paraded a glance around him, but saw nothing. He returned rapidly to the boudoir, and then went into another room, which was a library, without perceiving any living being.

Roll on tomorrow, he said to himself.

The Comte had the supreme pleasure of not writing books, which might have given rise to the supposition that, strictly speaking, he did not like them very much. He did not like them at all, in fact, for he did not deign to cast a single glance at the dusty shelves on which the hand off a bibliophile had patiently arranged two or three thousand volumes in Greek, Latin, Hebrew, Arabic and French. He passed on and found himself in a vast gallery of black and white marble, the vault of which was supported by colonnettes of yellow marble. Windows of Gothic stained-glass were doubtless designed to light it by day, but at this hour, it was illuminated by resinous torches held by bronze hands that emerged from the walls. The walls in question were covered in family portraits.

But what family? the Comte wondered. It must have been illustrious and well-connected, at any rate, for there were none but lords in gallant costumes, ladies on courtly robes, mitered prelates, cardinals in red garb, knights in the robes of Malta and commanders of all the Orders of the Christian World.

"I am indeed in good company," the Comte murmured. "It remains to be seen whether the stables and kennels are as proper as everything I've just seen. Let's go down."

The Comte got his bearings without overmuch difficulty, went back to the large staircase at the end of the gallery, went down to the ground floor, the courtyard and the commons, and ended up finding the stables. The stables were maintained in fabulous luxury; forty horses were eating, side by side from an aloe-wood trough in a sandalwood frame; the finest rice-straw was extended as litter on the marble-paved floor; the reins were not made of vulgar leather but superb Abyssinian shagreen. The beauty of the noble animals astounded the Comte; all the breeds of celebrated chargers were worthily represented there, from Arab and Andalusian stallions to Tartarian fillies.

The same voice that had already vibrated in the Comte's ears made itself heard again, proclaiming: "Monsieur le Comte may choose the one he will mount tomorrow."

"Very well," said the Comte—and, after hesitating for a few minutes, he decided on an ebony-black Arab stallion with an iron-gray mane and tail.

From the stables the Comte passed on to the kennels. There were about three hundred dogs there—which is to say, a pack for each hunted beast, from the bear, to which were reserved enormous Norwegian mastiffs, to the hare, for which the unknown castellan had procured a Swiss pack of small orange and white dogs, as rapid as lightning, with superb low-pitched voices that must have resonated delightfully in the brushwood and low thickets

"What beast does Monsieur le Comte desire to hunt tomorrow?" asked the voice.

"An elk," the Comte replied.

"Very well; the woods will be beaten right away."

At that moment, an invisible clock whose topographical situation the hunter could not specify exactly sounded midnight.

"Well now," murmured the Comte, "what if I want to go to bed."

"Monsieur le Comte's apartment is ready," said the voice.

The Comte left the kennels, went back up the steps of the broad staircase, and, having no idea where his bedroom was, decided to go through the room in which he had eaten supper. The tablecloth, the dishes and all the remaining food had disappeared. Tea had been set out on the table, accompanied by Oriental jams, sorbets and liqueurs. A hookah was nearby, stuffed with golden Levantine tobacco.

"Decidedly," said the Comte, with a slightly ribald laugh, "the enchantress of the abode is a charming woman."

"You think so!" said a soft and harmonious voice—a woman's voice, which bore no resemblance to the one that the Comte had already heard.

The Comte looked around again; the room was deserted.

"Damn it!" he cried. "I find her adorable, but I'd dearly like to see her."

"Would you permit her to take tea with you?"

"Oh, Madame!" exclaimed the Comte. "Permission granted—but the decision is hers."

"Well, turn around."

The Comte turned around, hoping finally to see his mysterious hostess behind him. There was no one there, and he sought in vain—but on resuming his initial stance, he found himself face to face with a being so singularly beautiful that he uttered a cry of admiration.

It was a woman of twenty-two or twenty-three, dazzlingly white in the face and hands, with jet-black hair and the profound and velvety gazelle-like eyes of the women of the Levant. She wore an Oriental costume of marvelous richness, white silk trousers tightened at the ankle with golden rings; an embroidered and braided black velvet basquine enclosed a waist as slim and supple as that of a panther. The wavy tresses of her long hair escaped profusely from a small red toque, and ruby and emerald bracelets sparkled on her rounded arms, as white as those of a statue.

She gazed at the Comte with a charming smile, arching her red and voluptuous lips slightly, and the Comte gazed at her, with a naïve astonishment that was almost a stupor. And as his tongue seemed to be stuck to his palate, rendering him unable to pronounce a single word, she was the first to speak.

"Are you content with your supper, Comte?" she said.

That question, simple and almost vulgar, caused the Comte to shiver and recover a little of his self-composure. "Yes, Madame," he stammered.

She perceived his embarrassment and continued; "You may make yourself at home here, Monsieur, and I'm very happy to welcome you." She expressed herself in French with a slightly languid accent, which suited her cool and velvety voice admirably.

The Comte finally succeeded in mastering his emotion; he even recovered the witty assurance of the gallant gentlemen of his era, and replied: "We had in France, nearly a century ago, a very clever man named Perrault...."

"I know him," said the young woman. "I've read his fairy tales."

"Very good," said the Comte. "I was about to ask you whether he might not have forgotten your story in his book."

The young woman began to laugh. "You believe in fairies, then?" she said.

"Since an hour ago, Madame."

"Don't believe in them any longer; I'm a mere mortal."

"Enchanted, perhaps?"

"Not in the least."

"In that case," said the Comte, straightening up and putting his hat under his arm, as he would have done in a drawing-room at Versailles, "Whoever you are, Madame, permit me to offer you my thanks for the charming hospitality that I have received in your home, so unexpectedly."

"I accept them, Monsieur le Comte, for I hope that the hospitality in question can seduce you for a few hours more."

The Comte bowed. "If I were the master of my destiny, Madame," he said, gallantly, "I would venture to desire that that hospitality might be endless."

"Yes," murmured the young woman, with a mocking smile, "that's very pretty and sincere, but you have an important diplomatic mission to fulfill, and you're awaited in Constantinople."

The Comte shivered. "How do you know that?" he asked.

"You were kind enough to compare me to a fairy; suppose that I really am one, and don't ask my secret..."

"But still, Madame...."

"Don't you want to take tea, Monsieur le Comte?"

The Comte bit his lip. "May I offer you some cream, Madame?" he said, in a piqued tone.

"Indeed," replied his beautiful hostess, putting her red lips to the amber of her hookah.

There was a moment of silence, during which the Comte admired the young woman's arms and hands, her smooth forehead and black hair. Eventually, he continued. "I don't want to be indiscreet, Madame, but...."

"But?" she said, in an encouraging tone.

"Might I ask you in whose home I have the honor of finding myself?"

"Hmm," she murmured, with an adorable little moue. "You're curious, Comte."

"I'm astonished, Madame."

"Truly?"

"I'm mistaken—I'm wonderstruck."

"And what is it here that astonishes you, Monsieur?"

"First of all, your beauty, Madame."

"Let's pass on."

"Secondly, the luxury of your house, doubtless served by a population of great and small genies."

"In the house of an enchantress, that's perfectly simple."

"Didn't you just tell me that you were mortal?"

"That's true. Well, I'm an Indian princess."

"I suspected as much."

"And my servants possess the ring of Gyges, which, as you know, renders one invisible when one turns the bezel in a certain fashion."

"That's very ingenious. Might I ask where they found it?"

"In the ruins of Nineveh, Comte."

The Comte bowed. "I see," he said, "that you're enveloping yourself in an impenetrable mystery."

"Impenetrable—yes and no. Yes, if you want to know at any price; no if you have patience and can wait....."

"That's difficult."

"Monsieur le Comte," said the young woman, gravely, "you have the impetuosity of your age and your nation, and you're forgetting that we Orientals have elevated patience above other virtues. What are you asking me? Of what are you complaining?

You had gone astray, like the heroes of Monsieur Perrault's tales; the rain was falling, you were hungry; you sought shelter and food at hazard, and hazard has given you both. What more do you want?"

The Comte bowed his head, and seemed ashamed. "You're right, Madame," he said, sadly. "I'm indiscreet, and stupidly indiscreet, for I have no right to want to penetrate your incognito—and stupid because I resemble the man in the Arabian tale to whom a genie gave two bags of rubies and who, not satisfied, wanted to carry away a further handful. The roof of the cavern into which he had come to enrich himself collapsed and swallowed him up. You are beautiful, like no other woman I have ever seen; you have put your home at my disposal; you have smiled at me admirably; you have given me a charming welcome, and I am not content; I want even more...."

The expression of sad gravity that had spread over the young woman's face disappeared; the smile returned to it and she held out her hand to him. "You have," she said, "such a naïve frankness in excusing yourself that it is necessary to forgive you, a little. Be patient; you shall know everything, and perhaps...."

"Perhaps?"

"Perhaps," she said, with a certain hesitation, "You are destined by hazard to save me from a danger."

"Oh!" exclaimed the Comte, excitedly. "Speak, Madame—speak, I implore you!"

"Child," she murmured, smiling. "Always in a hurry...."

"Oh, tell me...."

"Have I not told you to wait?"

"That's true—I shall wait."

Two o'clock chimed on the stonework clock in the drawing-room.

"You know that we're going hunting tomorrow, Comte?" said the young woman, immediately.

"With whom, Madame?"

"Always indiscreet. With me, Monsieur."

"No one but you?"

"Again!" She shrugged her shoulders imperceptibly, with a small gesture of impatience. The Comte perceived it, took her hand and kissed it.

"I'm an incorrigible villain," he said, "but what do you expect? I'm so afraid of seeing the shadow of a human being other than me beside you...."

"Ever gallant!" she said, laughing.

She fell silent, studying her admiringly.

"We'll hunt alone," she said.

"Oh! Thank you."

"But as we'll set out at eight o'clock, and it's necessary for you to be able to get up, I urge you to go to sleep as soon as possible. Take that sorbet and follow me."

The Comte swallowed the sorbet in a single gulp and put his hand in the beautiful hand of his hostess.

"Come," she said to him.

She took him through the half dozen rooms that he had already gone through, arrived in the blue and white boudoir that he had admired so much, opened a door hidden in a fold of the tapestry and showed him into a bedroom furnished as brightly and elegantly as any nobleman of the Regency ever possessed.

"You are at home," she said to him.

The Comte looked at her admiringly. "I believe in fairies," he said.

"I permit you to."

"Will you be far away? The grotto that you inhabit...."

"The grotto that I inhabit, my fine gentleman, is two paces from here—or, rather, a simple partition wall separates us."

The Comte shivered.

"If you need anything," she added, "call me, and one of my invisible servants will come to your aid. Good night...."

The Comte remained immobile in the middle of the room, considering her with the naïve enthusiasm of a nascent amour.

"Good night!" she repeated—and before he had time to reply, to bow or to say a word, she disappeared like a true fairy and the door closed again.

Once again the Comte found himself alone. A flood of thoughts assailed him, and in that flood, one above all was dominant, and took possession of his mind.

"I'm there, next door," she said.

The Comte was a pupil of Richelieu and Lauzun; if the word "impossible" was not French for him, it was especially so in the matter of love. He belonged to the school of slightly indecent great lords accustomed to undertaking an intrigue at the gallop, and he doubtless thought about putting together a plan of attack immediately. Unfortunately, a sudden drowsiness, which he attributed to an excessive abuse of his beautiful hostess's fine vintages, combined with the fatigues of the day, immediately took possession of him.

* * * * * * *

It is rather difficult to recount the dreams that one has just had; awakening always throws a veil over them that obscures the majority of the details. We cannot, therefore, describe those that agitated the Comte's sleep; all that we know is that they possessed a very pronounced Orientalism. When he awoke, he perceived the mysterious chatelaine seated at the foot of his bed, and, doubtless believing that his dream as continuing, he uttered a cry of joy and reached out for her....

Alas, the sunlight entered the room in a great flood, and the denouement of the dream became impossible.

"Did you sleep well, Comte?"

"I must have slept for fifteen hours, Madame."

"Only four, Comte."

"Impossible!"

"Take a look." She pointed at the clock. The hands had only just reached six o'clock.

"That's odd!" he said. "I seem to have slept for a century."

"Are you still curious?"

"Oh, certainly."

"Would you like to know my name?"

"I'm begging you on my knees."

"And my history?"

"I'm all ears."

"Will you be discreet?"

"As the tomb."

"The word is ambitious, but no matter. We have two hours before us; listen to me."

"First, give me your hands to kiss."

"You're greedy; one alone will suffice."

She applied her white hand to his lips, and began: "I'm Persian in origin, and the daughter of a Grand Vizier...."

The Comte made a gesture of astonishment. "You can see," he said, "that we're in the midst of an Arabian tale."

"Don't be so impatient! Before being a Vizier, my father was the Shah of Persia's ambassador to the French court, and I was born in Paris, in the Rue Saint-Honoré, near the Palais-Royal. I lived for fifteen years in France, and that explains why, in spite of my origin, I speak your language so purely."

"And I understand," said the Comte, "why, in spite of your costume, you're so scrupulously Parisian, and courtly."

"Monsieur le Comte?"

"Madame?"

"Do you know that my story is a long one?"

"So much the better, Madame."

"So much the worse, for if you keep interrupting me, we'll never get to the end."

"A thousand pardons, Madame; I'll keep quiet."

"I'm twenty-three. It's five years since I left Paris and my father was promoted by the Shah to Grand Vizier. Two months after our return to Ispahan, my father received a letter from Paris signed by the Austrian ambassador, which recommended energetically to him a young Magyar by the name of Ban Rodstock."

The Comte shivered. "I know him," he said.

"I know," she continued. "Wait. The Magyar was traveling and intended to go to India, traversing Persia, where he counted on staying for a year. My father had adopted European habits in

Paris and had renounced a considerable number of the customs of our country—among others, that of carefully veiling women, sequestering them in their apartments and never showing them to any man. My mother and I frequently wore the costume of French ladies. The Magyar found an entirely European hospitality in my father's house; he lived in our intimacy for two months, and hardly noticed that he was in Persia. He found me beautiful and fell in love with me.

"If my father had renounced Persian mores, however, he had remained faithful to the law of the prophet that forbids any alliance with giaours or infidels. The Magyar was a Christian. To marry me it would have been necessary to abjure his religion and embrace that of Mohammed. He did not consider that for an instant, and thought it much simpler to abduct me.

"I was a credulous and naïve child; all that I knew of the world was what I had read in the books of Monsieur Crébillon *fils* and other romancers of your country. Besides which, I could not see myself, without shuddering, destined for a rich Persian friend of my father's, one of the great dignitaries of the Empire. My future husband was descended from one of the mage-kings who went to salute the prophet Jesus; he wore the ring of Solomon on the little finger of his left hand, and for any Persian woman other than me it would have been the most illustrious of alliances. Unfortunately, he had a white beard, and when he passed through the streets the faithful were constrained to kneel down, with their forehead in the dust.

"All that would have been nothing, but his wife was not emancipated from that adoration—entirely to the contrary; she was obliged to bow down before him and kiss his feet every time he deigned to visit her. Now, you can imagine that my European education and my recent memories of Paris, where men, instead of having themselves adored by women, have the custom of spending half the day at their knees, made no contribution at all to my seeing a Persian marriage in an agreeable light.

"The Magyar was handsome; he was elegant and rich; fine pearls and rubies sparkled in his dolman; he had a seductive, poetic speech, a gaze that fascinated...I fell in love with him.

"It happened that one day, my father, in his capacity as Grand Vizier, was obliged to leave for a coastal province that had rebelled, and as a great Persian lord always takes his family with him, my mother and I made the journey. The Magyar asked my father for permission to accompany him, and my father consented.

"We established our residence by the sea, not far from the mouth of the Ganges. Then my father was constrained to set himself at the head of an army and to march against the insurgents. His absence was to last a week. That doomed me.

"One evening, the Magyar was more eloquent and more persuasive than ever; he spoke to me about the half-Oriental, half-European life of his country—a life that would render me the luxury and indolent sumptuousness of my own without imposing its prejudices upon me. He shook me, but I tried to resist....

"Then he offered to marry me according to European law and without obliging me to change religion. I was already indecisive, and was vanquished by that final offer. There was a Dutch ship in the harbor. We took advantage of a dark night; I bribed two of my father's servants, they found a launch and we reached the Dutch ship, which was preparing to sail at dawn. At that point my misfortunes began. The Magyar was brutal, carried away; he loved me with a furious passion, long contained by the narrow bounds of respect, that burst forth violently as soon as I was in his power. We had not yet reached European territory when I no longer loved him. Alas, it was too late....

"We disembarked in France, and initially came to Paris. There, Michael—that's his name—displayed a ferocious and unparalleled jealousy. He hid me away from all eyes. He had bought a small town house in the Rue de Bac, isolated between a courtyard and a garden. It was there that he locked himself away with me, there that he found the means of concealing my existence, so that none of his friends—and you were in that number—ever suspected that he did not live entirely alone...."

"What?" the Comte interjected. "You were there in Paris, in the Rue de Bac!"

"Yes, Comte."

"He was very jealous, then?"

"Listen: one day I had the misfortune to show myself at the window, framing my head for a minute in a clump of clematis that was climbing over the shutters. Do you know what he did?"

"Closed the window no doubt."

"He stabbed me with a dagger—which, thanks to a diamond brooch that I had on my neck, only grazed me."

"Horror!" exclaimed the Comte.

"My boudoir was next door to the drawing room; the partition wall was thin. I could easily hear what was said there. Thus, my dear Comte, I have known you for some time; twenty times over I've heard you sustaining paradoxes, crazy and chivalrous theories; I loved your intelligence; I loved your bravery; I loved...."

"Oh!" the Comte interjected, swiftly. "Enough, Madame—I'm going mad."

"So be it. I'll continue: we spent three months in Paris, me locked away, him conducting some tenebrous intrigue, which doubtless had no result, for he came into my room abruptly one evening and said: 'We're leaving in an hour.'

"Several times, since I had belonged to that man, I had reminded him of his promise and asked him: 'When will you marry me?' 'In my own country,' he had replied.

"We left. It was here that he brought me. He still had land in Hungary, but he rarely lived there, he told me. He loved me, it's true; his love was a perpetual adoration. He surrounded me with this splendid luxury, these delicate cares, these small attentions of which the great noblemen of the French court seem to possess the secret. Numerous servants obeyed my slightest gesture, anticipated my most futile desires. I hardly had time to formulate a wish before it was accomplished.

"After a few days I asked him again: 'When will you marry me?'

"He frowned and said: 'That's impossible.'

"I got to me feet indignantly. 'For the moment, at least,' he added. And as I looked at him with dolorous amazement, he added: 'Do you know that I'm married?'

"'Married!' I exclaimed, beside myself, and weak at the knees.

"'Yes, married,' he repeated, "but not for long.'

"I didn't understand. I looked at him with dull and haggard eyes.

"'My wife will die within six moths,' he went on—and when I still remained silent, he added: 'I've subjected her to a sure treatment; she'll inevitably die.'

"That was an enigma to me; I didn't have the strength to ask him for an explanation. He gave me one on his own accord. 'My wife,' he said, 'has been consumptive for some time. I've sent her to my schloss on the banks of the Danube, a river whose fogs are fatal for those with afflicted lungs. She doesn't suspect, and is dying with a smile on her face.'

"I uttered a cry of horror.

"'I don't love her,' he told me, coldly. I recoiled, fearfully. 'But I love you,' he added.

"Oh, as you can imagine, since then the man has horrified me, and I thought of escaping—but I hid it; I became once again—I had the courage to become once again—tender and affectionate, submissive to his jealous caprices, mute before his fits of excess. He hunted every day, and took me with him. One day, I pretended to be ill and he left without me. When I was alone I had a horse saddled and fled at a gallop, running at hazard through a country that was unknown to me, only escorted by one of the two Persian servants we had brought with us.

"After traveling for five hours, we went to knock on the door of a woodcutter's cottage in the middle of a forest. He gave us hospitality. I was exhausted, and fell sleep on a crude bed, profoundly. When I woke up, I uttered a scream of fright; the Magyar was standing beside my bed.

"'Madame, he said to me, calmly, 'you have tried to run

away from me; your hope was insane; my wife will be dead in three months; afterwards, I will marry you. Until then, you belong to me body and soul; I am your master, and if you try to escape from me again I will kill you.'

"I shivered. He went on: 'As for the servant who accompanied you, you shall see how I will be able to make it impossible for him to do so again.'

"He called and the Persian appeared. The Magyar did not say a word, but he took a pistol from his belt, aimed at the unfortunate man, and fired. The Persian collapsed, and died without uttering a cry. I fainted. The Magyar carried me away, I know not how, and when I opened my eyes again I was lying across his saddle.

"From that day on he did not address any reproach to me; he absented himself quite often, without the slightest dread—except that two Hungarians, his damned souls, never left me for a moment, and had orders to kill me if I made any attempt to escape. I was a prisoner forever."

"Well," said the Comte, impatiently, "how is it that you're free?"

"I'm not, yet. Listen: you know the sinister name of this valley, the infernal reputation of this schloss?"

"Yes."

"The Magyar prepared it thus for me; he was quite certain that the local inhabitants would never prowl around it, and it was to maintain that chronic terror that he had it illuminated from top to bottom every night, to give it an infernal color."

"Very good."

"Now, the Magyar is the colonel of a Hungarian Imperial regiment; the war broke out and it was necessary for him to march and fight. The army of which his regiment is a part is on campaign fifty leagues from here. In consequence, he cannot come to see me very often, and had even been constrained to remove some of the servants from the schloss, whom he has incorporated into his regiment, and he left me in the custody of his two Hungarians, a dozen Slav domestics, my Persian and his valet, who is French and whom he brought from Paris. His is the voice that you have already heard."

"Ah!" said the Comte. "And?"

"Yesterday, I had a visit from the Magyar; he left again a few hours later, and won't come back for ten days—but I heard a singular conversation that he had with his two Hungarians.

"A spy had warned him that a French gentleman would go all the way to Constantinople, hunting, and carrying a message for the Sultan. That gentleman is you. The Magyar knew that you would inevitably pass through the valley, and he had instructed that you be kept prisoner in the schloss and treated with the greatest respect. In addition, he forbade me to show myself, and ordered that the schloss ought to be, so far as you were concerned, the Devil's abode."

"And that," said the Comte, "is why I found it deserted?"

"Yes," said the young woman. "The Hungarians had given their orders—except that, aided by the French valet, whom I won to my cause, and my Persian, who is devoted to me, I tricked the Hungarians."

"Ah!" said the Comte, intrigued.

"In my country," the daughter of the Grand Vizier continued, "the use of opium is frequent; we smoke it in our pipes in small doses, and we always have it at our disposal; the Magyar has never refused it to me. Yesterday, the Hungarians, after having prepared everything for your reception, announced that you would be hunting today, and the beaters have gone into the woods to flush out an elk. Then they gave me the order to go to my room and lock myself in, after which they went to bed themselves. They had eaten well and drunk a good deal—they'll sleep for at least forty-eight hours."

"Thanks to the opium, presumably?" the Comte asked.

"My Persian put it into all the food. Come and see."

The Comte had gone to sleep fully dressed, so he did not have to put his clothes on, and he followed his beautiful hostess, who opened a door and introduced him into a room where two tall bearded grim-faced fellows of athletic build were snoring like church organs.

"Damn!" murmured the Comte. "They're terrible guardians!"

"You think so? Well, we're going to cage them for a few days."

"How?"

"Are you strong?"

"As a Turk."

"Then put one of these fellows over your shoulder and follow me."

The Comte obeyed. The young woman opened another door, which unmasked a dark spiral staircase, and picked up a torch.

"Where are we going?" asked the Comte.

"Into the cellars of the schloss," she replied.

They went down for ten minutes, by the pale light of the torch, and arrived in a narrow tunnel with a steep slope. The took another dozen paces and finally found themselves in front of a iron door fitted with solid hinges and a triple lock, which the chatelaine opened with a single key, with marvelous dexterity. The Comte then found himself in a sort of damp cellar, receiving a trickle of air through a narrow ventilation-shaft.

There was a crude bed in the cellar, on which, at a sign from his guide, he deposited the unconscious Hungarian.

"Go and fetch the other," she told him.

The second of the chatelaine's jailers was laid down in the same manner alongside his companion.

Then the chatelaine added: "The Magyar's valet will bring enough food down for ten days. They won't wake up before tomorrow, anyway, and when they wake up they can swear and rage as much as they like, shout and batter at the door, but no one will hear them."

"But when their food runs out," the Comte objected, "they'll die of starvation."

"Not at all."

"Why is that?"

"The Magyar comes here every ten days. I'll leave him a note, in which I'll notify him of my flight and indicate the temporary retreat of his aides-de-camp."

"Very well—and in ten days?"

"We'll be in Constantinople, my dear Comte."

The Comte looked at the chatelaine her face radiant with beauty, malice and intelligence; she was a demon who had put on the most seductive of her forms.

"And in Constantinople?" he asked.

"In Constantinople, Comte, you'll put me aboard a Persian ship or procure me an escort, and I'll go back to my father."

The Comte shivered. "Is that an unshakable resolution?"

She looked at him and hesitated.

"Shall I have met you only to lose you forever?"

"What does it matter?"

"But I love you!" cried the Comte.

She burst out laughing. "What folly!" she murmured.

He threw himself at her knees, took her hands, kissed them deliriously, and continued: "You had consented to marry the Magyar."

She blushed and lowered her head. "I am pure," she said, in a low voice.

"You are the most beautiful and most noble of women!" he cried, excitedly.

"You'd marry me, then?"

"I'm asking you on my knees."

"Well," she said, planting a kiss on his burning forehead, "we'll see."

It was almost a promise. The Comte got to his feet and, uttering a cry of joy, took her in his arms and carried her through the subterranean tunnels and staircases all the way to the Hungarians' room.

There she recovered her composure and said to him: "We don't have any time to lose; we have to go."

"Go!"

"The Magyar's men know that you're going hunting today; they don't know that the Hungarians have received orders not to let me appear, and to bring you back here this evening whether you like it or not. Perhaps they'll have some suspicion on not seeing them, but fortunately, the Magyar's valet has full authority over them and will persuade them that the Hungarians have left during the night to their master's orders."

"Very well. So we'll lead them all the way to Constantinople?"

"Why not?"

"But they'll end up realizing that the Magyar has been duped...."

"No, for we'll stay, on the way, at the Magyar's three residences...."

"And everywhere, they'll believe...."

"No one, except for the Hungarians and the valet, knows about the tyranny that he exercises over me; everyone has orders to surround me with cares and respect, to obey me in all matters; they al imagine that I have an excessive empire over the Magyar, and in Bohemia as in Hungary, feudalism exists in all its rigor; there isn't one of his vassals who doesn't shiver at the thought that he might displease his lord and master by refusing my blind obedience. Let's be on our way, Comte; the signal for departure is being sounded."

"One moment, Madame."

"What is it?"

"You've forgotten to write to the Magyar."

"That's true."

"Would you like me to do it myself?"

"Oh—that would be funny."

"Wait."

The Comte went into the chatelaine's boudoir, where he found paper and quills, and be wrote the following letter to the Magyar:

> *My dear Count, there is a proverb about eels, which I don't have time to quote, but which you'll guess. I'm sure. You have a treasure of which you keep a tight hold, but it's slipping through your fingers—and I*

confess that I have helped somewhat in that. The future Countess Rodstock feels the need to breathe the air of Constantinople, and I shall accompany her; I hope that she will want to follow me to Paris where I shall have the honor of introducing her to you, in a month's time, under the name of the Comtesse de Main-Hardye.

Yours devotedly,

P.S. By the way, you left two rather badly brought-up Hungarians with our beautiful chatelaine, who would have opposed the voyage to Constantinople for bad reasons; I have little liking for debates of that sort, and thought it simpler to shut them up in one of your cellars. The Devil alone, your co-proprietor in the Manor of the Red Valley, will be able to get them out before your return, and I have some reason to believe that he would rather wait for you,

Yours once again,

P.P.S. Thank you for the excellent and magical hospitality that I've received in your home; I compliment you on your cynegetic collection, stable and kennels, which are irreproachable.

Still yours,

Le Comte de Main-Hardye.

The chatelaine cast her eyes over the letter and let slip a frank and impudent burst of laughter, which laid bare the thirty-two pearls that a Persian genie had given her in the guise of teeth. At that moment the Magyar's valet presented himself and bowed to the Comte with the respectful familiarity of the Frontins made fashionable by the Duc de Richelieu.[21]

"Ah, there you are, fellow!" said the Comte, smiling. "I'm taking you into my service."

"Monsieur le Comte honors me."

"Will you steal much from me?"

"As little as possible, Monsieur le Comte."

"There's a witty fellow who will suit me very well," Monsieur de Main-Hardye murmured. "Take this letter to the Magyar' room."

The Comte offered his arm to the chatelaine, who had donned hunting costume while he was writing, and they both went into the dining room, where they ate some cold pâté and drank a stirrup cup. Then they went down into the courtyard, where their horses were waiting for them ready-saddled, and the dogs, tethered in pairs.

The Magyar's servants made up a dozen beaters and kennel-grooms, mostly well-built Hungarians and Bohemians, wearing goatskin cloaks, leather mountain gaiters and fur hats. In the midst of them, speaking German, which he understood well enough, was the Magyar's valet, who explained to them briefly that their master had summoned the two Hungarians to whom they were usually obedient, and that Madame's desire was to go, while hunting in the company of the French gentleman, to the schloss that the Magyar owned in the vicinity of Pest. The horn was sounded; the chatelaine and the Comte mounted up, and they departed.

An hour hater, they arrived at the hunt rendezvous, and the connection was made. The elk that had been flushed was a good size, and promised to hold out all day, but the Magyar's dogs were first rate, and seven hours later, the elk faced up to them at bay, and received the Comte's bullet in its head.

The Comte was too much a hunter not to have put his diplomatic mission out of his mind to some extent thanks to the

---

21. Frontin is a valet whose numerous avatars are featured in Classical French comedy, perhaps most notably in Lesage's *Turcaret* (1709).

excitement of the day, along with the dangers he was running by thus abducting a chatelaine and her servants, and even the love he felt for her. He made the kill methodically, set aside the elk's sirloin and kidneys, cut off its right foot and offered it to the chatelaine, who accepted it with a smile on her lips.

"Oh, damn it!" cried the Comte. "That reminds me of something."

"What?"

"I've forgotten my huntsman, Bouquin."

"Bah!" said the chatelaine. "You'll find him tomorrow."

The Comte frowned anxiously, but she took his hand and said to him: "you've lost your huntsman and found a wife; there's compensation."

The dogs were tethered again, the elk was dead, the sun was setting; the enthusiasm of the hunter vanished; love returned— and the Comte forgot about Bouquin. They stayed the night three leagues away, in a German hostelry where the supper was passable. The Comte and the chatelaine ate together in private, and Monsieur de Main-Hardye's amorous Oriental whimsy gripped him even more tenaciously than the previous evening—but at the end of the meal, he felt an imperious need to sleep, and scarcely had time to undress. The chatelaine spent the night in the next room.

* * * * * * *

"That's odd," murmured the Comte, on waking up. "I feel as if I've slept for a week."

"Not a week," replied the chatelaine, whom he perceived sitting at the foot of his bed, "but fourteen hours. It's one o'clock in the afternoon, and it's too late to hunt now."

"Fourteen hours!" exclaimed the Comte. "You should have woken me."

"That would have been difficult."

"Why?"

"Because I was asleep myself, and have only just got up."

The chatelaine was right; it was too late to go hunting. They postponed their departure until the following day; they had ten days before them until the Magyar was alerted. The Comte took the chatelaine into a little arbutus bower; dinner was served to them there and they spent the day beneath a tree, on a lawn on the edge of a babbling stream, hand in hand, like a schoolboy and a schoolgirl stammering the first hymn of love.

When evening came they returned to the hostelry, after having ordered that the woods be carefully beaten and a bear flushed out, if possible.

The Comte woke up at six o'clock in the morning, after seeming, as on the day before, to have slept for an infinite interval.

The valet came in. "Should I wake Madame?"

"Yes, certainly!"

"She must still be asleep, for she went to bed late."

Those words, pronounced with a perfect bonhomie, dispelled all suspicion from the Comte's mind. He got dressed and went into the chatelaine's room, where he found the latter putting the final touches to her costume, mounted up with her, and set forth on the hunt. A bear had been flushed, and they chased it for several hours; then the Comte killed it with a thrust of his hunting-knife.

That evening, they stayed in a village where there was a Hungarian garrison. The Comte felt slightly anxious at first, but the Magyar's livery was familiar and no officer came to question him. That night again, the Comte promised himself to realize his dreams in part, but as on the previous nights he fell asleep, did not awake until daylight, and claimed, once again, that he had slept for a incalculable number of hours.

The chatelaine laughed in his face, gave him her hand to kiss, told him that she loved him, and made him set out again.

That day they chased a wolf, and stopped in a woodcutter's hut. The Comte could not think, for the moment, at least, of renewing his attempts of the previous days. In a woodcutter's hut? Fie! Then again, he was beginning to get used to this mode of existence, which permitted him simultaneously to fulfill a diplomatic mission, hunt, and make love according to the maxims of Plato, the wisest and most inoffensive of Greek philosophers.

The bed he was given was very hard, but as on previous days, he slept very well and had the strangest dreams.

"Do you know, Madame," he said to his beautiful Persian the next day, "that I've had a strange idea?"

"Really?"

"Can you imagine that I'm wondering...." The Comte hesitated.

"What?" she said.

"I'm wondering whether you've played the same trick on me as on your Hungarian jailers."

"What trick?"

"Administering opium to me every evening."

"What an idea!"

"Which," the Comte continued, "is making me sleep a little too heavily."

"But it seems to me," said the chatelaine laughing, "that you've still been getting up at six o'clock."

"That's true—but how do I know that I didn't go to bed two days ago?"

The chatelaine shrugged her shoulders. "How do you know," she said, disdainfully, "that I'm not leading you directly to my tyrant the Magyar, so that he can thank you for stealing me from him?"

The Comte looked at the chatelaine. Her argument was unanswerable, and her face had such an expression of honesty that he was ashamed of his absurd supposition, took her hands and said to her: "Forgive me; I'm crazy."

"I fear so," she said to him, coldly.

The Comte was ill at ease for the rest of the day. Fortunately toward evening, the chatelaine's forehead cleared, and she said to him: "I forgive you, and I believe that I love you."

"Is that true?" he exclaimed.

"In a fortnight, I shall be your wife, and you'll see."

"By the way," said the Comte, "I've written to Baron von Hollingen."

"Why?"

"To tell him that I'll be hunting on his estate."

"Well, let's go, then."

"Do you think so?"

"We'll spend twenty-four hours with him, and we'll tell him that you've met he Magyar and that he's asked you to go to wait for him in his manor in Hungary with his servants and his mistress, whom he's placed in your safe keeping."

"That's a good idea."

"That way, we can take the Baron with us as far as Pest; we'll only have a few more leagues to cover to reach the Ottoman frontier—and with the aid of opium, we'll do that without him."

"Bravo!"

At the overnight stop, the Comte learned that he had covered sixty leagues, and that they only had another five days' travel to reach to reach Baron von Hollingen's schloss.

"Damn," he said, "five days is a lot; it will then be ten since we left the valley, and the Magyar will be after us."

"Well, said the chatelaine, "as long as we stay five days ahead of him, we'll be safe."

The chatelaine evidently bore little resemblance to those fearful young women who, fleeing with the lover, look round every minute, fearing that they might be pursued, urging the weary horse carrying them to go faster. But the Comte paid little heed to that reflection on the chatelaine's part. He had been occupied for a few moments in making a new strategic plan for that evening.

When he sat down at table he was amiable, cheerful and witty, opening the treasure-chest of gallantry and seduction that he had penitently accumulated at Versailles over four or five years, supping with Monsieur de Richelieu and the Duc de Chartres, who was still young. The chatelaine displayed a ravishing coquetry; she had the worldliness and affectation of a pretty she-cat born in a boudoir and well brought-up. For a while the Comte was radiant and enjoying in advance the honors of his triumph—which did not prevent him, at the end of the supper, from feeling drowsiness gradually exhausting him and nailing him to his chair. Then he forgot his clever schemes and staggered to his room.

"Word of honor," he mumbled, while the Magyar's valet undressed him, "one of three things must be true: either I'm not the hunter I once was and am undermined by some unfamiliar illness; or the chatelaine's making fun of me; or these accursed Bohemian wines are diabolically intoxicating."

That final reason was the most plausible; the Comte took it aboard without overmuch difficulty and fell asleep. There was the same awakening the following day; it seemed to him that his sleep had lasted an eternity. However, a certain haste that the chatelaine appeared to put into their departure, and the desire she manifested to press on that day as far as possible chased away the vague suspicions that were besieging him once again. The hunt was superb and a bear fell to the Comte's bullet, while the cubs became the huntsmen's prey.

Another three days, and the same incidents and phenomena were renewed; the Comte ended up getting used to them and saying to himself: *it seems that in Bohemia the nights are interminable and the wines inebriating.*

On the evening of the fourth day, through the mists of the gathering dusk, they perceived the spires of a schloss lost in the middle of a clump of woodland and licked to the south by a pond. It was Baron von Hollingen's manse.

"Finally!" exclaimed the Comte, with a sigh of relief. They spurred their horses and rode the breathless animals out, but no matter what efforts they made, the Comte and the beautiful Persian only reach the manor's drawbridge after nightfall.

The Comte raised his trumpet to his lips and sounded a fanfare well known in the land of Bohemia—the fanfare of the "Black Huntsman." He got all the way to the end without anything seeming to move within the schloss, but on the final note, a trumpet roared inside and repeated the fanfare mockingly.

"Oho!" said the Comte. "Our host is here; I recognize his trumpet."

Indeed, the manor immediately lit up, the drawbridge was lowered, and a rude and joyful voice, as Germanic as can be, shouted in the Bohemian language: "Welcome are belated hunters!"

"Especially when they come from far away," replied the Comte, in French.

The Baron appeared, the Comte dismounted and they embraced by the light of a torch in the most fraternal manner.

"My dear Baron," said the Comte. "I introduce to you a lady of my acquaintance; soon, when we're at table, I'll tell you her name."

The Baron bowed. "Come," he said. "My supper is served, and I already have a guest."

He offered his hand to the chatelaine and climbed the broad staircase side-by-side with the Comte. The dining room was illuminated as if for a fête and a delicate aroma was escaping from the already-set table that promised marvels.

A tall man in a Hungarian colonel's uniform was already at the table and rose to his feet as the newcomers approached. At the sight of him, however, the Comte took a step back and put his hand on the hilt of his sword. In the colonel he had jut recognized...the Magyar!

"Ah!" the latter exclaimed. "What a pleasant surprise, Monsieur de Main-Hardye."

The Comte made no reply, but he stood in the doorway, with the evident intention of masking the beautiful Persian who was still behind him.

"What!" cried the Magyar. "You haven't brought my sister"

"Your sister!"

"Of course."

The Comte was stupefied.

"Here I am," said the beautiful Persian, moving the Comte

gently to one side. "Good day, Brother...."

"Am I drunk?" exclaimed the Comte,. "Or am I dreaming?"

"Not in the least, my dear Comte," replied the Magyar joyously. "I don't know what little story Mademoiselle de Rodstock can have told you, but she's surely given me a villainous reputation."

The Comte was dumbfounded, unable to say a single word.

"Can you imagine," the Mahyar continued, "that I met the Znapan who was bringing your letter to me in Hungary. My soldiers had stopped him, along with the companion that was coming here. Then, as I had a few days' leave, I came to wait for you with my friend von Hollingen, leaving my sister the care of putting my dogs, my servants and my schloss at your disposal."

The Comte turned to the beautiful Persian; she came to him, smiling, and said to him: "It's a joke—forgive me."

"So," said the Comte, still not knowing whether to laugh or be angry, "you're his sister?"

"Undoubtedly; and am I to be married, Comte?"

"Would you like to be my brother-in-law, Comte?"

The Comte ended up laughing and replied: "You can assure me that she's your sister?"

"Of course."

"Well, in that case, give the order to let your two Hungarians out."

"Bah!" said the Magyar. "they've been free for a long time. One of them will serve us at table."

The Comte frowned. "This," he said, "is beginning to resemble a hoax."

"No," said the Baron von Holingen, "But it's a stratagem of war."

"What do you mean?"

"Don't you have a month's leave signed by the Maréchal de Belle-Isle?"

"Of course."

"And during that leave, weren't you counting on going all the way to Constantinople to discover what beasts are usually hunted on the shores of the Bosphorus?"

The Comte reddened, and put his hand on the hilt of his sword a second time.

"Oh," said the Magyar, tranquilly, "Don't get carried away, Comte—we're gentlemen, and incapable of arresting you while you're on leave, and we don't want to know what you're going to do in Constantinople."

The Comte took a step backwards, and looked at the Magyar, who was still mocking.

"Except," added the Baron von Hollingen, "that your leave expires this evening."

"My leave expires this evening?" cried the Comte. "You're mad."

"Not at all. You think you've been traveling for ten days, but you've been traveling for a month."

The Comte put his hands to his head. "I'm losing my mind!" he murmured.

"Let's see," said the Magyar—and he shouted: "Bouquin! Bouquin!"

The huntsman appeared, with a consternated expression. "I'm not unhappy, Monsieur the Comte, to see you at last. I've been searching for you for three weeks."

The Comte tottered and spun around like a drunkard.

"My dear Comte," the Magyar said to him, "you know by what dark means the faithless woman you see succeeded in escaping her husband by putting her jailers to sleep?"

"Oh!" said the Comte, beginning to understand.

"Well, she made use of the same procedure ever evening with you, and you slept for two or three days at each lodging—your nights were forty-eight hours long."

Anger colored the Comte's cheeks. "I've been tricked!" he exclaimed.

"You're our guest, and to some extent our prisoner, Comte. We lead a joyful life, however, and during your captivity, we shall depopulate all the Baron's forests and some of mine.

"I shan't depopulate anything," said the Comte, with terrible self-composure. "I promised to reach Constantinople or die trying; I haven't arrived, and it's therefore necessary to kill myself if I'm not to be dishonored. Long live the King!"

And the Comte drew his sword....

But at that moment, the gallop of a horse resounded in the courtyard, and the Comte hesitated. The young woman threw herself on his sword, and while Monsieur de Main-Hardye struggled, gripped as he was by the iron hands of the Magyar woman, a mud-spattered courier came into the room and presented a dispatch to the Baron.

The Baron opened it precipitately and uttered a cry. "Comte," he said, radiantly, "you can live tranquil; you won't be dishonored and you shall go to Constantinople."

"What do you mean?" demanded Monsieur de Main-Hardye stupefied.

"Look," said the Baron, holding out the dispatch. "Peace has been made; you can go to Constantinople now; you're no longer a prisoner here."

"Well," said the Comte, "I can go hunting."

The false Persian, who was none other than the Magyar's sister, advanced then and took his hand.

"Since I've done you a bad turn," she said, "I'll try to repair it. Do you still want to marry me?"

"Yes," the Comte replied, "but on one condition."

"What?"

"That I don't take any opium...on my wedding night."

AFTERWORD
HOW MYSTERIOUS
IS *LE CHAMBRION*?

Le Chambrion is advertised as a "mysterious story," but if it is taken at face value, it does not seem so very mysterious, in that the protagonist already believes that he knows what really happened on the night when the Baron and Baronne de Méreuil died. If we consider his presumed version of what happened that night with the modern eyes of readers to whom murder mysteries are familiar, however, we will soon see that it makes no more sense than the absurd version accepted by the agents of the law and the local gossips—or, at the very least, leaves several crucial questions unanswered.

No modern detective, confronted with the evidence that the Chambrion had available to him, would conclude so readily that Jérôme Véru really had killed the Baron and the Baronne. The only thing of which the Chambrion can really be sure is that his father recovered the receipt that Père Clappier had given the Baron, because had Jérôme not handed that receipt over, he would not have been acquitted of his own debt. Jérôme's blood-stained hands and possession of the satchel also demonstrate that he was in the presence of the Baron's dead body—but not that he actually murdered anyone, and there are several signifi-cant objections to be raised to the assumption that he did.

First of all, why would he? If he were going to murder anyone, and then disappear forever, would it not have been far simpler and far more appropriate to murder Père Clappier, thus having only one guilty victim to his discredit rather than two innocent ones. Even if he were stupid enough not to think of that (and he does, admittedly, seem to be as utterly stupid as everyone else in the story), why would he murder the Baronne in her bedroom, given that he could have murdered the Baron and stolen the receipt without her ever seeing him? In which order did he commit the murders, and how did he commit them both without occasioning any resistance? Is it not more likely that he found them both already dead, but that he realized that he would be sure to be blamed for the crime if his presence at the scene were discovered, and thus did what he had been commissioned to do—recover the receipt—and then made himself scarce?

A further complication arises by virtue of the most obvious unanswered question: why did Armand de Verne commit suicide? Surely one does not commit suicide because local gossip has accused one of a sin of which one is innocent?

If Armand was on his way to Paris when the murders were committed, it surely cannot be difficult for him to establish that he was not in the Baronne's bedroom when the Baron returned home, and that the footprints found beneath the open window were not his. He must have an alibi of some sort, and even if his feet are the same size as Jérôme Véru's, his boots cannot be similar in the imprints they would make. It makes no sense at all that Armand would blow his brains out, instead of simply demonstrating that the rumors concerning his presence at the scene were false.

How then, can we begin to make sense of all this? Firstly, and most obviously, we must conclude that Armand de Verne did not commit suicide, but was murdered, presumably in order to stop him talking, and probably by the Baron's actual murderer. Given that Jérôme Véru's body was never fished out of the Saule, and that he does not reappear in the climax of the book (as many readers must surely have expected him to do) in order to enlighten his confused son as to what really happened at the Sapinières that night, there is surely a strong possibility that he was murdered too. But by whom, and why?

We would, I suppose, like to believe that it was Maupert, who disappears from the story in a rather unsatisfactory manner without his account being settled. It is, in a sense, surprising that it was not Maupert to whom Père Clappier turned, given the latter's aptitude for dirty work, but if Maupert had committed the murders he would certainly have taken the receipt, and as the receipt ended up with Jérôme Véru, it cannot have been him. It must, therefore, have been someone unglimpsed within the story, whose very presence in the plot is unsuspected by the main players. It must, in fact, have been someone sufficiently intelligent to leave no trace: a genuine criminal mastermind, or a whole company of masterminds.

We can be reasonably certain that the evil masterminds who planned the four murders were not the Habits Noirs, not so much because they were Paul Féval's intellectual property rather than Ponson's, but because they would certainly have framed Père Clappier for everything and appropriated all his ill-gotten gains—but it must have surely been some similarly tenebrous organization, clever enough to operate entirely in the shadows.

We must remember, of course, that even though the gossips of the Sologne are a bunch of evil-minded, bigoted fools, that does not mean that they were *entirely* wrong in their malevolent suspicions. Although they were completely mistaken about Armand de Verne's relationship with the poor Baronne, there is still some basis for their suspicion of the Baron de Méreuil. Why, indeed, did he buy the Sapinières, in a godforsaken location like the Sologne, unless he were running away from something that made it difficult for him to reside in his own native region or in Paris? Surely he must have had a secret in his past—and a past of the kind that can sometimes catch up with a man in an unfortunate manner. Is it not likely that someone had a mortal grudge against him, which was eventually and cleverly paid off, in no uncertain terms, so ruthlessly that the only two people who might have been able to put the police on the track of the assassin—Jérôme Véru and Armand de Verne—were dispatched with similar ruthlessness? We do not know enough about the Baron's murky past to point the finger at Venetian *bravi*, German *vehmgerichte*, the Union Corse or the Camorra (the real Camorra, not the Habits Noirs), but it is surely more likely that some such semi-secret society was involved in a crime that gives every evidence of being that kind of handiwork than it is that the poor benighted Chambrion has jumped to the right conclusion.

In the event, Ponson du Terrail did not introduce any such plot-twist into his story, but that probably has more to do with the fact that he got hung up on other concerns than with any intrinsic hostility to the possibility. Perhaps he simply did not think of recomplicating his plot in that fashion, or perhaps he was not given the scope to do it—*Le Chambrion* is considerably shorter than most of his serial novels, and he might have been put under pressure to end it sooner than he had initially hoped or vaguely planned—but whatever the reason might be, he certainly set up all kinds of narrative potential that he ultimately left undeveloped.

The text remains as it is, and nothing more, but that does not mean that readers cannot go any further, in reasoning and speculating, and we too owe something of an obligation to the Chambrion, by virtue of having involved ourselves in his mental torments and drawn some entertainment therefrom. We cannot say anything to him, because he is, after all, merely an item of fiction, but we are perfectly at liberty to imagine what we might say if we could—and what we surely ought to say, if we were given an opportunity, is: "Your father was innocent of murder; your lifelong shame is unnecessary."

On reflection, though, perhaps it is as well that he never knew that, because that is, after all, his motive for becoming the guiding light of the Utopian community that replaced the miseries of Sologne in the futuristic epilogue of Ponson's story. As writers of popular literature has been striving to demonstrate ever since its inception, the road to virtue is sometimes boggier and more convoluted than simple-minded moralists would have us believe.

ABOUT THE TRANSLATOR

BRIAN STABLEFORD has translated more than a hundred volumes of French prose into English. His principal interests are the French Romantic Movement and its Decadent/Symbolist aftermath, with particular reference to the evolution of the *conte cruel*, and the evolution of the *roman scientifique* from its origins in the eighteen-century *conte philosophique* to the aftermath of the Great War of 1914-18.

www.ingramcontent.com/pod-product-compliance
Lightning Source LLC
Chambersburg PA
CBHW020313260626
47156CB00004B/1210